W9-CMJ-203

CUENTOS

CUENTOS

An Anthology of Short Stories from Puerto Rico

Edited and with a Preface by

KAL WAGENHEIM

SCHOCKEN BOOKS • NEW YORK

First published by SCHOCKEN BOOKS 1978

10 9 8 7 6 5 4 3 2   79 80 81

Library of Congress Cataloging in Publication Data

Main entry under title:

Cuentos: an anthology of short stories from Puerto Rico.

With Spanish and English on facing pages.
CONTENTS: Belaval, E. S. Monsona Quintana's purple child. Spectralia.—Marqués, R. Three men by the river. Purification on Cristo Street.—Soto, P. J. The champ. The innocents. [etc.]
1. Short stories, Puerto Rican—Translations into English. 2. Short stories, Puerto Rican. 3. Short stories, English—Translations from Spanish. I. Wagenheim, Kal.

PZ1.C8963 [PQ7436.S5] 863′.01   78-54399

Manufactured in the United States of America

CONTENTS

INTRODUCTION

As recently as 1940, the seventy thousand Puerto Ricans living in the United States were only a small offshoot of the island's society, which numbered two million persons. Today, however, largely due to the mass migration that took place in the two decades after World War II, nearly two million *puertorriqueños* reside in the United States, compared with three million in their Caribbean homeland. In other words, more than one-third of the Puerto Rican people live in the "Diaspora."

Puerto Rico is now a divided nation. On the one hand there is the island itself, which in many respects is like a Third World country locked within the political and economic sphere of the United States. And on the other, we have nearly two million Puerto Ricans dispersed throughout the fifty states of the Union, with the largest concentrations in the United States Northeast and Midwest. Roughly half of those in the "Diaspora" were either born there, or arrived at an early age.[1] The existence of two Puerto Ricos has caused severe cultural tensions.

In Puerto Rico's multiracial, Spanish-speaking society, people are bound together by four centuries of Hispano-Antillean culture. In the United States, not only do Puerto Ricans lose their language, but tremendous forces also pull at them, to identify with either the white or black parts of American society. Total surrender to such forces is, of course, equivalent to a kind of ethnic suicide.

1. Of the one million students in New York City's public schools, for example, about 250,000 are of Puerto Rican birth or descent, mostly the latter.

Samuel Betances, the Harlem-born publisher of *The Rican* magazine, has written that "the single most crucial issue burning deep in the souls of many young second-generation Puerto Ricans in the United States is that of . . . the search for ethnicity." And Professor Frank Bonilla, who directs the Center for Puerto Rican Studies at the City University of New York, has said, "If we choose to go beyond survival as a community, then our creativity must be fed by a collective vision that reaches out to Puerto Ricans everywhere."

A nation's literature can help to define, and nurture, such a collective vision.

This book of twelve short stories, by six Puerto Rican writers, is by no means a definitive survey of contemporary short fiction in Puerto Rico. But most of the stories reflect a critical period in the island's history—the 1940s and 1950s—when chronic poverty, coupled with vertiginous social change, caused great anguish and confusion.[2] It was also a time when an entire generation of Puerto Rico's young writers broke with the traditional Spanish style of the *estampa* (folklore sketch, or vignette) and burst forth with an unprecedented quantity of powerful, socially conscious fiction.

But, before discussing the stories at hand, let's first step back for a brief historical overview.

The first literary accounts of Puerto Rico were written by Spanish friars and government officials who—in letters, memoirs, and chronicles—documented the island's conquest and colonization. Among the best of these is the *Historia general y natural de las Indias,* by Gonzalo Fernández de Oviedo, which was published in 1535, only four decades after Columbus' historic voyages to the New World.

Perhaps the first Puerto Rican to contribute to this body of letters was Alonso Ramírez, a poor carpenter's son who left San Juan at the age of thirteen, traveled the world, and became involved in thrilling episodes of piracy and shipwreck. When the young Puerto Rican mariner stopped off in Mexico, he was referred to the scholar *don* Carlos Sigüenza y Góngora, who took down the colorful narration, which was first published in 1690, under the title *Los infortunios de Alonso Ramírez.*[3]

2. This process has by no means run its course in Puerto Rico, but has entered a new, different phase.

3. This was reprinted in booklet form, in 1967, by the Institute of Puerto Rican Culture, San Juan.

In a sense, Puerto Rico "came of age" during the nineteenth century, after 300 years as a small, neglected Spanish colonial outpost. Between 1800 and 1900, the island's population exploded from 150,000 to nearly a million, largely due to an influx of immigrants from Spain and South America. This resulted in a dramatic flowering of political, economic, and cultural life. A true creole literature blossomed forth as the island began to assert its own national personality.

The foremost writers of this time included playwright Alejandro Tapia y Rivera (1826–82); poets Lola Rodríguez de Tió (1854–1924), José de Diego (1866–1918), and José Gautier Benítez (1848–1880); and essayists Salvador Brau (1842–1912), Cayetano Coll y Toste (1850–1930), Manuel Fernández Juncos (1846–1928), and Eugenio María de Hostos (1839–1903).

Among the earliest major works of that period was *El gíbaro,* published in 1849, which sketches the characteristics of the island's rural, agrarian society. The author was Manuel A. Alonso, who was at the time studying medicine in Barcelona. In vivid poetry and prose, Alonso wrote of dancing, cockfighting, marriage, slang, music, and many other topics. This work is a picaresque, humorous, and highly useful source for the student of Puerto Rico's past.

It was not until the 1890s that Puerto Rico produced its first full-fledged novel. But *La charca,* by Manuel Zeno-Gandía, has remained in print ever since, because of its memorable description of the harsh life in Puerto Rico's remote, mountainous coffee country.[4]

Life took a radical, new course in 1898 when, as a consequence of the Spanish-American War, Puerto Rico became a possession of the United States. Although many of the island's native sons had a long list of grievances against Spain, and sought some form of political distance, they still viewed that country as *la madre patria* in cultural terms. But the language of the conquerors was that of Shakespeare, not Cervantes. And suddenly, in their own land, Puerto Ricans were faced with a ruling government and a set of institutions that were totally foreign. By 1917, political ties with the United States were further strengthened, when United States citizenship was imposed, en masse, on all natives of the island.

4. Zeno-Gandía, a prominent doctor, had traveled widely and was fluent in several languages. *La Charca* was the first in his tetralogy of four novels, which he called "Chronicle of a Sick World."

These elements—of political and cultural conflict—have been major issues, not only in the daily life of Puerto Rico, but also in its literature.

After the United States takeover of the island, Puerto Rico during the first four decades of this century remained much as it was—a poor, agrarian, semi-feudal society. In 1940, for example, per capita income was about $120 per year. Most workers labored on farms—cultivating sugar cane, tobacco, and coffee—and earning about 6 cents an hour, when there was work. The "elite" workers, those in the small construction industry, earned about 22 cents per hour. Seven of every ten adults were illiterate, and only half the children were in school. Life expectancy was only 46 years, as thousands of infants perished from malnutrition or disease, and countless thousands of young and old were disabled by parasites. Life was harsh. But, in the cultural sense, since traditions passed on from one generation to the next, there was a sense of stability. As René Marqués writes in one of the stories in this volume, in another context, "there was order in the affairs of men and of the gods. . . . Everything in the universe had made sense, and that which did not was the doing of the gods."

But after World War II, a tidal wave of social change literally engulfed the island. Factories displaced farms as the chief source of earning a living (for those who found jobs). Air travel revolutionized lifestyles. Television brought new, strange images into remote hamlets. The decline of farm jobs spurred the growth of festering slums on the cities' fringes, and when migrants found nothing there, many traveled north, to find snow, crumbling tenements, and hostility.

The distinguished Peruvian novelist Mario Vargas Llosa, in an interview some years ago, commented that writers of fiction are a "bit like vultures, and the food they need most is carrion, the carrion of history. . . . Societies in crisis, corroded by internal struggle and contradictions, stimulate the imagination."

Puerto Rico in the first half of this century was certainly a society "in crisis," and a number of island writers responded to the stimuli with plays, poems, and essays. Among these artists were Luis Palés Matos (1898–1959), Julia de Burgos (1916–1953), Antonio S. Pedreira (1898–1939), Luis Llorens Torres (1878–1944), and Nemesio Canales (1878–1923).[5]

5. Even by the 1930s there was some literary interest in the Puerto Rican migration to New York, which was the theme of Fernando Sierra Berdecía's play, *Esta noche juega el joker*.

Perhaps the first Puerto Rican to describe this period of transition in novel form was Enrique Laguerre (1906–). Laguerre, the author of eight novels, was born in the countryside near Aguadilla, and now teaches at the University of Puerto Rico. He once wrote in an essay, "I am conscious of a wide world, inhabited by millions of humans, but each of us needs a friendly place to stand upon." And Puerto Rico, assaulted by change, was hardly that place, as many of its inhabitants were swept about like leaves in a storm.

Most of the stories in this volume reflect the creative response of Puerto Rican writers to these menacing winds of change.

In the 1940s, when the first waves of affluent tourists were being attracted to Puerto Rico, Emilio S. Belaval published a short story collection with the ironical title *Cuentos para fomentar el turismo (Stories to Promote Tourism)*. One of these, "Monsona Quintana's Purple Child," included in this volume, tells of the heroic struggle of a poverty-stricken mother to keep alive a dying newborn child.

At about that time, Abelardo Díaz Alfaro (1917–) published *Terrazo,* a book of sketches and stories of rural life that is full of vitality, poetry, humor, and poignancy. Two stories from *Terrazo* are included here. "Josco" is an allegorical account of a Puerto Rican bull, whose owner plans to put him out to pasture and import an American stud that will "improve the breed." The other is a comical tale of Peyo Mercé, a country schoolteacher, and his bumbling attempts to introduce the English language to the bewildered, barefoot children of the *barrio*.

By the 1950s, as the migration to the United States gathered full steam (averaging 50,000 persons a year), more fiction began to appear about the challenge of life in New York. One of the earliest of this genre was the short novel *Paisa,* an acerbic comment on racial discrimination, by José Luis González (1926–). González, who lived both in Puerto Rico and the United States, is the author of two stories in this volume. One of these, "There's a Little Colored Boy in the Bottom of the Water," touchingly recounts the fate that befalls an innocent child who lives in a ramshackle slum in San Juan. The second story, "The Night We Became People Again," takes place in New York, and is a seriocomic monologue by a factory worker.

Pedro Juan Soto (1928–) is another writer who has observed Puerto Rican life both in the United States and on the island. Soto, who was born in Cataño and raised in New York, returned

to Puerto Rico about twenty years ago. His first book, *Spiks,* is a hard-hitting collection of stories, in Spanish and "Spanglish," about life in El Barrio. Two of those stories are included here: "The Champ," about a youth who seeks to prove his manhood in a pool hall; and "The Innocents," about a mother's anguish when she is faced with the painful task of sending her mentally ill son to an institution.

René Marqués (1919–) also wrote of the migration in *La carreta (The Oxcart),* a play which has been translated into several languages. For this volume, however, I have selected two stories that deal with other themes. In the first, "Three Men by the River," Marqués reaches back to early Spanish colonial times, when the Taíno Indians were conquered and enslaved by invaders whom they believed to be gods. In his second story, "Purification on Cristo Street," Marqués writes of three elderly spinsters in a decrepit San Juan townhouse, surrounded by the menace of a world that "had lost its equilibrium."

Emilio Díaz Valcárcel (1929–) is the youngest writer represented in this collection. Although pessimism saturates much of his work, Díaz is one of the few Puerto Rican writers of his generation to translate this into effective black humor. One of his most memorable stories, included in this volume, is "Grandma's Wake," about a shopkeeper who flies from New York to Puerto Rico to attend his mother's funeral—only to find that she is not quite dead.

Puerto Ricans on the island and those in the United States write in different languages, and from a different geographic and cultural perspective. But they share a common dilemma: the challenge presented to them and their people by the United States. In the United States, the Puerto Rican is part of a so-called "minority group" seeking some form of psychic adjustment to a new culture. In Puerto Rico, that same culture threatens to overwhelm the island. More than a decade ago, in an essay, René Marqués aptly summed up the perspective from Puerto Rico:

> This is a really schizophrenic society. Puerto Ricans have two languages, two citizenships, two basic philosophies of life, two flags, two anthems, two loyalties. It is very hard for human beings to deal with all this ambivalence.

Not all of the stories in this volume, or in the main body of

Puerto Rican literature, deal with these political-cultural tensions. But such concerns are, perhaps, the most consistently voiced theme, in the same way that much of the new writing by Puerto Ricans in the United States deals with the question of identity and roots, and of adjustments, or resistance, to a different, often hostile society. Miguel Piñero, Pedro Pietri, Nicolasa Mohr, Piri Thomas, J. J. González, Jesus Colón, Edwin Torres, Victor Hernández Cruz—to name just a few Puerto Rican writers in the United States—have written ably and eloquently, in English, about this dramatic phase in the history of their people.

This emerging literature is a valuable addition to the large body of writing created by all of the racial and ethnic groups that now comprise the United States. But it is even more closely related to Puerto Rico's rich literary tradition. However, since most young Puerto Ricans in the United States do not read Spanish, they are cut off from that tradition, and, therefore, from a vital link with their roots.

Only time can tell how, or when, the political and cultural dilemmas of the Puerto Rican people will be resolved. But I hope that this small collection of stories sheds at least some light on the subject, and that it helps to strengthen the bonds of understanding between the two Puerto Ricos.

I am particularly pleased that this edition is bilingual, providing both the Spanish and English texts, since translations are rarely more than a dim facsimile of the original.

In conclusion, I wish to thank the authors of these stories for granting permission to have them reprinted here. Special thanks go to Pedro Juan Soto, for his extra help in this project, and to Ricardo Alegría, former director of the Institute of Puerto Rican Culture, who early on recognized the need for reaching out to his compatriots in the "Diaspora."

KAL WAGENHEIM
New York City, 1978

NOTES ON THE AUTHORS

Emilio S. Belaval (1903–72), a former judge in Puerto Rico's Supreme Court, was born in Fajardo, on the island's northeast coast. During his long career, he wrote many short stories, essays, and plays. His short story collections have appeared in book form under the following titles: *Cuentos de la universidad* (1935), *Cuentos para fomentar el turismo* (1946), and *Cuentos de la plaza fuerte* (1963).

René Marqués, born in Arecibo in 1919, is perhaps Puerto Rico's best-known literary figure abroad, since his works have been translated into several languages. Primarily a playwright, Marqués has also written short stories, poetry, essays, and literary criticism. *La carreta,* one of his plays, has been staged in New York, in English, and was also produced in English on television in the United States. His novel *La víspera del hombre* was awarded the Faulkner Foundation Prize in 1962. Marqués' short stories have appeared in two published collections: *Otro día nuestro* (1955) and *En una ciudad llamada San Juan* (1960). His latest novel is *La mirada* (1975). After heading the editorial unit of the government's Community Education Division for many years, Marqués joined the faculty of the University of Puerto Rico.

Pedro Juan Soto, born in Cataño in 1928, spent his youth in

New York City, where he received his college education, and returned to the island in 1954. His first book, the short story collection *Spiks* (1957), and his novel *Ardiente suelo, fría estación* (1962) have been translated and published in English. Other books by Soto include *Usmaíl* (1958), *El francotirador* (1969), *Temporada de duendes* (1970), *A solas con Pedro Juan Soto,* a "self-interview" (1973), *El huésped, las máscaras y otros disfraces* (1974), and *Un decir* (1976). Soto for several years wrote film scripts for the government's Community Education Division, and now teaches at the University of Puerto Rico.

Abelardo Díaz Alfaro was born in Caguas in 1917. His first book, *Terrazo* (1948), is still widely read, and is considered a modern classic. Its thirteen stories and sketches, dealing with rural Puerto Rico, are among the richest in the island's literature. His second book, *Isla soñada* (1966), is now in its fifth edition. One of Díaz Alfaro's short stories, *"los perros,"* has been included in *The Eye of the Heart,* an anthology of "great short stories by Latin American writers." Díaz Alfaro has worked for many years as a script writer for WIPR and WIPR-TV, the Puerto Rican government's radio and television stations, and has written hundreds of brief folklore dramas.

José Luis González was born in 1926 in Santo Domingo of a Dominican mother and a Puerto Rican father, and at the age of four went to Puerto Rico, where he was educated and began his writing career. He has lived in New York, and resided in Mexico for many years. Gonzalez's first book of short stories was *En la sombra* (1943), published when he was only seventeen years old. His other short story collections include *Cinco cuentos de sangre* (1945) and *El hombre en la calle* (1948); they were followed by the short novel *Paisa* (1950), and another book of short stories, *En este lado* (1954). His recent works include *Veinte cuentos y Paisa* (1973) and *En Nueva York y otras desgracias* (1973). He is now at work on a novel.

Emilio Díaz Valcárcel, born in Trujillo Alto in 1929, is the youngest writer represented in this collection. Two of his short story collections, *El asedio* (1958) and *Proceso en diciembre* (1963), illustrate the profound impact of the Korean War upon him and other Puerto Ricans who served in that conflict. Díaz

Valcárcel has lived in New York and in Spain (as the recipient of a Guggenheim Fellowship), and is now back in Puerto Rico. His other books include *El hombre que trabajó el lunes* (1966), *Napalm* (1971), *Panorama* (1971), *Figuraciones en el mes de marzo,* his first novel (1972), and *Inventario* (1975). His latest book, *Harlem todos los días,* is due to be published this year.

The Translations. The translators of the stories in this volume are: Patricia Vallés, "Monsona Quintana's Purple Child"; Bob Robinson, "Spectralia"; Charles Pilditch, "Purification on Cristo Street"; Pedro Juan Soto, the author, "The Champ"; Barbara Howes with Pedro Juan Soto, the author, "The Innocents"; C. Virginia Matters, "Josco," "Black Sun"; Pedro Juan Soto, "Peyo Mercé: English Teacher"; Lysander Kemp, "There's a Little Colored Boy in the Bottom of the Water," and Kal Wagenheim, "Three Men by the River," "Grandma's Wake," "The Night We Became People Again."

CUENTOS

EL NIÑO MORADO DE MONSONA QUINTANA

Emilio S. Belaval

Para el doctor José S. Belaval y Veve

POR la mañana, Monsona Quintana le dijo a su marido Anacleto Quintana:

—Anoche nos nasió otro. Yo no quise dispeltalte. Me las emburujé yo sola como púe.

El padre no se conmovió mucho que digamos con el nacimiento del nuevo hijo. Eran dieciséis picos pidiones que tenía bajo su techo y los hijos no se alimentan con pepitas de cundiamor.

—Haberá que compral algo, me imagino—indagó recelosamente.

—Ya le he remendao el coy y le he jecho unas batinas pa vestil. No te apures.

—Endispué idré a vello—respondió el padre, un tanto aliviado, tirando para sus abrojales.

A Monsona Quintana le dolió más el despego de su hombre que el parto: "Este canijo no me va a querel a mi guimbo. ¡Mía que ilse sin mirallo!" Ella que está desesperada por acabar con el café de la mañana, para darle una mirada de tres yardas de largo a su guimbo precioso. Los picos pidiones de la casa estaban agolpados alrededor del coy, velándose los ojos al recién nacido:

—¡Mai, qué chiquitito es!

—Entoavía no ha estirao una patita.

—¿Cuándo abririá los sojos, mai?

Oyendo el cotorreo do los picos, Monsona Quintana se desesperaba sin poder echarle a su guimbo esa primera mirada donde una mai busca con qué hilos de lucero le han bordado a su niño.

MONSONA QUINTANA'S PURPLE CHILD

Emilio S. Belaval

To Doctor José S. Belaval y Veve

IN the morning, Monsona Quintana told her husband, Anacleto Quintana:

"Last night another was born. Didn't want to wake you. Managed alone best I could."

The father was not greatly moved, let's say, by the birth of the new child. He had sixteen other hungry mouths under his roof, and you can't feed children on flower seeds.

"Have to buy something, I guess," he ventured cautiously.

"I already mended the cloth-cradle, and made him some little shirts. Don't you worry."

"I'll go see him later," the father answered, a bit relieved, heading for his weedy patch of a garden.

Monsona Quintana was hurt more by her man's indifference than by her labor pains. "He ain't going to love my kid. Goin' away without lookin' at him!" Yet she was anxious to finish preparing the morning coffee, so she could give her precious baby a long look, three yards long. The children of the house were crowded around the cradle, watching the eyes of the newborn.

"Mamma, how tiny he is!"

"He ain't moved a leg yet."

"When's he going to open his eyes, mamma?"

Hearing their chatter, Monsona Quintana fretted, unable as she was to give her son that first look which tells a mother with what starry threads has her child been adorned. But not even

Pero ni siquiera esa sensiblería le está permitida a una jíbara de mi tierra, cuando pare por la madrugada. Dale que dale a la paleta del café para que tueste la hedionda, más pendiente el ojo del coy que del humero, más llena de curiosidad la cara que de entuertos la cintura; por fin pudo servir el café, cargar su latón de agua, apagar las tres piedras, y con el corazón echando llamas, ir a mirarle la carita a su guimbo.

El niño de Monsona Quintana era uno de esos niños morados de nuestra montaña, pobre motete de cera escrofulosa, cañamazo trágico donde borda la tuberculosis, a quien nunca se le conoce otra color que no sea la color de la muerte. Al contemplar aquel pellejito humano se embraveció el alma amorosa de Monsona Quintana.

—¡Guimbo bonito, más que bonito, precioso, más que precioso, divino!—cantaleteó su corazón de mai, agarrando su lío morado.

Monsona Quintana es una jíbara estracijada de mi tierra, que ha parido diecisiete veces; tiene la barriga tan dilatada que ya su marido nunca sabe cuándo su mujer está embarazada. La maternidad se ha tragado la juventud de la jíbara, que una vez tuvo colores de camándula y pechos de tórtola dormilona. Ahora sólo queda una mai imaginera, agotada de tanto cargar la quebrada hasta la casa, sin más cintas que los pequeños cintajos que siempre lleva colgados en el alma, una mai jíbara de mi tierra. Esta vez el cielo ha querido hacer un escarmiento en el bohío de Monsona Quintana. El último hijo le ha nacido tan raquítico, que es casi una sobraja de hijo.

—Si al menos entuviera leche pa éste—suspiró la jíbara, tentándose el colgajo.

El guimbo se decidió a estirar una piernecita y la mai se olvidó de toda su miseria. Aquella mezquindad de hijo, que se atrevía a moverse entre un montón de harapos, volvió a poner a la mai imaginera:

—¡Mía que piese más bonito que me ha sacao mi guimbo!—, voceó Monsona Quintana, coleteando su goce de paridora. —Tié colol de indio el angelito.

Se fue a prepararle una agüita de tautúa para que soltara la borra. Se había sacado una botellita y un teto nuevo de su propio buche, a fuerza de un ahorrillo de granos, sin que el marido husmeara que estaba la sopa corta. El guimbo se la bebió sin

that tiny concession to sentimentality is allowed a countrywoman of my land who has given birth at dawn. Turning and turning the wooden spoon to toast the fragrant coffee, her eye more attentive to the cradle than to the smoke, her face more filled with curiosity than her back was with after-pains, at last she was able to serve the coffee, fill and carry the water can back to the house, cool the three stones on which she cooked, and with heart aflame, go to look at the tiny face of her new son.

Monsona Quintana's child was one of those purple babies so common in our mountains, a poor bundle of scrofulous wax, a pathetic warp to be woven by tuberculosis, a child whose color is never anything but the color of death. Contemplating that tiny human scrap, Monsona Quintana's loving soul became aroused.

"Pretty baby, more than pretty, precious, more than precious, deevine!" sang her mother's heart, as she embraced her purple bundle.

Monsona Quintana is an emaciated countrywoman of my land who has given birth seventeen times; her belly is so stretched that her husband can no longer tell when she is pregnant. Childbearing has devoured the youth of this countrygirl who once had the color of *camándula* seeds and the breasts of a sleepy turtledove. Now she is only a dreamy mother, exhausted from carrying so much creek water to the house, bare of ribbons other than the tawdry shreds which, in my land, are suspended in a mother's soul. This time heaven has seen fit to inflict punishment upon Monsona Quintana's hut. The newborn is so sickly that he is almost like a left-over child.

"If there was only some milk for him," the countrywoman sighed, trying her sagging breast.

The baby decided to stretch one little leg and his mamma forgot all her misery. That pathetic child who dared to stir about among the pile of rags made his mamma a dreamer again.

"Look at the pretty feet my boy got from me!" cried Monsona Quintana, giving vent to her maternal joy. "The little angel is indian-color!"

She went to make him a drink of *tautúa* to move his bowels. She had bought a little bottle and a new nipple out of her house-money, by saving on the beans, without letting her husband notice that the soup was short. The baby drank it without

apretar el bembe. Estaba dormido en un sueño de caracol, un sueño de niño morado, el sueño que casi se parece a la muerte, pero que para Monsona Quintana era como el reposo de un serafín a quien le están remendando el ala: "¿Pol qué me haberé encariñao tanto con este guimbo?," se preguntaba con indomable alegría, una mujer a quien la maternidad no podía ya darle un solo goce, una mujer que había apurado, año tras año, el romance de la barriga.

Cuando llegaron las otras piponas del barrio, Monsona Quintana les presentó a su guimbo morado con la soberbia de haber parido el hijo más fino de su comisariado. Una de las barrigonas alzó el niño, soplando su sinfonía de boca:

—¡Mía que mono es, Monsona! Aojalá el mío me salga asina.

—A mí me está un poco amorotao. ¿Tendrá frío?—inquirió una, menos entusiasta.

—Vas a tenel que criarlo con leche maúra. Pa mí que éste te ha nasío delicao—la previno otra, tragándose un poco la repugnancia.

Monsona Quintana les arrebató el guimbo con una furia alegre, para matar el augurio. ¡Bah!, chinches que son las mujeres cuando tienen barriga. ¿Qué iba a estar amorotado su guimbito precioso? Aquella era color de indiecito, color de gallito morado de palizada jíbara. Bien podría ella quitarle el frío, si lo tenía, con su calor de mai, bien apretujado su guimbo en el nido hondo de su vientre adiposo. Aquel niño venía del cielo, con un pico de pitirre, a ser el hombrecito que le sirviera a su mai, cuando el guimbo fuera comisario y tuviera una mai impedida.

Pero la charla de las piponas dejó durante todo el día una roncha en el alma de Monsona Quintana; una de ellas apenas se había atrevido a mirar el guimbo de Monsona Quintana, como si tuviera miedo de que se le pegara el mal de ojo al por nacer. ¿Estaría de verdad enfermo su guimbo? ¿Tendría frío? El nene era de tiempo y había coronado en un solo dolor; apenas se le había hinchado una vena para parir. El guimbo quiso ahuyentar la zozobra de su mai, tirándose el primer berrido. Monsona Quintana brincó, más riscosa que una cabra, a desnatar la primera hambre de su guimbo.

Vino una comadrona, de ojos viejos y manos sucias, a verle el ombligo al niño morado de Monsona Quintana.

—Me han dicho que lo de anoche fue ligero.

closing his lips. He was sleeping like a snail, a purple baby's sleep, an almost deathlike sleep, but which seemed, to Monsona Quintana, like the peaceful repose of a seraph whose wing is being mended. "Why am I so fond of this kid?" she asked herself with uncontrollable happiness, a woman to whom motherhood should no longer offer a single joy, a woman who, year after year, had exhausted the romance of the belly.

When the other big-bellied women of the neighborhood arrived, Monsona Quintana presented her purple child with the haughtiness of one who has borne the finest son in the county. One of the pregnant women lifted the boy, breathing her mouthy symphony:

"Look how cute he is! Hope mine will be just like that!"

"He looks a little purple to me. Is he cold?" inquired another, less enthusiastic.

"You'll have to raise him on fresh milk. Looks like this one's born delicate," another warned, just barely veiling her disgust.

Furiously, but happily, Monsona Quintana grabbed the baby to dispel the omen. Bah! Women get stupid when they grow a belly. How could her precious child be purple? His color was that of a little indian, the color of a lovely red and violet vine on a country fence. She could very well take the cold away from him, if he felt any, with her mother's warmth, pressing him tight in the deep nest of her fleshy belly. This child, with the beak of a *pitirre,* was sent from heaven to be the little man who would take care of her when he became the political leader around this place and found his mamma feeble.

But the chatter of the fat-bellied women left a welt on Monsona Quintana's soul which lasted the entire day; one of them had hardly dared to look at the child, as if she were afraid her unborn might catch the evil eye. Could her baby be really sick? Was he cold? The baby was on time and had emerged in only one pain; she had hardly swollen a vein to give birth. The baby tried to dispel his mother's worry by uttering his first wail. Monsona Quintana leaped, wilder than a goat, to skim her baby's first hunger.

A midwife came, with old eyes and dirty hands, to examine the belly button of Monsona Quintana's purple baby.

"They told me it happened fast last night."

—Casi sin dolol. No tuví que dispeltal a Anacleto. Adigame usté, ¿me le vé usté algo malo a mi guimbo?

—Yo no le vedo ná malo. El colol que no es de salú. Ya te he dicho que no calgues tanta agua cuando estés asina. Esas cosas jacen mal.

—Pero, ¿ha veído usté algunos como éste?

—Sí, mujel. Sólo que se crían esmirriaos y dan mucha fatiga. Yo te trairé algo pa tu guimbo.

La fatiga que pudiera ocasionarla el nuevo nene no le importaba nada a Monsona Quintana. Fatiga de madre estaba ella dispuesta a padecer por su guimbo desde la mañana hasta la madrugada. Ya verían aquellas piponas melindrosas, de lo que era capaz una mai jíbara, para matarle el frío a un guimbito enfermizo. Ella estaba dispuesta a despezuñarse por salvar a su comisarito. Se quitó sus naguas nuevas para hacerle unos buenos pañales, se puso los ojos en el coy, y la oración en Santa Rita, patrona de los niños jíbaros. Dos o tres días más tarde, le pidió a su marido:

—Tráigame una sobrina pa que atienda la casa. Yo, dende agora, quieo estal pindiente del guimbo na más.

—¿Está enfelmo?

—Asina me han dicho. ¿Quiés tú velo que eres pai?

Anacleto Quintana se acercó al coy y miró al guimbo pedazo a pedazo. El marido estaba francamente nublado. Era la primera vez que le veía a su jíbara una calenturita en el mirar, que desmadejaba el brío sublime de su criandera.

—Yo no le vedo ná. Un chis flacuenco, sí.

—¿Tú crees que esté enfelmo?

—¡Njú! El colol paese como de mosesuelo. Algunos se mueren casi nacíos.

La verdad no podía entrarle por los moños a Monsona Quintana. Tenía susto de que su guimbo le hubiera nacido un poco ñangilucho, pero su corazón alentaba una esperanza insobornable. Lo que su guimbo necesitaba era su calor de mai, para criarse más lindo que un gallito morado, y allí estaba ella, más estracijada que un cuero de becerra, pero más brava que un mayoral, dispuesta a no dormir, ni a cabecear, para que su guimbo sanara.

Anacleto Quintana tuvo que traerle una sobrina que atendiera los piches y la marota. Monsona Quintana se arremangó bien la esperanza, para disputarle su guimbo a la muerte. El

"Almost without pain. Didn't have to wake Anacleto. Tell me, you see anything wrong with my kid?"

"I don't see nothin' bad. Only his color ain't so healthy. I already told you not to carry so much water when you're like that. Them things is bad for you."

"But you seen any like this?"

"Yes, woman. Only they grow up pretty thin and give a lot of trouble. I'll bring something for your kid."

The trouble the new baby might give didn't matter at all to Monsona Quintana. She was ready to suffer a mother's trouble for her baby from morning to dawn. Those fussy fat-bellies would see what a country mother could do to keep the cold from a sickly child. She was ready to do anything to save her little politician. She took off her new petticoats to make some good diapers, kept her eyes on the cradle and prayed to Santa Rita, patron of country children, Two or three days later, she told her husband:

"Go get your niece to take care of the house. From now on, I want to take care of the kid, nothin' else."

"He sick?"

"That's what they tell me. Want to take a look at him, you bein' his pa?"

Anacleto Quintana went close to the cradle and looked the baby over bit by bit. The husband was frankly dazed. It was the first time that he saw his woman with a fever in her look, which sapped the sublime vigor from her maternal cares.

"Don't see nothin'. A little skinny, sure."

"Think he's sick?"

"Well . . . His color ain't good. He looks burned. Some die just born."

Monsona Quintana wouldn't let the truth get through her matted braids. She feared that perhaps her baby had been born a little scrawny, but her heart nourished an unflagging hope. What he needed was his mamma's warmth, and she was there, more worn than the hide of a calf, but stronger willed than an overseer, willing to go without sleep, not even nodding, to make her baby get well.

Anacleto Quintana had to bring her a niece, to cook the green bananas and the flour. Monsona Quintana pulled up the sleeves of her hope to save her child from death. The husband

marido la miraba, más asustado de la calentura de ella, que de la color de su último hijo.

—Te estás matando, Monsona. Arrecuéstate un rato.

—La muelte no se lo pué lleval mientras yo le tenga un ojo puesto ensima—murmuraba la jíbara, sacudiéndose la fatiga.

El guimbo se había sepultado en el vientre de Monsona Quintana, como si otra vez se le quisiera extravasar en las entrañas. No había forma de separar el uno del otro, mirándose a los ojos, morado él, a pesar del lindo almidón de marungüey con que Monsona Quintana le empolvaba los pellejitos para taparle el color; amarilla ella, con ese color que da un insomnio cuando se junta con otro.

Algunas veces el cielo, compadecido de aquellos ojos hinchados, de los tobillos sonámbulos de la estracijada, decidía descoser al guimbo del vientre adiposo de la madre. Le entraba un fogaje al nene, que se sabía que estaba vivo, por el ronquido metálico que profería cuando boqueaba. Monsona Quintana clavaba los ojos en el cielo, con una mirada tan hosca, que bajaba despavorido el ángel de la guarda en persona, temiendo una blasfemia. El marido protestaba, convencido de que nada podían contra aquel color, que en los niños jíbaros de mi tierra, es casi un tizne de la muerte.

—Se te va a pegal un mal como sigas asina, mujel.

—La muelte no se lo pué lleval, mientras yo le tenga un ojo puesto ensima—perjuraba la madre en espera del milagro, impasible ante los sufrimientos de su matriz macerada.

Noche tras noche, se ponía al sereno la cernada, de donde se tomaba el pellizco de ceniza para la leche madura del guimbo; día tras día, fallaba una nueva yerba, hasta entonces infalible para desaventar el atolillo; hora tras hora se agrandaba la ojero agónica de la mai. Ya Monsona Quintana no es la jíbara imaginera, con cintajos alegres colgados en el alma; es una mai terrible que no se rinde ante la acechanza espectral de la muerte, con un pañal de llorosa tendido sobre su barrigona dilatada, con una oración implacable crujiéndole en los labios, para que el cielo no pudiera olvidarse de ella.

Porque el martirio de Monsona Quintana no debía terminar en un mes, ni en dos, ni en tres. El guimbo se moría lentamente, cosido aún a las entrañas de la mujer, como si quisiera llevarse con él a su mai, para dormir juntos un sueño de canto, bajo sábanas moradas. ¡Monsona Quintana, jíbara desgraciada de mi

watched her, more frightened by her fervor than by the color of his latest son.

"You're killin' yourself, Monsona. Lay down awhile."

"Death can't take him away while I got my eye on him," the countrywoman murmured, shaking off her fatigue.

The baby had buried itself in Monsona Quintana's belly as if it were trying to get back inside her. There was no way to separate one from the other, both looking into each other's eyes; he was purple, in spite of the nice *marunguey* starch with which Monsona Quintana powdered him to cover his color; she was the kind of yellow which a sleepless night induces when it is blended with another such night.

At times heaven, pitying the exhausted woman's swollen eyes and somnambulent ankles, would decide to tear away the baby from his mother's fleshy belly. The child would be taken with such a fever that she could only tell he was alive by the metallic snore he uttered when he gasped. Monsona Quintana fixed her eyes on heaven with a look so hostile that the terrified guardian angel himself came down, fearing a blasphemy. The husband protested, convinced they could do nothing against that color, which in the country children of my land is almost like a smudge of death.

"You'll catch a sickness if you keep up like this, woman."

"Death can't take him away, while I got an eye on him," swore the mother, awaiting a miracle, impassive under the agony of her macerated womb.

Night after night, she placed the sieve in the cool of the evening, from which she took the pinch of ash for the baby's milk; day after day, a new herb was used to dispel the child's internal gases, and failed; hour after hour, the agonized shadows grew under the mother's eyes. Monsona Quintana is no longer a fanciful countrywoman with happy ribbons strung in her soul; she is a terrible mamma who will not surrender to the spectral snare of death, a cloth wet with tears hung over her dilated stomach, an implacable prayer twisting her lips so that heaven might not forget her.

Monsona Quintana's agony would not end in a month, nor two, nor three. The baby was dying slowly, still sewn to the woman's entrails, as if he wished to take her with him, to sleep blissfully together under purple sheets. Monsona Quintana, luckless peasant of my country, worn-out mamma whose milky little

patria, máter estracijada, a quien le falla con la teta exhausta su ambicioncilla láctea de mai, con la oración inflexible la voluntad del cielo, con la miseria del bohío el auxilio de la tierra!

Llegó el momento en que el guimbo empezó a quejarse con su quejido de niño morado, a quien la muerte le va dando poco a poco sus tironcitos, para irlo descosiendo del vientre que lo ampara. No hay tuna caliente que pueda con un frío, que le ha endurecido todos sus pellejitos; no hay baño aromático que pueda con un fogaje, que va derritiendo, gota a gota, la cera escrofulosa. La mai lo pasea con tranco medroso, con rabia de pasión, con la fe maltratada por un cielo inexcrutable hasta donde, a veces, no llega el rezo de una jíbara. La curandera no sabe cómo acallar aquel quejido, que ya Monsona siente salirle de su propio vientre sangrante.

El padre torvo esperando un doble entierro, los picos mudos por temor a que su risa ofendiera al niño que se moría, y el lamento monocorde de una madre cerrera, todavía con una súplica monstruosa prendida en la voz:

—No se muera mi guimbito precioso, no se me muera; míste que su mai se va a queal muy solita si usté se le muere— suplicaba la mai, apelando en último lloro, al soplito de conciencia que pudiera contener aquel cuerpecillo convulso, repitiendo cada palabra como si fuera la letra de una nana trágica, dándole el dulzor de veinte cálices plañideros al moribundo.

Pero el guimbo se murió; se le escocotó a la madre de los brazos, cuando ya Monsona Quintana estaba vidriosa de rencor y de fatiga. La muerte tenía que recaudar aquella piltrafa de amor que era casi una aberración de la vida. Nadie se atrevió a cantar ni a bailar, en el velorio del niño morado de Monsona Quintana, temeroso todo el barrio de la mirada blásfema de la madre, que no bajaba del cielo.

Yo vi el entierrito del niño morado de Monsona Quintana. Me lo topé una tarde en que iba en un carro del gobierno, tratando de venderle la policromía munificente de nuestro paisaje a unos turistas norteamericanos. Lo llevaban a enterrar Anacleto y sus compadres, en un cajoncito blanco, con tres coronas de flores de papel que portaban unos niños moquillentos, cundidos de piojos y de lágrimas; una mohina comparsita de ángeles de pies descalzos, que no se atrevían mirar hacia el cielo.

En mi tierra la que pare, cría, camaradas, aunque a muchas se les escocote el guimbo escrofuloso de los brazos.

motherly ambition fails in an exhausted tit, whose inflexible prayers cannot change the will of heaven, whose miserable shack offers no help on this earth!

The moment arrived when the child began to complain with his purple baby's cry, when death, bit by bit, gave little tugs to unstitch him from the body which protected him. There is no warm cactus able to conquer the cold which has hardened his meager flesh; there is no aromatic bath to cure the fever which melts the scrofulous wax drop by drop. His mamma walks him with fearful stride, with passionate rage, with a faith abused by an inscrutable heaven where, at times, the prayer of a countrywoman cannot reach. The medicine woman has no art to calm that cry, which Monsona Quintana now feels coming from her own bleeding insides.

The grim father expecting a double burial, the other little mouths mute with fear that their laughter may offend the dying child, and the monochord lament of a mountain mother, still holding a monstrous supplication in her voice: "Don't you die, my precious, don't you die on me; look, your mamma's goin' to be left so all alone if you go an' die on her," pleaded the mother, appealing in her last weeping to the breath of consciousness which that convulsed little body might contain, repeating each word as if it were the verse of a tragic lullaby, offering the sweetness of twenty tear-filled chalices to the dying one.

But the baby died; he was torn from his mother's arms when Monsona Quintana was already glassy with rancor and fatigue. Death had to sweep away that scrap of love which was almost an aberration of life. No one dared to sing nor dance at the wake of Monsona Quintana's purple child—the whole county was fearful of the mother's blasphemous gaze, which never left the heavens.

I saw the little burial of Monsona Quintana's purple baby. Came across it one afternoon while riding in a government car, trying to sell the munificent colors of our landscape to some American tourists. Anacleto and his *compadres* were taking him to burial in a little white box, with three wreaths of paper flowers carried by some boys, noses dripping, full of fleas and tears; a melancholy procession of barefoot angels who dared not look toward heaven.

In my land, friend, she who gives birth *rears,* although the scrofulous scrap of a child may be torn from many a mother's arms.

—tr. Patricia Vallés

ESPERPENTO

Emilio S. Belaval

PRIMERO iba el aullido lastimero del can; detrás la vieja con el pregón de culpas y su campanillo de cobre; por último, Pacita Soledad, con su cuerpecillo de yuca y dos trenzas rubias prendidas de su azoro:

—Vecinos, tres avemarías por el alma de la desventurada dama de esta plaza, doña Carlota Mariana Ayala de Vallesola.

—Dios te salve, María.

—Una limosna depare la gracia de Dios a su ingrata hija Paz Soledad Vallesola, condenada a cinco meses de exposición de culpas, a viva voz, sin probar otra vianda que no sea de limosna.

—Duro es el castigo y crueles las amonestaciones. ¿Qué ha hecho la niña para merecerlo?

—Abandonó a su madre en el momento de la agonía, yéndose al portalillo a platicar con un canastero.

Detrás del grupo expiatorio caminaban siete fantasmones con sus rubores de parientes ocultos en un embozo de seda negra. Eran los siete curadores de la penitente supuestos a presenciar el acto de la expurgación. La inocencia de la niña y sus lágrimas claras contrastaban con la dureza de los curadores y sus rostros tiesos.

—¿Por qué abandonaste a tu madre en la hora de la muerte, linda Pacita Vallesola?

—Un pastor con el pecho desnudo me trajo un ramo de gualdas amarillas y rosas blancas al portal. Tenía el cuerpo atravesado por tres saetas.

—¿No estarías soñando, criatura?

SPECTRALIA

Emilio S. Belaval

FIRST came the sad canine wail; an old woman with the banns of penitence and her small copper bell came after; finally, little Paz Soledad, with her yucca-like body and yellow tresses hanging from her look of dismay.

"Neighbors, three Hail Marys for the soul of the unfortunate lady of this city, *Doña* Carlota Mariana Ayala de Vallesola."

"Hail, Mary."

"Alms to shed God's grace on his ungrateful daughter Paz Soledad Vallesola, sentenced to expiate her guilt aloud in public for five months without receiving food other than alms."

"The punishment is harsh and the banns are cruel. What has the child done to deserve it?"

"She left her mother on her deathbed to chat with a basket-maker at the door."

Behind the expiatory gathering there came seven ghostly looking individuals who hid their blushing of relatives behind muffles of black silk. As curates of the penitent they were on hand to witness the act of expurgation. The girl's innocence and her sparkling tears contrasted with the stern looks of the stiff-faced curates.

Why did you leave your mother in the hour of her death, pretty Pacita Vallesola?"

"A shepherd without a shirt brought a bunch of yellow welds and white roses to the door for me. His body was pierced by three arrows."

"Wasn't that a dream, child?"

—Los sueños no tienen tibias las manos ni los ojos negros, madrina.

Las beatas de la calle; conocedoras de la virtud de la niña, llenaban el bolsón de la vieja de hogazas doradas, racimejos de uvas morenas y panes de pasas. Al pasar junto al Colegio de Párvulos, se acercó a la penitente una monjita menuda, con voz temblona y ojeras de duende:

—Este pastelito de almendras es para tu cena; cómelo recordando tus rezos de niña.

—Sor Tránsito que voy de culpas.

—Los pecados tuyos caben en el uñero de una cotorrilla, mi serafina.

Fue llegando a la Plaza del Mercado donde se armó la batahola. Los asnillos se escaparon por el ojo de los aldabones a patear; las aves dejaron sus plumas en las cestas buscando ojos de picar; los aceiteros de coco, de almendra y algodón echaron a rodar los cangilones en busca de pajuelas y candelillas, por si había carnes que achicharrar. Los matarifes, los polleros, los puyadores de tortugas estaban furiosos con los parientes y la vieja.

—No hay duda; es la niña rubia de doña Carlotita Ayala. Veinte veces he visto esas trenzas caminando dentro de mis piaras . . .

—El castigo ha tenido que ser obra de los papahuevos que van detrás de la niña.

—Cara de raposa tiene la vieja. Habrá que llenarle el bolsón para que no se coma a la niña. —Las panapeneras, las buñoleritas, las amuletistas se echaron al suelo a soplar en sus barrigas de paridoras:

—Desgraciada Pacita Soledad, niña Paz, ¿qué han hecho de tus cachetes de muñeca?

—De chicuela solía vestir las berengenas de ursulinas.

—La gente moza no gusta de contemplar la muerte en los ojos de la casa —La vieja iba verde y sudorosa, mascando su rabia de espantapájaros. Los siete compulgadores, resentidos del reto a su virtud, ordenaron seguir hasta la Plaza de San José, con la esperanza de encontrar una atmósfera más propicia a una exposición de culpas.

La Plaza de San José es una lonja adusta y misteriosa,

"Dreams do not have warm hands nor dark eyes, my godmother."

The devout ladies of the street, familiar with the girl's virtue, packed the old woman's bag with golden loaves of bread, bunches of dark grapes and raisin cakes. As they passed the parochial school for infants, a tiny nun with a faltering voice and elfish shadows under her eyes approached the penitent.

"This little almond cake is for your supper. Remember your child prayers as you eat it."

"Sister Tránsito, I am a penitent."

"My seraphim, your sins would fit under the nail of a little parakeet."

The hurly-burly arose in the market place, as they reached it. The crickets escaped through the openings of the door-latches; the fowls abandoned their feathers in the baskets to search for eyes to peck; the coconut oil-lamps, the almond oil-lamps and the oil-lamps with cotton wicks set in motion the dippers in search of kindling and matches, in case there was flesh to burn. The cattle-slaughterers, the chicken-dressers and the turtle-stabbers were furious with the relatives and the old woman.

"No doubt about it, that's *Doña* Carlotita Ayala's blonde girl. I must have seen those tresses twenty times among my pigs . . ."

"The punishment must have been the work of those louts walking behind the girl."

"The old woman looks like a fox. We'll have to fill her bag so that she won't eat the child."

The breadfruit-vendors, the bun-vendors and the amulet-vendors sat down on the floor to blow at their big bellies.

"Unlucky Pacita Soledad, little girl, what have they done to your doll-like cheeks?"

"When she was smaller she used to dress the color of eggplant, like the Ursuline nuns."

"Young people do not like to look at death when it comes to their house."

The old woman walked along green and sweaty, chewing on her scarecrow rage. The seven overseers, resenting the challenge to their virtue, ordered them to continue as far as the San José Plaza in the hope of finding there a more suitable atmosphere for the exposition of sins.

San José Plaza is a stern and mysterious meeting place, a

triángulo místico donde barban raíces de penitencia y ensueños de argonautas. Tiene un costal de Obispado, un convento de dominicos, una iglesia de ladrillos y una estatua de bronce. En sus alrededores hay casas de medallas, artesas de cerería y oraciones a los santos fuertes. Los frailes visten de blanco, las beatas de gris con vieses de moco de pavo, los velistas con blusones amarillos acanalados por la espelma. El aullido del perro, el campanillo de la vieja y los tientos de los siete rabadanes le sonaron demasiado groseros al eco del santuario. Cuando escuchó el pregón, la plaza frunció el entrecejo.

Las plazas guardan buenas memorias de los ancianos, los enamorados y de las niñas que juegan entre sus baldosines. La Plaza de San José se acordaba de Pacita Soledad por haberla visto de pasotera antes de entrar a sus oraciones. Empezó a soplar en el polvo de los ladrillos carcomidos, y a poco, los ojos de los parientes ardían entre una niebla de pimentón; sacudiéndose estuvieron los árboles esqueléticos hasta llenar de hojas secas el bolsón de la vieja. Los seminaristas eran más cándidos que la plaza, y creyendo a la niña endemoniada, entraron en congoja:

—Dios te salve, María, ayuda a la niña inocente a sacarse el demonio del cuerpo.

—Dios te salve, dulcísima María; sangre mía lleva en sus venas y es sangre de pecadores.

—Dios te salve, reina y señora; haz que se corte las trenzas y se lave la cara con cogollos de pringamosa. —La congoja de los seminaristas hizo temblar el corazón de la culpada; intentó arrodillarse a pedir perdón, pero un brazo fuerte, vibrando como un pino melodioso, la tomó por la cintura, obligándola a seguir sobre sus pies.

La calle se tornó lóbrega y atormentada. Era un angosto lecho de sombras tendido entre el Hospital Militar y un manicomio. Había allí salas de apestados, casas de tullidos, jaulas de delirantes. Mujeres enflaquecidas hasta el hueso, frailes con las sotabarbas chamuscadas por el rezo, loqueros membrudos con mañas de jaguares, iban por las parrillas, repartiendo lágrimas de cal, ofertas de perdón y camisas de lona:

—¿Quién te hizo pecar, hermosa niña?—le preguntó una ancianita desde sus arrugas de santera.

—Un pastor pelinegro con el cuerpo lacerado por las saetas.

mystical triangle where roots of penitence and dreams of argonauts grow beards. It is weighed down by the Bishop's residence, a Dominican convent, a church made of bricks and a bronze statue. Close to it there are medal shops, wax-workers' stalls and prayers for powerful saints. The friars dress in white, the church-going women in gray with trimmings the color of turkey wattles, the candle makers in coarse yellow shirts streaked by the sperm. The dog's howling, the old woman's little bell and the gropings of the seven shepherds were much too coarse for the echo in the sanctuary. The plaza wrinkled its brow when it heard the banns.

Plazas retain the good memories of old men, lovers and little girls who play among their stones. The San José Plaza remembered Pacita Soledad, for it had seen her stroll about before going for prayers at the church. Dust began to blow from crumbling bricks and soon the eyes of the relatives were burning under a peppery cloud; the frail trees shook all over until they filled the old woman's bag with dry leaves.

The seminarians were more candid than the Plaza and, thinking the girl bedeviled, they fell sad.

"Hail thee, Mary, help this innocent child to rid her flesh of the devil."

"Hail thee, sweetest Mary, my blood flows in her veins and it is the blood of sinners."

"Hail thee, queen and lady, make her cut her tresses and wash her face with the sops of nettles."

The sadness of the seminarians made the accused's heart tremble; she attempted to kneel for forgiveness, but a strong arm, vibrating like a melodious pine, caught her by the waist and forced her to continue on her feet.

The street turned dark and tormented. It was a narrow bed of shadows stretching between the Military Hospital and an insane asylum. In it there were wards for the plagued ones, houses for the maimed, cages for the delirious. Women thinned down to their bones, friars with their bearded jowls scorched by prayer candles, hulking keepers of the mad with all the tricks of a jaguar, went by the grillwork shedding tears of lime, offers of forgiveness and straightjackets.

"Who made you sin, beautiful child?" a wrinkled old lady who sold wooden saints asked.

"A dark-haired shepherd with his body pierced by arrows."

—Guarda en ropero de cedro tu cuerpo de moza y esconde tus miradas de los espejos. El espejo es el lago del pecado.

—Qué hermosa es, madre; tiene pechos de pitirrina y los ojos castos—comentó un adolescente con rodilleras de gutapercha.

—No apartes los ojos del cielo, hijo, hasta que te cure el mal.

—El mal que me aqueja tiene más gusanos en el alma que en las rodillas.

—Dale un empellón a la vieja para que caiga entre mis brazos, preciosa niña—le propuso un loco de ojos atizonados y risa de mortero—. Así era la bruja que le vendió los amores de mi casa a un levitas.

—La penitencia es mía y no de la señora—contestó la niña tristemente.

—Es ella la que ha puesto el diablo a colgar de tus trenzas.

La vieja llegó sulfurada y los siete curadores con las madres de la hiel sobre la cintura. Algo había funcionado mal en el pregón de culpas. La niña había recibido bendiciones y ellos insultos. La vieja estaba amoscada y el perro abochornado. La vieja se puso a matar su miedo junto a las piedras del fogón y los siete mirones montaron guardia cerca de las cacerolas.

—¿Dónde están mis espumillas de huevo?—preguntó la niña.

—Sembradas las vi en el fondo del mar—contestó la vieja, malhumorada. La niña empezó a quejarse de hambre y la vieja prometió hacerle una sopa con las cáscaras de las patatas y recalentarle la borra de lentejas pegada de la cazuela.

—¿No era la limosna pedida para mis hambres?

—Primero comen tus tíos; después yo de lo que sobre y tú de lo que a mí no me apetezca.

—Así padeceré hambre toda la vida.

La niña se puso a soñar que estaba sentada ante una mesa suculenta, servida por ama y copero; dos morcillas indignadas saltaron de la sartén y se le desmoronaron en la boca; el pastelito de almendras se puso en secreto con el pan de pasas y le jugaron a la vieja la misma treta. Los curadores impacientes sacaban sus pescuezos de los cuellos de celuloide, preguntando por la cena:

—Apura la candela, vieja; siento vértigos en la cabeza. Supongo que habrá para todos.

"Keep your body in a cedar locker and hide your glances from the mirrors. The mirror is the lake of sinfulness."

"She is beautiful, mother; she has breasts of *pitirre* and chaste eyes," said an adolescent who had rubber pads on his knees.

"Do not take your eyes off heaven, son, until you are free of your ailment."

"The evil that besets me has more worms in its soul than in its knees."

"Give the old hag a push so that she falls in my arms, beautiful," suggested a lunatic with eyes like burning coals and laughter like the clack of a mortar. "She reminds me of the witch that sold my darling to a blackcoat."

"The penitence is mine and not the lady's" the girl answered sadly.

"It was she that set the devil to hang from your tresses."

The old woman got to the house with her blood boiling and the seven curates with the worst of biles under their belts. Something had gone wrong in the proclamation of guilt. The child had received blessings while all they had gathered was insults. The old woman was irritated and the dog was embarrassed. The old woman went to stifle her fears beside the cooking fire and the seven lookers-on stood guard near the pots and pans.

"Where are my egg spumes" the girl asked.

"Stuck at the bottom of the sea, I saw them," the old woman replied with disgust.

The girl began to complain of hunger and the old woman promised that she would make her a soup from potato peelings and warm over for her the dregs of the lentils stuck in the kettle.

"Weren't the alms for my hunger?"

"First your uncles shall eat. From what is left I shall eat, and you may have whatever does not suit my taste."

"I shall be hungry all my life, then."

The girl began to dream that she was seated at a succulent table, served by a maid and a cupbearer; two angry blood-sausages leaped from the frying pan and crumbled in her mouth; the almond cake conspired with the raisin bread and played the same trick on the old woman. The impatient curates stretched their necks out of their celluloid collars, asking about supper.

"Quicken the fire, old one, I feel dizzy. There will be plenty for everyone, I suppose."

—La niña tomará puré de cascarones y rebañará las lentejas que sobraron de ayer.

—No le vendrá mal el ayuno. La gula es el peor pecado de la mujer virtuosa.

—Es pecado propio de viejas y de caballeros hambrones— rezongó la pregonera afilando sus porfías.

—Algo habrá que apartarle al can. Un pregón de culpas sin perro, daña la tradición. Dale de las lentejas de la niña.

Se sentaron ocho en la tocinera con los ojos conjurados y las manos de percheros. La vieja empezó por una sopa de fideos con las hueseras de un pollo melancólico. Uno de los hambrones destapó la fuente de las morcillas y lanzó un grito terrible:

—¡Alguien se ha comido dos morcillas!; bien contadas venían desde la plaza hasta el fogaril del patio.

—¿Habrá sido la niña? ¿Cómo se ha atrevido a violentar el voto de la penitencia?

—No ha sido la niña; no me despegué del caldero mientras se freían las morcillas.

—Huele en su boca, por si acaso.

—La boca le huele a anemia de pensionista.

—Entonces las tendrá escondidas . . .

—Miserable, babosilla, rata sabia, haberse atrevido a acortarnos la mesa después de la humillación que hemos recibido por sus culpas.

—A lo mejor las tiene todavía encima. Voy a arrancárselas del cuerpo a tiro de uña.

—Dejen la niña dormir sin buscar morcillas donde sólo hay cosas de mujer.

Los rabadanes estaban furiosos y la vieja arisca. En la algarabeta, el perro recibió una patada, lanzando un ladrido frenético. La vieja trató de amansarlo y cogió una mordida en un tobillo. La niña se despertó con los gritos, encontrando su boca cuajada de almendras, y brillando entre sus cabellos, clavos de especie. El buscón de la pezuña de cabrío se le acercó envuelto en rencores de basilisco:

—¿Dónde están las morcillas que estaban en la sartén? Confiesa que te las comiste.

—No he comido más morcillas que las que me sirvieran las manos de un pastor.

"The girl shall eat puree of peelings and the lentils left over from yesterday."

"Fasting will be good for her. Gluttony is the worst sin of a virtuous woman."

"A sin proper to old women and guzzlers," the old woman muttered, harping on her quarrels.

"Something will have to be put aside for the dog. A proclamation of sins without a dog harms tradition. Give him some of the girl's lentils."

With plotting glances and hands like clothes-hooks all eight sat down on the board used for salting the bacon. The old woman began with a noodle soup and the ruins of a melancholy chicken. One of the guzzlers uncovered the dish of bloodsausages and let out a terrible cry. "Someone has eaten all of two sausages! They were well counted from the plaza up to the fire in the patio."

"Could it have been the girl? How could she have dared to violate her penitential vow?"

"It hasn't been the girl. I did not move away from the kettle while the bloodsausages were cooking."

"Smell her breath, just in case."

"It smells of a boarder's anemia."

"Then she must have hidden them."

"Miserable, slobbering, snitching rat, to dare cut down our table after the humiliation that we have suffered for her guilt."

"She probably has them on her. I shall tear them out of her flesh with my nails."

"Let the girl sleep and do not go looking for sausages where there are only things fitting a woman."

The seven watchdogs were furious and the old woman fidgety. In the uproar the dog received a kick which made him bark frantically. The old woman tried to quiet him and was bitten on the ankle. The noise woke up the girl, who found her mouth covered by almonds and her hair shining with spice cloves. The clovenhoofed one who had wanted to search her before now approached her with a deadly look.

"Where are the sausages that were in the frying pan? Confess that you ate them."

"I haven't eaten any more sausages than those served to me by the hands of a shepherd."

—Manos de diablo azotarán tus carnes de lagartona. Has violado el voto de la penitencia. —La vieja llegó con la escudilla colmada de cáscaras, pero otro de los hambrones le arrancó las sopillas de la mano y se las sorbió de cuatro resoples.

—No dejéis a la niña sin comer que luego los insultos de la chusma serán para mí—protestó la vieja recordando los ojos del loco.

—Que se acueste sin comer; así aprenderá a respetar la cena de sus tutores.

—Esto merece un castigo ejemplar. Ponle tú salivillas al perro en lo que nosotros decidimos.

El caso era grave y la niña testaruda. No había forma de meterla en penitencia ni que su corazón se sintiera culpado. Los tutores, tratando de aventar sus escrúpulos, decidieron imponerle otro castigo más: ellos guardarían en sus casas los muebles, las lámparas, las alfombras, las vajillas, la plata de los aparadores, el joyero de doña Carlota Mariana, hasta el monumental crucifijo de oro ante el cual se arrodillaba la culpada. Así la niña se acostumbraría a sentarse en el suelo, dormir en el camastro del jardinero, comer en escudilla de barro, lamer las cucharas de madera y rezarle sus padrenuestros al almanaque.

Otra vez salió pregón de culpas, con el perro cojeando, la vieja añusgada y los siete estafermos con el embozo a mitad de nariz. La calle se sorprendió de ver a la niña vestida de andrajos, sin velo que tapara su rubor, y las mejillas tiznadas. Mayor era la sorpresa que la calle le había preparado a los tutores. Todos los niños de la calle se habían vestido de blanco a fin de acompañar a Pacita Soledad en su penitencia. Cada vez que la vieja intentaba levantar la voz proclamando la ingratitud de la hija, un nutrido avemaría modulado por cien gargantas adiestradas en el retozo de las chirinolas, apagaban los ayes de la vieja:

—Grita tú más, condenada, ¿no ves que te están tomando de chacota?—le ordenaban coléricos los estantiguados.

—Ni pasándome una plumilla de ron de caña y miel, llegaría a esos timbres.

—Grita más, grita más, aunque se te engorde la lengua.

La vieja gritaba y los niños rezaban; el perro empezó a mover la cola y a lamer las manos de Pacita Soledad. La niña resplan-

"May the devil's hands flail your lizardy hide. You have broken the vow of penitence."

The old woman came over carrying the bowl brimming with peelings, but another guzzler snatched the swill from her hand and downed it in four gulps.

"Do not leave the child without food or the insults of the mob will be for me," protested the old woman, who remembered the eyes of the lunatic.

"Let her go to bed without eating so that she can learn to respect her tutors' supper."

"This deserves a good punishment. Give the dog the pots to lick while we decide."

The case was serious and the girl was stubborn. There was no way to force her into penitence, nor of making her feel guilty at heart. The tutors, attempting to let go of their scruples, decided to impose another punishment on her; they would keep in their homes the furniture, the lamps, the rugs, the tableware, the silver from the cupboard, *Doña* Carlotita Mariana's own jewelbox, even the monumental crucifix of gold before which the sinful girl used to kneel. Thus the child would become accustomed to sitting on the floor, sleeping on the gardener's bunk, eating from a clay pot, licking wooden spoons and saying her paternosters to the calendar on the wall.

Once more the banns went forth with the dog limping, the old woman in anger, and the seven gorgons with their muzzles pulled up half-way over their noses. The street was surprised to see the girl dressed in rags, no veil to cover her blushes, her cheeks streaked with coal. But even greater was the surprise that the street had prepared for the tutors. The street children had dressed in white so that they might accompany little Paz Soledad in her penitence. Each time that the old woman tried to raise her voice to proclaim the ingratitude of the girl, a full-sounding Hail Mary, modulated by a hundred throats made skillful at bawling out in the open, drowned out the old woman's laments.

"Louder, damn you! Can't you see they are laughing at you?" the wrathful effigies ordered.

"Even if I licked a feather moistened in rum and honey I would not be able to reach that key."

"Louder, louder, even if your tongue grows fat."

The old woman shouted and the children prayed; the dog began to move his tail and to lick Pacita Soledad's hands. The

decía de virtud y sus ojos prendidos iban de la loa callejera. Los curadores llevaban el entrecejo como el humo de un farol envidioso, sin saber a quién alumbrar y a quién descabezar.

Al pasar frente a la Plaza del Mercado, tres anteriores revendonas de doña Carlotita Mariana se arrodillaron ante la niña; una con una taza de caldo, otra con una hoja de parra rebosando natillas y otra con una jícara de chocolate:

—Tómalas aquí Pacita Soledad, que sabemos cómo tus años se olvidan de comer. ¿Cuál fue tu desayuno?

—Una galleta sosa con agua de aljibe. Es todo lo que la penitencia me permite durante el día.

—Hola la vieja tragona; habrá que descoserle el buche a ver lo que esconde.

Hubo que hacer un alto, entre las rabias azules de los parientes y las ansias verdes de la vieja, hasta que la niña engullera las sabrosas limosnas. La confitería italiana de la calle del Sol envió un azafate con palitos de San Jacobo y capuchinos de harina nadando en almíbares de caramelo. La vieja trató de encestar las golosinas, pretextando el canon de la penitencia, pero los ujierillos de las chirinolas, le arrebataron el azafate volviéndolo a poner frente a los goces de la penitente. El bolsón llegó flaco y lleno de malicias callejeras. Traían rabos de bacalao, ñames jojotos y tripitas a poco soplar. Los parientes tuvieron que expulgar sus portamonedas antes de ordenar una tortilla de setas con chorizos:

—Parece que el pueblo no quiere entender nuestras limpias intenciones. A lo mejor creerán que somos nosotros los que disfrutamos de las limosnas.

—Yo lo que he tomado del bolsón es para ayudar a la niña en su penitencia. Si continúa esta fantasía, nunca acabará de cumplir la expurgación.

—Nuestra autoridad para imponer esa penitencia, no puede discutirse. Todo se ha consultado con el golilla y en lo único que puso reparo fue en mantener la niña bajo el manto de la vieja.

La penitencia había tomado piquete contrario y los parientes no sabían cómo apaciguar las siete iras dentro de sus envidias. Hasta la vieja andaba respondona y el can rabiscoso:

girl beamed with virtue and her eyes filled with stars at the praises she received along the street. The curates' brows darkened like the smoking of an envious streetlamp, knowing not whom to light upon and whom to behead.

As they walked in front of the Plaza de Mercado, three old vendors who had known *Doña* Carlotita Mariana knelt before the child—one with a cup of broth, another with a grape leaf loaded with custards, and one other with a small clay jar of chocolate.

"Take it all right here, Pacita Soledad, for we know that at your age you sometimes forget to eat. What did you have for breakfast?"

"An unsweetened cracker with water from the cistern. That is all that penitence will allow me during the day."

A halt was necessary, between the blue ire of the relatives and the green anxiety of the old woman, in order for the girl to eat the delicious alms. The Italian candy shop on Sol St. sent over a tray of eclairs and wheat-flour capuchins wading in caramel syrup. The old woman tried to put the sweets in her bag, mentioning the penitence canon as an excuse, but the small ushers from the bowling parties snatched the tray from her and placed it again in reach of the penitent. The black bag got home looking thin, full of pranks from the people in the street. It contained dried codfish tails, sick-looking yams and tripe quite unstuffed. The relatives had to search deep within their pocketbooks before ordering a mushroom and sausage omelet.

"It seems that the people do not want to understand our good intentions. They probably believe that it is we who enjoy the alms."

"What I have taken from the bag has been to help the child in her penitence. If this fancy keeps up, she will never be able to complete her purge."

"Our authority for imposing this penitence cannot be questioned. We consulted everything with the priest and the only thing he objected to was keeping the girl under the old woman's skirts."

The penitence had gone slightly askew and the relatives did not know how to pacify the seven wraths that dwelled within their envy. Even the old woman was beginning to talk back, and the dog had become snappish.

—Mejor sería enviarla a un convento a esperar que la trabaje la gracia.

—¿Y si a la fortuna de la niña también le da por profesar?— comentó el más candoroso de los curadores. Los otros seis parientes sintieron sus hambres replegarse hasta el último botón. Nadie había pensado desprenderse, a saltillo de rana, de los dineros. El séptimo se conformó en musitar:

—Más está ella de manicomio que de beaterio.

La frase quedó colgando como una araña peluda de las babas de los tutores. Un silencio de apagavelas los dejó sumidos en una insidiosa expectación. Cavilaron toda la noche con el dedo puesto en la nariz, y la nariz hundida en el barril de la codicia. La niña padecía de alucinaciones. Ella misma lo había confesado ante los vecinos. Tenía pegado al ombligo un pastor pelinegro, con los ojos ardidos y el pecho atravesado por una saeta. Los pastores no se hacen con migas de pan; ni atravesarse el pecho con una saeta, se estila entre las modas de los cuerdos. Lo primero que hicieron fue sentarse la pupila en las rodillas:

—Nos gustaría conocer a tu pastor. ¿Sabes dónde vive?

—Tiene puertas abiertas en todas las nubes y algunas noches se asoma por los entrepaños.

—Cómo se llama?

—Nunca ha querido decirme su nombre. Yo le llamo por Estéfano.

—¿No tienes miedo que sea un espíritu maligno?

—Una noche le hice la cruz, y me besó los dedos, sonriéndose.

La vieja no hacía más que cambiar de sustos y el can se meneaba inquieto. Hubo que empapar siete pañuelos con lágrimas y sangres antes que la vieja consintiera en salir otra vez a sus piropos. La niña se asomó a la ventana a contemplar las casas vaporosas de las nubes. Vio a su pastor cerrándole tranquilamente las puertas a la madrugada.

—Estéfano, ¡Estéfano!, baja que mis tutores quieren conocerte. ¡Estéfano! —Siete tutores y una vieja se agolparon en las ventanas, lívidos y despatarrados pero no vieron al pastor dibujado por los sueños virginales de la culpada. Uno de los tutores se le acercó a la niña con una ternura siniestra:

—Esta noche irás al pregón de rodillas y llamarás a tu pastor hasta que aparezca. Así todos sabremos si está vivo.

"It would be better to put her in a convent and wait for grace to work on her."

"And if the girl's inheritance also decides to take the vows?" the most candid of the curates commented. The other six felt their hunger reach down to the last button. None of them had thought of easing himself away from the money. The seventh found comfort in musing, "She seems more suited for the insane asylum than for the convent."

The phrase hung like a hairy spider from the pouting lips of the tutors. A graveyard silence left them deep in insidious expectation. All night they brooded with a finger along their noses, noses buried in the barrel of covetousness. The girl suffered from hallucinations. She herself had told the neighbors. Stuck to her navel there was a dark-haired shepherd with ardent eyes and the chest pierced by an arrow. Shepherds are not made out of breadcrumbs, nor is it the style among sane people to stick an arrow through one's chest. The first thing they did was to seat their ward on their knees.

"We would like to meet your shepherd. Do you know where he lives?"

"He has open doors in all of the clouds and some nights he looks out through the facings."

"What is his name?"

"He has never told me his name. I call him Estéfano."

"Are you not afraid that he might be an evil spirit?"

"One night I made the sign of the cross and he kissed my fingers, smiling."

The old woman could only trade one fear for another and the dog kept moving around. It was necessary to drench seven handkerchiefs in blood and tears before the old woman would consent to go out again on her errands. The girl looked out the window at the vaporous houses in the clouds. She saw her shepherd calmly closing the doors as the dawn came by.

"Estéfano, Estéfano! Come down, my tutors want to meet you, Estéfano." Seven tutors and an old woman crowded the windows, legs wide apart and faces all livid, but they did not see the shepherd sketched out by the virginal dreams of the guilt bearer. One of the tutors approached the girl with sinister tenderness. "Tonight you shall follow the banns on your knees and you shall call your shepherd until he appears. That way we all shall know if he is alive."

La tercera noche el perro salió envejigado, la vieja afónica y la niña de rodillas. Detrás iban los tutores con un solo ojo fuera del rebozo. El pueblo se sorprendió de ver a la niña descalza, con un caramillo en la boca soplando sobre cuatro ajises picantes. Pero mayor fue la sorpresa de los siete embaucadores. La niña encontró la calle alfombrada, velones rosados en manos de las beatas amigas, y en cada esquina, una batea de pechugas de aves, orejones de pajuil espolvoreados con azúcar de naranja y agua de panales.

—Pastor, pastor, ¿dónde estás?—imploraba la niña débilmente—pastor, no dejes que vuelvan a untarme ajises en los labios como a las niñas embusteras. —La vieja se iba agrietando y ya llevaba dos manchas en las sayas; las mantecas del terror le corrían por la barriga; el can cargaba demonio aparte pero los tutores no cesaban de acosar a la niña:

—Llámalo ahora, llámalo; estamos seguros que no te hará quedar mal ante las amistades de tu casa.

—Pastor, noble pastor; mis tutores no quieren creer que te he visto con carne tibia y los ojos completos.

—¡Pobrecita!—pregonaba la vieja recitando su cartilla—. Veinte horas lleva de enloquecida llamando a su pastor.

El rumor de la calle cortaba como navaja; las beatas zajaron el grupo expiatorio en tres, envolviendo a la niña en un círculo de luces, las comadres se ocuparon de estirarle los cueros a la vieja:

—Deja quieta a la niña, si quieres conservar la pelleja, matraquera; las visiones son cosas de mocitas.

—Yo sólo cumplo órdenes de mis señores—replicó la vieja, con la saliva más espesa que un emplasto de higuereta.

—Algún enredo se traen estos garrapatos entre manos.

La noche no estaba para enredos. Al pasar el pregón cerca de la Plaza de San José, había tres canónigos esperando a la niña con casullas de seda y bonetillos carmesíes. La niña trémula, desmoralizada, hizo un último esfuerzo y llamó de nuevo al pastor:

—Pastor, pastorcillo amigo, no me hagas pasar por embustera frente a los confesores de mi casa. —Se le acercó a la niña

The third night the dog went out all in blisters, the old woman hardly without a voice, and the child on her knees. Behind them walked the tutors with only one eye glaring from their cowls. The people were surprised to see the child barefooted, in her mouth a small flute to blow over four burning chili-peppers. But greater was the surprise of the seven extortionists. The girl found the street carpeted, pink candles in the hands of the friendly church-going women, and by each street corner a tray of breasts of chicken, *pajuil* slices powdered with orange sugar, and honey-comb water.

"Shepherd, shepherd, where are you?" the girl implored weakly. "Shepherd, do not let them rub pepper on my lips again, like they do to little girls who tell lies." The old woman was already cracking in places and there were a couple of stains on her skirt; the lard of terror ran down her stomach. The dog was afflicted by a demon all his own, but the tutors did not cease hounding the girl, "Call him now, call him. We are sure that he will not let you look bad in front of all the friends of your family."

"Shepherd, noble shepherd, my tutors do not want to believe that I have seen you in your warm flesh and full eyes."

"Poor child," the old woman proclaimed, acting her part. "For twenty hours she has been in madness, calling out for her shepherd."

The murmuring along the street cut like a knife; the devout women rammed through the group of expiators breaking it in three, enclosing the girl in a circle of light; the other women took the old woman to task.

"Leave the girl alone if you want to keep your hide, you old clacketyclack. Visions are things common among virgins."

"I only obey orders from my masters," the old woman answered, her spittle much stickier than a fig leaf poultice.

"These ticks are planning some dirty deal."

The night would not permit any dirty deals. When the banns came close to the San José Plaza, three priests in silk cassocks and crimson skullcaps were found waiting for the girl. The quivering, demoralized girl made a last effort and called the shepherd once more.

"Shepherd, little shepherd friend, don't make me a liar in front of my family's confessors." The oldest of the three priests

el más viejo de los tres canónigos y le preguntó:

—¿Quién es ese pastor por quien tanto clamas, linda Pacita Soledad?

—Es arrogante como un pino del bancal, con el pecho atravesado por una saeta.

—¿Tiene otra saeta clavada en la rodilla?

—¡Ay! Sí, señor; con ella puede encontrarse mi memoria; mas saber, no sé siquiera cómo se llama.

—Yo te diré su nombre; se llama Sebastián. La próxima vez que lo encuentres tienes permiso de tu iglesia para arrodillarte ante él.

—¿Por qué no quiso que viera morir a mi madre?

—A nadie le gusta ver la tristeza empañando los ojos de las niñas. Así ha debido pedírselo antes de morir, tu propia madre.

—Entonces, ¿limpia estoy de culpas?

—Culpas inventadas fueron las tuyas y habrán de ser investigadas por la iglesia.

Las levitas se fueron menguando hasta caer en el fondo de los zapatones. Nadie supo cómo lograron evadirse los siete curadores del amoroso cerco que les habían tendido los matarifes. Caminando iban los siete, y bien soplados, en busca de los últimos ochavos del jergón de la vieja, cuando se les apareció en el fondo de la calle, un pastor. Cada uno de ellos se agarró de un farol a sujetarse las quijadas. Los faroles sintieron asco de aquel miedo y sólo tuvieron que bajar un brazo y apretarlos por el cuello. Lo cierto es que en los faroles que tiene la calle de San Sebastián cabecearon siete levitones con las chisteras ahorcadas aparte. La vieja anduvo loca por el callejón del Grito:

—Visita de Santo tuve en mi casa y yo de ratera, salando esmeraldas en las aguas de las aceitunas.

El can alegó sus apretadas hambres, y después de las amonestaciones de rigor, le fijaron un hueso de la sopa del prior.

Lo mejor de todo fue cuando llegaron los alguacilotes de la Audiencia, con sus bigotes de estopa y sus ropillas de paño, a entregar muebles y joyas, y volvieron los niños a cantar sus chirinolas en el patio de Paz Soledad.

asked her, "Who is this shepherd for whom you cry so much, pretty Pacita Soledad?"

"He is as proud as a pine on a cliff, with an arrow through his chest."

"Does he have another arrow through his knee?"

"Ay! Yes, sir. With that, my memory comes back. But as far as knowing anything, I do not even know what his name is."

"I shall tell you. His name is Sebastián. Next time you see him you have permission from your church to kneel before him."

"Why did he not want me to see my mother die?"

"Nobody likes to see a child's eyes clouded with sadness. This your own mother must have begged him before she died."

"Then, am I rid of my guilt?"

"Your sins were inventions and they shall be investigated by the church."

The blackcoats shrunk until they dropped to the bottom of the big shoes. No one knows how the seven curates managed to escape the loving circle of the cattle-slaughterers. All seven were walking, ever with a good wind on their backs, to search for the last coins in the old woman's straw mattress, when the shepherd appeared at the end of the street. Each of them embraced a streetlamp in order to support his slack jaw. The streetlamps felt nauseous over such fright and they only had to lower an arm to wring their necks. The truth is that seven blackcoats nodded over the streetlamps found on San Sebastián St., their hats hung aside. The old woman, out of her wits, wandered through the Callejón del Grito, saying, "A saint came over to my house and I, such a cheap crook, spent the time salting emeralds in olive water."

The dog claimed his urging hunger and, after the warnings to be expected in the matter, he was sentenced to one bone from the Prior's soup.

The best that happened was when the big constables from the *Audiencia,** with their burlap moustaches and their wool suits, came over to return the furniture and the jewels, and the children once again appeared to carry on their frolic in the patio of Paz Soledad.

—*tr. Bob Robinson*

*Court.

TRES HOMBRES JUNTO AL RÍO*

René Marqués

Mataréis al Dios del Miedo, y
sólo entonces seréis libres.
PROFESIA DE BAYOÁN

VIO la hormiga titubear un instante y al fin subir decidida por el lóbulo y desaparecer luego en el oído del hombre. Como si hubiesen percibido el alerta de un fotuto, para él inaudible, las otras emprendieron la misma ruta, sin vacilar siquiera, invadiendo la oreja de un color tan absurdamente pálido.

Observaba en cuclillas, como un cacique en su dujo, inmóvil, con la misma inexpresividad de un cemí que hubiesen tallado en tronco de guayacán en vez de labrado en piedra. Seguía sin pestañear la invasión de los insectos en la oreja del hombre. No experimentaba ansiedad, ni alegría, ni odio. Observaba, sencillamente. Un fenómeno ajeno a él, fatal, inexorable.

El crepúsculo teñía de achiote el azul del cielo sobre aquel claro junto al río. Pero las sombras empezaban a alongarse en el bosque cercano. Toda voz humana callaba ante el misterio. Sólo las higuacas en la espesura ponían una nota discordante en el monótono areyto del coquí.

Alzó la vista y vio a sus dos compañeros. En cuclillas también, inmóviles como él, observando al hombre cuya piel tenía ese color absurdo del casabe. Pensó que la espera había sido larga. Dos veces el sol se había alzado sobre la Tierra del Altivo Señor y otras tantas la había abandonado. Sintió una gran gratitud hacia ellos. No por el valor demostrado. Ni siquiera por la paciencia en la espera, sino por compartir su fe en el acto sacrílego.

*Premio de Cuento Histórico del Instituto de Cultura Puertorriqueña, 1959.

THREE MEN BY THE RIVER*

René Marqués

Ye shall kill the God of Fear, and
only then shall ye be free.
PROPHECY OF BAYOÁN

HE saw the ant hesitate, then finally climb up the lobe and disappear into the man's ear. As though they had heard the alert from a seashell trumpet, which was inaudible to him, the other ants set off on the same route, without even hesitating, invading the ear, which was such an absurdly pale color

Squatting, in the ceremonial position of a cacique upon his wooden throne, immobile, he watched with the expressionless face of a *cemí* idol, that might have been carved from a rich brown guayacán tree trunk, rather than from stone. Unblinking, he watched the insects invade the man's ear. He felt neither concern, nor joy, nor hatred. He simply watched. It had nothing to do with him: it was inevitable, inexorable.

Dusk stained the blue sky with an *achiote* red above the clearing by the river. But the shadows were beginning to lengthen in the nearby forest. Every human voice was silenced by the mystery. Only the *higuaca* birds in the thicket added a discordant note to the monotonous song of the *coquí*.

He looked up and saw his two companions. Also squatting, immobile as he, watching the man whose skin was such an absurd cassava-white color. He thought to himself that they had been waiting for a long time. Twice the sun had gone up over the Land of the Noble Lord, and twice it had left. He felt deeply grateful to them. Not for their courage. Not even for their patience in waiting, but for sharing his faith in this sacrilegious act.

*Historical Short Story Prize, Institute of Puerto Rican Culture, 1959.

Tenía sed, pero no quiso mirar hacia el río. El rumor de las aguas poseía ahora un sentido nuevo: voz agónica de un dios que musitara cosas de muerte. No pudo menos que estremecerse. *El frío baja ya de la montaña.* Pero en verdad no estaba seguro de que así fuese. *Es el frío,* repitió para sí tercamente. Y apretó sus mandíbulas con rabia.

Era preciso estar seguro, seguro de algo en un mundo que súbitamente había perdido todo su sentido, como si los dioses se hubiesen vuelto locos, y el Hombre sólo fuese una flor de majagua lanzada al torbellino de un río, flotando apenas, a punto de naufragio, girando, sin rumbo ni destino, sobre las aguas. No como antes, cuando había un orden en las cosas de la tierra y de los dioses. Un orden cíclico para los hombres: la paz del yucayeke y el ardor de la guasábara, la bendición de Yuquiyú y la furia de Jurakán, la vida siempre buena y la muerte mala siempre. Y un orden inmutable para los dioses: vida eternamente invisible en lo alto de la Montaña. Todo en el universo había tenido un sentido, pues aquello que no lo tenía era obra de los dioses y había en ello uno sabiduría que no discutían los hombres, pues los hombres no son dioses y su única responsabilidad es vivir la vida buena, en plena libertad. Y defenderla contra los caribes, que son parte del orden cíclico, la parte que procede de las tinieblas. Pero nunca las tinieblas prevalecieron. Porque la vida libre es la luz. Y la luz ha de poner en fuga a las tinieblas. Desde siempre. Desde que del mar surgiera la Gran Montaña. Pero ocurrió la catástrofe. Y los dioses vinieron a habitar entre los hombres. Y la tierra tuvo un nombre, un nuevo nombre: Infierno.

Desvió la vista de sus dos compañeros y dejó escurrir su mirada sobre el cuerpo tendido junto al río. Sus ojos se detuvieron en el vientre. Estaba horriblemente hinchado. La presión había desgarrado las ropas y un trozo de piel quedaba al descubierto. Pensó que aquella carne era tan blanca como la pulpa del guamá. Pero la imagen le produjo una sensación de náusea. Como si hubiese inhalado la primera bocanada de humo sagrado en el ritual embriagante de la cojoba. Y, sin embargo, no podía apartar los ojos de aquella protuberancia que tenía la forma mística del la Gran Montaña. Y a la luz crepuscular le pareció que el vientre crecía ante sus ojos. Monstruosamente creciendo, amenazador, ocupando el claro junto al río, invadiendo la espesura, creciendo siempre, extendiéndose por la

He felt thirsty, but didn't want to look toward the river. The sound of the water was now something different: the agonizing voice of God musing over death. He could not stop from shuddering. *The cold is coming down from the mountain.* But he was not really sure if that was so. *It is the cold,* he repeated to himself, stubbornly. And he angrily clenched his jaws.

He had to be sure, sure of something in this world, which had suddenly lost all its meaning. As though the gods had gone mad, and Man were merely a *majagua* flower hurled into the river's rushing current, barely afloat, spinning, without a path or destiny. Not like before, when there was order in the affairs of men and of the gods. A cyclical order for men: the peace of the village, and the ardor of the *guasábara* ceremony preceding the battle; the blessing of the god *Yukiyú,* and the fury of *Juracán;* life ever good, and death ever bad. And an immutable order for the gods, who lived ever invisible in the heights of the Mountain. Everything in the universe had made sense, and that which did not was the doing of the gods; men did not discuss the wisdom of those things, since men are not gods, and their sole responsibility is to live the good life, completely free. And defend it against the Caribs, who are part of the cyclical order, the part which emanates from the dark shadows. But the shadows never prevailed. Because the free life is light. And the light shall put the shadows to flight. It has always been thus. Since the Great Mountain surged forth from the sea. But catastrophe came. And the gods came to dwell among men. And the land had a name, a new name: Hell.

He glanced away from his two companions and looked at the body stretched out next to the river. His eyes stopped at the belly. It was terribly swollen. Pressure had torn the clothing open and left a patch of skin in view. He thought how the flesh looked as white as the pulp of the *guamá* fruit. But the image made him feel nauseous. As though he had inhaled the first mouthful of sacred smoke during the intoxicating ritual of the *cohoba.* Nevertheless, he could not remove his eyes from that protuberance, which had the mystical shape of the Great Mountain. And in the crepuscular light it appeared as though the belly grew before his eyes. Monstrously growing, menacingly, filling the clearing next to the river, advancing to the thicket, ever growing, extending across the land, destroying, flattening,

tierra, destruyendo, aplastando, arrollando los valles, absorbiendo dentro de sí los más altos picos, extinguiendo implacable y para siempre la vida . . . ¿La vida?

Cerró los ojos bruscamente. *No creo en su poder. No creo.* Volvió a mirar. Ya el mundo había recobrado su justa perspectiva. El vientre hinchado era otra vez sólo eso. Sintió un gran alivio y pudo sonreír. Pero no lo hizo. No permitió que a su rostro se asomara el mínimo reflejo de lo que en su interior pasaba. Había aprendido con los dioses nuevos.

Ellos sonreían cuando odiaban: Tras de su amistad se agazapaba la muerte. Hablaban del amor y esclavizaban al hombre. Tenían una religión de caridad y perdón, y flagelaban las espaldas de aquellos que deseaban servirles libremente. Decían llevar en sí la humildad del niño misterioso nacido en un pesebre, y pisoteaban con furiosa soberbia los rostros de los vencidos. Eran tan feroces como los caribes. Excepto quizá por el hecho de no comer carne de hombre. Eran dioses, sin embargo. Lo eran por su aspecto, distinto a todo lo por el hombre conocido. Y por el trueno que encerraban sus fotutos negros. Eran dioses. *Mis amigos son dioses,* había dicho Agüeybana el Viejo.

Sintió sobre sí la mirada de los otros, y alzó sus ojos hacia ellos. Se miraron en silencio. Creyó que iban a decir algo, a sugerir quizá que abandonaran la espera. Pero en los rostros amigos no pudo discernir inquietud o impaciencia. Sus miradas eran firmes, tranquilizadoras. Casi como si fuesen ellos los que trataran de infundirle ánimo. Otra vez tuvo deseos de sonreir. Pero su rostro permaneció duro como una piedra.

Alzó la cabeza para mirar a lo alto. Las nubes tenían ahora el color de la tierra. Más arriba, no obstante, había reflejos amarillos. Y era justo que así fuese, porque ése era el color del metal que adoraban los dioses nuevos. Y allá, en lo alto invisible llamado Cielo, donde habitaba el dios supremo de los extraños seres, todo, sin duda, sería amarillo. Raro, inexplicable dios supremo, que se hizo hombre, y habitó entre los hombres, y por éstos fue sacrificado.

—¿Pero era hombre? ¿Hombre de carne y hueso, como nosotros?—sorprendió con su pregunta al consejero blanco de nagua parda, y cabeza monda, como fruto de higuero.

—Sí, hijo mío. Hombre.

—¿Y lo mataron?

crushing the valleys, swallowing up the tallest peaks, extinguishing life . . . life?

Quickly, he closed his eyes. *I do not believe in his power. I do not believe.* He looked again, and the world had returned to its proper perspective. The swollen belly was now just that. He felt greatly relieved, and was able to smile. But he did not. He did not allow his face to reflect even slightly what he felt inside. He had learned with the new gods.

They smiled when they hated: behind their friendliness lurked death. They spoke of love, and enslaved a man. Theirs was a religion of charity and forgiveness, and they whipped the backs of those who wished to serve them freely. They said they were as humble as the mysterious child born in a manger, yet with furious arrogance they trampled upon the faces of the vanquished. They were as fierce as the Caribs. Except perhaps for the fact that they did not eat human flesh. They were gods, nevertheless. They were, because of how they looked, different from all others known by man. And for the thunder encased in their black trumpets. They were gods. *My friends from beyond the sea are gods,* Agüeybana the Elder had said.

He felt the others looking at him and raised his eyes towards them. They looked at each other in silence. He thought they were going to say something, perhaps suggest they abandon the vigil. But in their friendly faces he could detect neither concern nor impatience. Their looks were firm and assuring. Almost as though they were trying to hearten him. Again, he felt like smiling. But his face remained hard as stone.

He raised his head to look upward. The clouds were now earth-colored. Up higher, though, were yellow gleamings. And it was right that this be so, because that was the color of the metal which the new gods worshipped. And up there, in the invisible heights called Heaven, where the supreme god of these strange beings reigned, everything, doubtlessly, must be yellow. Strange, inexplicable supreme god, who became a man and dwelt among men, and because of this was sacrificed.

"But was he a man, a flesh-and-bone man like us?" he had asked the white adviser, who wore a long, dark gray cloak, and whose head was as bare as the higuero gourd.

"Yes, my son. A man."

"And they killed him?"

—Sí, lo mataron.

—¿Y murió de verdad? ¿Como muere un hombre?

—Como muere un hombre. Pero al tercer dia había resucitado.

—¿Resucitado?

—Se levantó de entre los muertos. Volvió a la vida.

—¿Al tercer día?

—Resucitado.

—Y si a ustedes los matan, ¿volverán a estar vivos al tercer día?

—Sólo resucitaremos para ser juzgados.

—¿Juzgados?

—En el Juicio del Dios Padre.

—¿Y cuándo será ese día?

—Cuando no exista el mundo.

—¿Tardará mucho?

—¿Mucho? Quizá. Cientos, miles de años.

Y el dios de nagua parda había sonreído. Y posando la mano derecha sobre su hombro desnudo, le empezó a hablar de cosas aún más extrañas con voz que sonaba agridulce, como la jagua.

—Tú también, hijo mío, si vivieras en la fe de Cristo, vivirías eternamente . . .

Él oía la voz, pero ya no percibía las palabras. Ciertamente no tenía interés en vivir la eternidad bajo el yugo de los dioses nuevos. Agüeybana el Viejo había muerto. Le sucedía ahora Agüeybana el Bravo. Eran otros tiempos. Y si la magia de los dioses blancos no tenía el poder de volverlos a la vida hasta el fin del mundo . . .

La idea surgió súbita como un fogonazo lanzado por Jurakán. Su ser, hasta las más hondas raíces, experimentó el aturdimiento. Casi cayó de bruces. Sintió un miedo espantoso de haberlo pensado. Pero simultáneamente surgió en él una sensación liberadora. Se puso en pie con ganas de reír y llorar. Y echó a correr dando alaridos. Atrás quedó la risa de los seres blancos. Y entre carcajadas oyó cómo repetían las voces: ¡Loco! ¡Loco!

Bajó la vista y observó la marcha implacable de las hormigas. Ya no subían por la ruta inicial del lóbulo. Habían asaltado la oreja por todos los flancos y avanzaban en masa, atrope-

"Yes, they killed him."
"And he really died? As a man dies?"
"As a man dies. But by the third day he had risen."

"Risen?"
"Yes, from the dead. He returned to life."
"The third day?"
"Returned to life."
"And if you are killed, will you rise again by the third day?"

"We shall only live again to be judged."
"Judged?"
"In the Judgment of the Holy Father."
"And when shall that be?"
"When the world no longer exists."
"Shall that be long from now?"
"Long? Perhaps. Hundreds, thousands of years."

And the god with the dark gray cloak had smiled. And, resting his hand upon his naked shoulder, he began to speak to him of even stranger things, in a voice that sounded bittersweet, like the jagua fruit.

"You, too, my son, shall live forever, if you live in the faith of Christ . . ."

He heard the voice, but no longer perceived the words. He certainly had no interest in living forever under the yoke of the new gods. Agüeybana the Elder had died. He was now succeeded by Agüeybana the Brave. Things were different now. And if the magic of the white gods was unable to bring them back to life until the world came to an end . . .

The idea came suddenly, like a flash of lightning hurled by Juracán. He was totally stunned by it. Down to his deepest roots, he felt bewilderment. He nearly fell to his knees. He felt dreadfully afraid for having thought of it. But at the same time he felt a liberating sensation. He stood up, wanting to laugh and cry. And he began to run, letting out loud howls and whoops. Left behind him was the laughter of the white man. And amidst outbursts of laughter he heard how the voices repeated: Loco! loco!*

He looked down and observed the implacable march of the

* Juracán, from which is derived the word "hurricane," was the Taino Indian word for the God of Evil.

lladamente, con una prisa desconcertante, como si en el interior del hombre se celebrase una gran guasábara.

—Necesito una prueba, una prueba de lo que dices.

—Yo te traeré la prueba—dijo él a Agüeybana el Bravo.

Obtenerla era un riesgo demoníaco. Lo sabía. Pero había fe en su corazón. El insufló su fe segura en dos naborías rebeldes. Cruzaron los tres el bosque se pusieron en acecho, dominando aquel paraje junto al río. Esperaron. Terminaba el día cuando llegó a la orilla el hombre color de yuca. Intentó dos veces vadear el río. Podría creerse que no sabía nadar. O quizá sólo trataba de no echar a perder sus ropas nuevas. Miedo no sentiría. Era uno de los bravos. Él lo sabía.

Hizo seña a los otros de que estuvieran listos. Y salió de la espesura. Saludó sonriendo. Él podía conducir al dios blanco por un vado seguro. El otro, sin vacilar, le extendió la mano.

La mano color de yuca era fina como helecho. Y tibia como el casabe que se ha tostado al sol. La suya, en cambio, ardía como tea encendida de tabonuco. En el lugar previsto, dio un brutal tirón de la mano blanca. Aprovechando la momentánea pérdida de equilibrio, se abalanzó sobre el cuerpo. Y hundió sus dedos en el cuello fino, y sumergió la dorada cabeza en el agua, que se rompió en burbujas. Los otros ya habían acudido en su ayuda. Aquietaban tenazmente los convulsos movimientos, manteniendo todo el cuerpo bajo el agua. Y fluyó el tiempo. Y fluyó el río. Y el fluir de la brisa sorprendió la inmovilidad de tres cuerpos en el acto sacrílego.

Se miraron. Esperaban una manifestación de magia. No podían evitar el esperarlo. Surgiría de las aguas como un dios de la venganza.

Pero el dios no se movía. Lo sacaron de las aguas. Y tendieron sus despojos en un claro junto al río.

—Esperemos a que el sol muera y nazca por tres veces—dijo él.

Esperaban en cuclillas. Se iniciaba el día tercero y la cosa nunca vista aún podía suceder.

Desde el río subió súbito un viento helado que agitó las yerbas junto al cuerpo. Y el hedor subió hasta ellos. Y los tres as-

ants. They no longer followed the initial route of the lobe. They had attacked the ear from all sides and advanced en masse, with disconcerting haste, as though a great war council were being celebrated in the man's interior.

"I need proof, proof of what you say."

"I shall bring you proof," he said to Agüeybana the Brave.

He planned it by himself. He transmitted his faith to two fellow tribesmen. The three of them crossed the forest and prepared their ambush. They waited. The day was waning when the yucca-colored man came to the river bank. Twice he tried to wade across. One might believe he didn't know how to swim. Or perhaps he didn't want to ruin his new clothing. He could not be afraid, for this god was one of the brave ones. He knew it.

He signaled to the others to be ready. And he emerged from the thicket, greeting him with a smile. He could lead the white god to a shallower place. The other, without hesitating, put his hand out to him.

The yucca-colored hand was as delicate as fern. And lukewarm, like cassava toasted in the sun. His, in contrast, burned like a lit torch of tabonuco wood. At the planned spot, he tugged brutally at the white hand. Taking advantage of the momentary loss of balance, he threw himself upon the body. He dug his fingers into the thin neck, and submerged the golden head into the water, which erupted in bubbles. The others had already come to his aid. Tenaciously they held onto the body which moved in convulsions, keeping it completely under water. And time flowed by. And the river flowed. And the flow of the breeze caught the three men, immobile, in the midst of their sacrilegious act.

They looked at each other, They were expecting some manifestation of magic. They could not help but expect it. He would surge up from the waters like a vengeful god.

But the god didn't move. They pulled him from the water. And they stretched him out in a clearing by the river.

"Let us wait for the sun to die and be born three times," he said.

Crouched there, they waited. The third day was beginning, and unimaginable things could still happen.

From the river, a sudden cold gust of wind came up and shook the weeds next to the body. And the stench floated up to

piraron aquel vaho repugnante con fruición, con deleite casi. Las miradas convergieron en un punto: el vientre hinchado.

Había crecido desmesuradamente. Por la tela desgarrada quedaba ya al desnudo todo el tope de piel tirante y lívida. Hipnotizados, no podían apartar sus ojos de aquella cosa monstruosa. Respiraban apenas. También la tierra contenía su aliento. Callaban las higuacas en el bosque. No se oían los coquíes. Allá abajo, el río enmudeció el rumor del agua. Y la brisa se detuvo para dar paso al silencio. Los tres hombres esperaban. De pronto, ocurrió, ocurrió ante sus ojos.

Fue un estampido de espanto. El vientre hinchado se abrió, esparciendo por los aires toda la podredumbre que puede contener un hombre. El hedor era capaz de ahuyentar una centena. Pero ellos eran tres. Sólo tres. Y permanecieron quietos.

Hasta que él se puso en pie y dijo:

—No son dioses.

A una seña suya, los otros procedieron a colocar los despojos en una hamaca de algodón azul. Luego cada cual se echó un extremo de la hamaca al hombro. Inmóviles ya, esperaron sus órdenes.

Los miró un instante con ternura. Sonriendo al fin, dio la señal de partida.

—*Será libre mi pueblo. Será libre.*

No lo dijo. Lo pensó tan sólo. Y acercando sus labios al fotuto, echó al silencio de la noche el ronco sonido prolongado de su triunfo.

them. And the three of them breathed in that repugnant odor with relief, almost with delight. Their eyes all converged upon one spot: the swollen belly.

It had grown tremendously. The strained, livid dome rose nakedly through the shredded cloth. Hypnotized, they could not look away from that monstrous thing. They barely breathed. Even the earth held its breath. The *higuacas* fell silent in the forest. The *coquís* could not be heard. Down below, the sound of the river was muted. And the breeze stopped to let the silence by. The three men waited. Suddenly it happened, it happened before their eyes.

It was a frightful sound. The swollen belly split opened, scattering into the air all the rottenness a man can hold. The stench was enough to frighten off a hundred men. But they were three. Just three. And they remained still.

Until he stood up and said:

"They are not gods."

At his signal, the others began to put the remains into a blue cotton hammock. Then each of them lifted an end of the hammock to his shoulder. Standing motionless, they awaited his orders.

For an instant, he looked at them tenderly. Finally, smiling, he gave the signal to depart.

My people will be free. Free.

He didn't say it. He only thought it. And putting his lips to the seashell trumpet, he flung into the silence of the night a hoarse, prolonged sound of triumph.

—tr. Kal Wagenheim

PURIFICACIÓN EN LA CALLE DE CRISTO*

René Marqués

—LA casa está sola—dijo Inés. Y Emilia asintió.

Aunque no era cierto. Allí también estaba Hortensia, como siempre, las tres reunidas en la gran sala, las tres puertas de dos hojas cerradas como siempre sobre el balcón, las persianas apenas entreabiertas, la luz del amanecer rompiéndose en tres colores (azul, amarillo, rojo) a través de los cristales alemanes que formaban una rueda trunca sobre cada una de las puertas, o un sol tricolor, trunco también, cansado de haber visto morir un siglo y nacer otro, de las innumerables capas de polvo que la lluvia arrastraba luego, y de los años de salitre depositados sobre los cristales una vez transparentes, y que ahora parecían esmerilados, oponiendo mayor resistencia a la luz, a todo lo de afuera que pudiera ser claro, o impuro, o extraño (hiriente en fin).

—¿Recuerdas?—preguntó Inés. Y Emilia asintió.

No era preciso asentir a algo determinado porque la vida toda era un recuerdo, o quizá una serie de recuerdos, y en cualquiera de ellos podía situarse cómodamente para asentir a la pregunta de Inés, que pudo haber sido formulada por Hortensia, o por ella misma, y no precisamente en el instante de este amanecer, sino el día anterior o el mes pasado o un año antes, aunque el recuerdo bien pudiera remontarse al otro siglo: Estrasburgo, por ejemplo, en aquella época imprecisa (impreciso

*Cuento publicado originalmente en la Revista del Instituto de Cultura Puertorriqueña (número 37 de 1958). En este cuento basó el autor su drama *Los soles truncos,* estrenado en San Juan en 1958.

PURIFICATION ON CRISTO STREET*

René Marqués

Time is the fire in which we burn.
Delmore Schwartz
(Time is the Fire)

"THE house is lonely," Inés said. And Amelia assented.

Although it was not true. Hortensia was also there, as usual, the three of them gathered in the big parlor, the three double doors leading to the balcony shut as usual, the slats barely open, the early morning light splitting into three colors (blue, yellow, red) through the panes of German glass which formed a truncated circle above each of the doors, or a tricolored sun, also truncated, tired from having seen one century die and another born, from the innumerable layers of dust which the rain would later wash away, and from the years of saltpeter deposited on the once transparent panes of glass, which were now clouded over, offering greater resistance to the light, to everything from without that might be clear, or impure, or strange (harmful, in short).

"Remember?" Inés asked. And Amelia assented.

It was not necessary to assent to something definite because her entire life was a memory, or perhaps a series of memories, and she could easily place herself in any of them in order to assent to Inés' question, which could have been asked by Hortensia, or by Amelia herself, and not necessarily this morning at the present moment but yesterday or last month or a year ago, even though the memory might well go back to the previous century: Strasbourg, for example, during the imprecise era (impre-

*Short story originally published in the *Revista del Instituto de Cultura Puertorriqueña* (no. 37, 1958). This story was later adapted by the author into his play, *Los soles truncos,* first performed in San Juan in 1958.

era el orden cronológico, no el recuerdo ciertamente), en que las tres se preparaban en el colegio para ser lo que a su rango correspondía en la ciudad de San Juan, adivinando ella e Inés que sería Hortensia quien habría de deslumbrar en los salones, aunque las tres aprendieran por igual los pequeños secretos de vivir graciosamente en un mundo apacible y equilibrado, donde no habría cabida para lo que no fuese bello, para las terribles vulgaridades de una humanidad que no debía (no podía) llegar hasta las frágiles *fräulein,* protegidas no tanto por los espesos muros del colegio como por la labor complicada de los encajes, y los tapices, y la bruma melodiosa de los *lieder,* y la férrea caballerosidad de los más jóvenes oficiales prusianos. ¡Hortensia! Hortensia, en su traje de raso azul, cuando asistió a la primera recepción en La Fortaleza (el Gobernador General bailando una mazurca con su hermana mayor bajo la mirada fría de papá Bukhart). Eso es. Hortensia ya en San Juan. El colegio, atrás en el tiempo. Y ella, Emilia, observando el mundo deslumbrante del palacio colonial en esa noche memorable, al lado de la figura imponente de la madre. (Mamá Eugenia, con su soberbio porte de reina; su cabello oscuro y espeso como el vino de Málaga sobre el cual tan bien lucía la diadema de zafiros y brillantes; con su tez pálida y mate que el sol del trópico inútilmente había tratado de dorar, porque el sol de Andalucía le había dado ya el tinte justo; con su traje negro de encajes y su enorme pericón de ébano y seda, donde un cisne violáceo se deslizaba siempre sobre un estanque con olor a jazmín.) Y ella, Emilia, con sus trenzas apretadas (odiosas trenzas), hecha un ovillo de rubor cuando el alférez español se inclinó galante a su oído para murmurar: *Es usted más hermosa que su hermana Hortensia.*

Inés vio a Emilia asentir a su pregunta y pensó: *No puedes recordar, Emilia. Los más preciosos recuerdos los guardo yo.*

Porque a su pregunta, *¿Recuerdas?,* supo que Emilia iría a refugiarse en el recuerdo de siempre. Que no era en verdad un recuerdo, sino la sombra de un recuerdo, porque Emilia no lo había vivido.

Emilia, con sus trenzas apretadas (hermosas trenzas), se había quedado en casa con la vieja nana. (Emilia, con su pequeño pie torcido desde aquella terrible caída del caballo en la hacienda de Toa Alta, obstinada en huir de la gente, aún en el

cise was the chronological order, certainly not the memory), when the three girls were in boarding school preparing for whatever would correspond to their social position in the city of San Juan, when she and Inés guessed that Hortensia would be the belle of the ball, although all three learned equally well the little secrets of graceful living in a peaceful, well-adjusted world, where there was no room for ugliness, for the terrible vulgarities of humanity, which ought not (could not) reach these delicate *fraülein,* protected not so much by the thick walls of the school as by the intricate labor of the laces, and the tapestries, and the melodious haze of the *lieder,* and the staunch chivalry of the youngest Prussian officers. Hortensia! Hortensia in her blue satin gown when she attended the first reception in La Fortaleza (the Governor General dancing a mazurka with her older sister under Papa Bukhart's cold stare). Yes. Hortensia already in San Juan. The school, farther back in time. And she, Amelia, observing the dazzling world of the colonial palace on that memorable night, beside the imposing figure of her mother. (Mama Eugenia, with her regal bearing; her hair, dark and thick like the wine from Málaga, upon which she displayed so well the sapphire and diamond tiara; with her pale complexion which the tropical sun had tried in vain to gild, because the Andalusian sun had already lent it just the proper tint; with her black lace dress and her enormous ebony and silk fan with its violet swan gliding forever upon a jasmine-scented pool.) And she, Amelia, with her tight braids (awful braids), melted from shame and embarrassment when the Spanish ensign bowed gallantly to whisper in her ear: *You are prettier than your sister Hortensia.*

Inés saw Amelia assent to her question and thought: *You cannot remember, Amelia. The most precious memories are mine to keep.*

Because to her question, *Remember?* she knew that Amelia would seek refuge in the same memory as always. It was not really a memory, simply the shadow of a memory, because Amelia had not lived it.

Amelia, with her tight braids (pretty braids) had remained at home with the old nursemaid. (Amelia, with her tiny foot twisted from that terrible fall from the horse on the estate at Toa Alta, determined to avoid people, even at boarding school, al-

colegio, siempre apartada de los corros, del bullicio; haciendo esfuerzos dolorosos por ocultar su cojera, que no era tan ostensible después de todo, pero que tan hondo hería su orgullo; refugiándose en los libros o en el cuaderno de versos que escribía a hurtadillas.) Y ella, Inés, no logrando lucir hermosa en el traje color perla que hacía resaltar su tipo mediterráneo, porque tenía el mismo color de tez de mamá Eugenia, el mismo cabello espeso y oscuro, pero inútilmente, porque nada había en sus rasgos que hiciese recordar la perfección helena del rostro materno (era francamente fea: desde pequeña se lo había revelado la crueldad del espejo y de la gente) y su fealdad se acentuaba entre estos seres excepcionalmente hermosos: papá Bukhart, con su apariencia de dios nórdico, Hortensia, mamá Eugenia, y aún la lisiada Emilia, con su belleza transparente y rítmica, como uno de sus versos. No debió entonces sorprenderle el haber escuchado (¡sin proponérselo, Dios Santo!) las palabras que el joven alférez deslizara al oído de Hortensia: *Es usted la más deslumbrante belleza de esta recepción, señorita Hortensia* (fue poco después de haber bailado Hortensia la mazurca con el Gobernador General). Y en realidad no le sorprendió. Le dolió, en cambio. No porque ella dejase de reconocer la belleza de su hermana, sino porque las palabras provenían de *él*.

Emilia se levantó y, cojeando lastimosamente, fue a pasar con suavidad su pañolito de encajes por la mejilla izquierda de Hortensia.

—Le pusiste demasiados polvos de arroz en este lado— explicó, al sorprender la mirada inquieta de Inés. Luego volvió a sentarse.

Las tres permanecían silenciosas e inmóviles (Emilia e Inés sin apartar los ojos de Hortensia).

—¿Verdad que está hermosa?—preguntó Emilia en voz baja.

Lo estaba. Amorosamente la habían vestido con sus galas de novia. Bajo la luz del cirio todo lo blanco adquiría un tinte maravilloso. O era quizá el tiempo. El velo se había desgarrado. Pero los azahares estaban intactos. Y las manchas del traje pudieron disimularse gracias a los pliegues hábilmente dispuestos por Inés. Lástima que la caja no fuese digna de su contenido: un burdo ataúd cedido por Beneficencia Municipal.

Emilia suspiró. Esperaba. Pero Inés no parecía tener prisa.

ways away from the groups, the noise; making painful attempts to hide her lameness, which was not so noticeable after all, but which deeply wounded her pride; seeking refuge in books or in the notebook of verses that she was secretly writing.) And she, Inés, never able to look pretty in the pearl-colored dress that brought out her Mediterranean type, because she did have the same color complexion as Mama Eugenia, the same thick, dark hair, but to no avail, for there was nothing in her features that recalled the Hellenic perfection of the mother's face (she was downright unattractive: since she was a little girl the cruelty of her mirror and of other people had revealed this fact to her) and her ugliness stood out all the more among these exceptionally handsome beings: Papa Bukhart, looking like a Nordic god, Hortensia, Mama Eugenia, and even the lame Amelia, with her beauty as transparent and rhythmic as one of her verses. She should not have been surprised then on overhearing (accidentally, of course!) the words which the young ensign whispered to Hortensia: *You are the most dazzling beauty at this reception, Miss Hortensia* (it was shortly after Hortensia had danced the mazurka with the Governor General). And actually it did not surprise her. Instead, it pained her. Not because she failed to recognize her sister's beauty, but because the words came from *him.*

Amelia got up and, limping pitifully, went over to touch Hortensia's left cheek ever so lightly with her little lace handkerchief.

"You put too much rice powder on this side," she explained, noticing Inés' anxious glance. Then she sat down again.

The three of them remained silent and motionless (Amelia and Inés never taking their eyes off Hortensia).

"Doesn't she look truly beautiful?" Amelia asked quietly.

She did. They had lovingly dressed her in her wedding gown. Beneath the light from the single candle the white took on a marvellous glow. Or perhaps it was from time. The veil had been torn, but the orange blossoms were intact. And the stains on the dress could be concealed thanks to the folds which Inés had arranged so cleverly. What a pity that the casket was not worthy of its contents: just a crude coffin donated by Public Welfare.

Amelia sighed. And waited. But Inés did not seem in a hurry.

Estaba allí, encorvada, con su escaso pelo gris cayéndole sobre la frente, el rostro descuartizado por una red implacable de arrugas profundas, terriblemente fea en su callada determinación. Y a Emilia se le ocurrió pensar qué hubiese hecho Inés en el lugar de Hortensia. Aunque de inmediato se vio forzada a rechazar la proposición porque *nadie* pudo haber estado en el lugar de Hortensia. (Hortensia dijo *no* a la vida. Quienquiera que le hubiese revelado la verdad había sido cruel en demasía. ¿Hubo alguien que en realidad conociese a Hortensia? ¿Hubo alguien que *previese* su reacción?)

De todos modos lo supo: el rapacillo de la mulata (la mulata que tenía su puesto en un zaguán de la Calle Imperial), el que gateaba entre los manojos de saúco y albahaca y yerbabuena, tenía azules los ojos. Un alférez español puede amar hoy y haberle dado ayer el azul de sus ojos al rapacillo de una yerbatera. Hasta la imponente mamá Eugenia dio sus razones para excusar el hecho. (Papá Bukhart, no. Papá Bukhart siempre dejó que el mundo girara bajo su mirada fría de naturalista alemán convertido en hacendado del trópico.) Pero Hortensia dijo *no,* aunque antes había dicho *sí,* y aunque los encajes de su traje de novia hubiesen venido de Estrasburgo. Y la casa de la Calle del Cristo cerró sus tres puertas sobre el balcón de azulejos. El tiempo entonces se partió en dos: atrás quedóse el mundo estable y seguro de la buena vida; y el presente tornóse en el comienzo de un futuro preñado de desastres, como si el *no* de Hortensia hubiese sido el filo atroz de un cuchillo que cercenara el tiempo y dejase escapar por su herida un torbellino de cosas jamás soñadas: La armada de un pueblo nuevo y bárbaro bombardeó a San Juan. Y poco después murió mamá Eugenia (de anemia perniciosa, según el galeno; sólo para que papá Bukhart fríamente rechazase el diagnóstico porque mamá Eugenia había muerto de dolor al ver una bandera extraña ocupar en lo alto de La Fortaleza el lugar que siempre ocupara su pendón rojo y gualda). Y cuando el lujoso féretro de caoba desapareció por el zaguán, todos tuvieron conciencia de que el mundo había perdido su equilibrio. Como lo demostró papá Bukhart al pisar ya apenas la casa de la Calle del Cristo. Y pasar semanas enteras en la hacienda de Toa Alta, desbocando caballos por las vegas de caña. Hasta que un día su cuerpo de dios nórdico fue conducido por cuatro peones negros a la casa de los soles truncos (casi no podía reconocérsele en su improvisado sudario de polvo y

She was there, stoop-shouldered, with her sparse gray hair falling upon her forehead, her face crossed by an implacable network of deep wrinkles, terribly ugly in her quiet determination. And Amelia happened to think about what Inés would have done had she been Hortensia. She was forced to reject the idea immediately, however, because *no one* could have been in Hortensia's place. (Hortensia said *No* to life. Whoever had revealed the truth to her had been extremely cruel. Did anyone really know Hortensia? Could anyone have *foreseen* her reaction?)

One way or another she did find out: the mulatto woman's little boy (the same mulatto woman who had her stall in a doorway on Imperial Street), the child who crawled about among the bunches of elder, sweet basil, and peppermint leaves, had blue eyes. A Spanish ensign can love today and still have given yesterday the blue of his eyes to the child of a peddler woman. Even the imposing Mama Eugenia gave reasons for excusing the deed. (But not Papa Bukhart. Papa Bukhart always let the world go its way beneath the cold stare of a German naturalist transformed into a tropical landowner.) But Hortensia said *No,* even though earlier she had said *Yes* and the laces for her wedding gown had already arrived from Strasbourg. And the house on Cristo Street shut its three doors on the tiled balcony. Time was then divided in two: behind remained the safe, unchanging world of the good life; and the present became the beginning of a future fraught with disasters, and though Hortensia's *No* had been the cruel edge of a knife rending time and allowing a whirlwind of unimaginable things to escape through the wound: the armada of a new and barbaric people bombarded San Juan. And shortly thereafter, Mama Eugenia died (from pernicious anemia according to the physician, just so Papa Bukhart might coldly reject this diagnosis, because Mama Eugenia had died from the sorrow of seeing a strange flag occupying the spot above La Fortaleza where her flag of red and gold had always flown). And when the ornate mahogany casket disappeared through the street hallway, they all became aware that the world had lost its equilibrium. As evidenced by Papa Bukhart, who hardly ever set foot anymore in the house on Cristo Street. He would spend weeks at a time on the estate in Toa Alta breaking in horses in the cane flats. Until one day four colored peons brought his body like that of a Nordic god to the house of the

sangre). Y el mundo se hizo aún más estrecho, aunque a su estrechez llegaran luego noticias de una gran guerra en la Europa lejana, y cesara entonces la débil correspondencia sostenida con algunos parientes de Estrasburgo, y con los tíos de Málaga. Pero habrían de transcurrir dos años más para que en San Juan muriera la nana negra, y en Europa, Estrasburgo pasara a manos de Francia, y el mundo fuese ya un recinto cerrado al cual sólo tuviese acceso el viejo notario que hablaba de contribuciones, de crisis, de la urgencia de vender la hacienda de Toa Alta a los americanos del Norte, y Hortensia pudiese acoger siempre la proposición con su sonrisa helada: *Jamás nuestras tierras serán de los bárbaros.*

Inés casi se sobresaltó al ver a Emilia levantarse e ir a pasar su destrozado pañolito de encajes por la mejilla de Hortensia. Le pareció pueril la preocupación de Emilia por los polvos de arroz. Si ella le había puesto más polvos en la mejilla izquierda a Hortensia había sido sencillamente para ocultar la mancha negruzca que desde hacía años había aparecido en aquella zona de la piel de su hermana. Nunca hacía cosa alguna sin motivo. Nunca.

Emilia estaba nerviosa (era obvio que estaba nerviosa) y, sin embargo, se mostró decidida cuando le comunicó su plan. Había temido alguna resistencia de parte de su hermana. Pero Emilia había alzado hacia ella su mirada color violeta y había sonreído al murmurar: *Sí. Purificación.* Sin duda interpretaba el acto de un modo simbólico. Era una suerte. Hacía tanto tiempo que Emilia no escribía versos. En el cofre de sándalo descansaba el manojo de cuartillas amarillentas. Mamá Eugenia siempre sonrió leyendo los versos de Emilia. (Papá Bukhart, no. Y es que Emilia jamás osó mostrarle su cuaderno.) A ella, a Inés, le producían en cambio un extraño desasosiego. *Soy piedra pequeña entre tus manos de musgo.* Le desconcertaba la ausencia de rima. Y, sin embargo, sentía como el vértigo de un inasible ritmo arrastrándola a un mundo íntimo que la producía malestar. Emilia nunca explicaba sus versos. Y ese misterioso estar y no estar en el ámbito de un alma ajena la seducía y la angustiaba a la vez. *Tu pie implacable hollando mis palabras, tu pie de fauno sobre una palabra: amor.* No podía precisarlo, pero había algo obsceno en todo esto, algo que no era posible relacionar con el violeta pálido de los ojos de Emilia, ni con su pie lisiado, ni con su gesto

truncated suns (he was scarcely recognizable in his improvised shroud of dust and blood). And the world became even narrower, although to this narrowness there arrived news of a great war in far-off Europe; and then the slight correspondence maintained with a few relatives in Strasbourg and the aunts and uncles in Málaga ceased. But two more years would have to pass before the old colored nursemaid would die in San Juan, and in Europe Strasbourg would become French, and the world would be but a closed confine accessible only to the old notary who spoke of taxes, of crises, of the urgency of selling the estate at Toa Alta to the North Americans, and Hortensia, with her icy smile, could harbor the assertion that *Our lands will never belong to the barbarians.*

Inés was startled to see Amelia get up and go over to wipe Hortensia's cheek with her frayed lace handkerchief. Amelia's concern for the rice powder seemed childish. She had put more powder on Hortensia's left cheek simply to cover the blackish stain which had appeared years ago on that part of her sister's skin. She never did anything without a reason. Never.

Amelia was nervous (it was obvious that she was nervous), nevertheless she appeared determined when she heard about her plan. She had feared some resistance from her sister, but Amelia had raised her violet-colored glance and had smiled as she murmured: *Yes. Purification.* She undoubtedly interpreted the act symbolically. It was better that way. Amelia had not written any verses for such a long time now. The handful of yellowed pages rested in the sandalwood coffer. Mama Eugenia always smiled when reading Amelia's verses. (But not Papa Bukhart. Amelia never dared to show him her notebook.) They produced a strange uneasiness in Inés, on the other hand. *I am a tiny pebble between your hands of moss.* The lack of rhyme disconcerted her, but still she felt the vertigo of some unseizable rhythm pulling her toward an intimate world which caused her to be upset. Amelia never explained her verses. And that mysterious being and not being within the confines of another's soul attracted and tormented her at the same time. *Your implacable foot trampling upon my words, your faun's foot upon a single word: love.* She could not express it precisely, but there was something obscene in all this, something impossible to reconcile

de niño tímido y asustadizo. O quizá lo obsceno era precisamente eso, que fuese Emilia quien escribiese versos así. Lo peor había sido el *tu* innombrado, pero siempre presente en las cuartillas amarillentas. *Soy cordero de Pascua para TU espada, Valle del Eco para TU voz.* ¡La angustia de ese *tu* . . . ! ¿Podía ser otro que *él?*

No tenía prisa. Sabía que Emilia estaba impaciente. Pero ella no *podía* tener prisa. Necesitaba esos minutos para volcarse toda dentro de sí misma. Porque habían sido muchos los años de convivencia y miseria, de frases pueriles y largos silencios, de hambre y orgullo y penumbra y vejez. Pero nunca de estar a solas consigo misma. Viviendo Hortensia había sido imposible. Pero ahora . . .

El tiempo era como un sol trunco (azul, amarillo, rojo) proyectando su esmerilada fatiga sobre la gran sala. Sin embargo, el tiempo había sido también transparente. Lo había sido en el instante aquel en que viera allí a Hortensia con su bata blanca de encajes. Estaba casi de perfil y el rojo de un cristal daba sobre su cabeza produciendo una aureola fantástica de sangre, o de fuego quizá. Ella la observaba a través del espejo de la consola. Y deseó de pronto que la vida fuese un espejo donde no existieran las palabras. Pero las palabras habían sido pronunciadas. La fría superficie de la luna había rechazado su voz, y las palabras flotaban aún en la gran sala, irremediablemente dispersas, sin posibilidad alguna de recogerlas (de aprisionarlas de nuevo en su garganta), porque la vida no cabía dentro del marco del espejo, sino que transcurría más acá, en el tiempo, en un espacio sin límites, donde otra voz podría responder a sus palabras:

—Gracias por decírmelo—y era la voz de Hortensia. Luego un silencio corto y agudo como un grito, y de nuevo la voz—: No me casaré, desde luego.

Sus ojos se apartaron entonces del perfil reflejado junto al piano y resbalaron por la imagen de su propio rostro. Y toda su carne se estremeció. Porque jamás había sido su fealdad como en aquel instante. Y vio a Hortensia (su imagen en el espejo) apartarse del piano de palo de rosa y acercarse a ella lentamente. Y en su movimiento había abandonado la zona del cristal rojo y pasado por la zona del cristal azul, pero al detenerse a sus espaldas ya había entrado en la zona del cristal amarillo, de modo que

with the pale violet of Amelia's eyes, or with her own injured foot, or with her mannerisms of a timid, easily frightened child. Or perhaps the obscene thing was simply the fact that it was Amelia who wrote such verses. Worst of all was the unnamed *your* ever present in the yellowing sheets. *I am a paschal lamb for YOUR sword, Echo Valley for YOUR voice*. The anguish of that *your* . . . ! Could it be anyone but *he*?

She was not in a hurry. She knew that Amelia was impatient; but she *could* not hurry. She needed those minutes to reflect upon herself, because the years of misery and living together, of childish remarks and long silences, of hunger and pride and darkness and old age had been many. But never had she been alone with her own self. It had been impossible while Hortensia was alive. But now . . .

Time was like a truncated sun (blue, yellow, red) projecting its burnished fatigue over the big parlor. Nevertheless, time had also been transparent. It was thus at that moment when she saw Hortensia there in her white lace dressing gown. She was almost in profile and the red light from one of the panes shone upon her head producing a fantastic aureola of blood, or perhaps of fire. She observed her in the mirror over the pier table. And she suddenly wished that life were a mirror where words did not exist. But the words had been pronounced. The cold surface of the glass had repelled her voice, and the words still floated in the big parlor, irremediably dispersed, without any possibility of retrieving them or imprisoning them once more in her throat, because life did not fit within the mirror frame but moved closer, in time, where another voice would respond to her words:

"Thank you for telling me." It was Hortensia's voice. Then a silence short and sharp like a scream, and again the voice: "I shan't marry, of course."

Her eyes then turned from the profile reflected beside the piano and fell upon the image of her own face. And all her flesh shuddered, for never had she seen her ugliness as in that instant. She saw Hortensia (her reflection in the mirror) move away from the rosewood piano and slowly approach her. As she moved, she left the area of red glass, passed through the area of blue glass, and then she moved into the slanting beam streaming from the yellow glass, so that her face appeared enveloped in

su rostro parecía envuelto en un polvillo de oro como si después del tiempo de la vida y del tiempo del sueño entrase en un tiempo que podía ser de eternidad, desde el cual sus ojos fuesen capaces de romper el misterio del espejo para buscar los otros ojos angustiados, y aunque la voz de Hortensia no tuviese el poder de traspasar la superficie límpida, no era preciso que así fuese porque las palabras, de ser pronunciadas, rebotarían como imágenes para penetrar en su fealdad reflejada, y hacerla sentir el pavor de esa fealdad (o acentuar el pavor ya desatado):
—Es mejor así. Porque jamás *compartiría* yo el amor de un hombre. ¡Jamás!

Y ella sintió verdadero espanto, pues le pareció que Hortensia no se refería a la yerbatera de la Calle Imperial. Y pensó en Emilia. Pero el espejo no contenía en su breve mundo la imagen de Emilia, sino la suya propia. Y de pronto todas las palabras pronunciadas, las suyas también: *Tiene una querida, Hortensia; y un hijo en esa mulata,* le golpearon el pecho con tal ímpetu que le impidieron respirar. Y el espejo fue convirtiéndose en una bruma espesa que crecía, y crecía, y su cuerpo empezó a caer en un abismo sin límites, cayendo, cayendo más hondo, hasta chocar bruscamente contra un suelo alfombrado de gris.

El cuerpo de Hortensia permanecía en una zona a la cual no llegaba la luz tricolor del alba. Sólo el cirio derramaba su débil claridad de topacio sobre el rostro enmarcado en azahares y tul.

Inés observaba los labios secos, petrificando la sonrisa enigmática, los mismos labios que en tantos años de miseria (y soberbia, y hambre y frases pueriles) jamás abordaron la palabra que hubiese dado sosiego a la eterna incertidumbre, la palabra que hubiese hecho menos infernal su tarea de proteger el orgullo de Hortensia y la invalidez de Emilia, de fingirse loca ante los acreedores, y vender las joyas más valiosas (y la plata), de cargar diariamente el agua del aljibe desde que suspendieron el servicio de acueducto, y aceptar la caridad de los vecinos, y rechazar las ofertas de compra por la casa en ruinas, e impedir que los turistas violaran el recinto en su búsqueda bárbara de miseria (alejando los husmeantes hocicos ajenos de la ruina propia y el dolor).

Emilia no podía apartar su mirada de la tenue llama del cirio, y le parecía la manecita dorada de un niño que se abría y cerraba así, a intervalos caprichosos, y le vinieron a la memoria

a fine golden dust. It was as if after the time of life and the time of dreams she had entered a time that could be eternal, from which her eyes might be able to pierce the mystery of the mirror in order to seek out those other anguished eyes; and although Hortensia's voice lacked the power to go beyond the limpid surface, it was not necessary to do so because the words, once uttered, would rebound like reflections in order to penetrate Inés' mirrored ugliness and make her feel the terror of that ugliness (or accentuate the terror already unleashed): "It's better this way. Because never would I *share* a man's love. Never!"

And Inés was truly afraid, for it seemed to her that Hortensia was not referring to the peddler woman on Imperial Street. And she thought of Amelia. But the glass did not contain Amelia's image within its brief confines, but rather her own. And suddenly all the words that had been pronounced, including hers, *He has a mistress, Hortensia; and a child by that mulatto,* beat upon her breast with such force that she could scarcely breathe. And the mirror was becoming a dense mist that grew and grew, and her body began to sink into a limitless abyss, sinking, sinking deeper, until it struck sharply against a gray-carpeted floor.

Hortensia's body remained in an area untouched by the tricolored light of dawn. Only the candle shed its faint, topaz clarity upon the face framed in orange blossoms and tulle.

Inés observed the dry lips, petrified in an enigmatic smile, the same lips that through so many years of misery (and pride, and hunger, and puerile phrases) never formed the one word that would have appeased the eternal uncertainty, the one word that would have lessened her infernal task of protecting Hortensia's pride and Amelia's invalidism, of feigning insanity in front of creditors, of selling the most valuable jewels (and the silver), of carrying water from the cistern every day since their service was suspended, of accepting charity from neighbors, of refusing offers to sell the ruined house, and of preventing the tourists from violating the premises in their barbarous search for misery (driving the strange, prying faces away from her own ruin and sorrow).

Amelia remained staring at the faint flame of the candle, which seemed to her like a child's tiny golden hand opening and closing at capricious intervals, and she recalled some incom-

unas palabras incomprensibles: *Sólo tu mano purificará mi corazón.* ¿Isaías? No era un texto sagrado. Algo más próximo (¿o remoto?) en el tiempo. *Sólo tu mano . . .* ¡Si! En las cuartillas amarillentas del cofre de sándalo. ¡Eran palabras suyas! Sonrió. Su corazón en el cofre de sándalo. Donde no habría de llegar la sonrisa helada de Hortensia ni la mirada inquisitiva de Inés. (El único lugar donde puede sobrevivir el corazón en un mundo sin razón alguna para la vida.)

Volvió sus ojos hacia Inés. Esperaba la realización del acto. Un bello acto, ciertamente. ¿Cómo pudo ocurrírsele a su hermana? Bien, se le había ocurrido. Y ella aprobaba aquel acto de purificación. Porque todo lo bello, lo que había sido hermoso, estaba contenido en aquella caja tosca que proveía la Beneficencia Municipal. (Todo lo que es bello y debe perecer, había perecido.)

Vio en ese instante a Inés ponerse de pie y tuvo un ligero estremecimiento. Le pareció más alta que nunca y creyó descubrir en su gesto y su mirada algo terriblemente hermoso que hacía olvidar momentáneamente su horrible fealdad. *¡Al fin!*, pensó, y poniéndose de pie, preguntó, sonriendo:

—¿Ya?

Inés vio la sonrisa de Emilia y sintió una punzada en un lugar remoto de su pecho porque, inexplicablemente, aquellos labios de anciana habían sonreído con la frescura y el encanto de una niña. Oyó luego la voz cascada decir:

—Espera por mí.

Y vio a Emilia alejarse, con su horrible cojera más acentuada que nunca, hacia la habitación de la izquierda. Sola ya con Hortensia, echó una ojeada a la sala. Sus ojos se detuvieron en la enorme mancha irregular que, como el mapa de un istmo que uniera en la pared dos mundos, partía desde el plafón hasta el piso. Sobre el empapelado, que una vez fuera gris y rosa, el agua había grabado su huella para hacer eterno en la sala el recuerdo del temporal. Y fue en ese mismo año de *San Felipe* cuando ella supo de la otra catástrofe. Y es que el viejo notario le ahorró en esa ocasión todos los preámbulos: la hacienda de Toa Alta había sido vendida en subasta pública para cubrir contribuciones atrasadas. Desde entonces la miseria fue el girar continuo de un remolino lento, pero implacable, que arrastraba y arrastraba, por lustros, por décadas, hasta llegar al tiempo en que los revolucionarios atacaron La Fortaleza, y se descubrió el cáncer en

prehensible words: *Only your hand will purify my heart.* Isaiah? It was not a sacred text. Something closer (or more remote?) in time. *Only your hand* . . . Yes! Among the yellowing pages in the sandalwood coffer. They were her words! She smiled. Her heart in the redwood coffer. Where neither Hortensia's icy smile nor Inés' inquisitive glance could enter (the only place where the heart can survive in a world bereft of any reason for life).

She turned her eyes toward Inés and awaited the realization of the act. A beautiful act, indeed. How could it have occurred to her sister? Well, anyway, it had. And she approved of that deed of purification. Because everything beautiful, all that had been so lovely was contained in that crude casket provided by Public Welfare. (All that is beautiful and must perish, had perished.)

At that moment she saw Inés rise and shudder slightly. She seemed taller than ever and she thought she discerned something terribly beautiful in her gestures, that made one forget momentarily her horrible ugliness. *At last!,* she thought; and getting to her feet, asked with a smile: "Now?"

Inés saw Amelia's smile and felt a sharp pain deep within her breast because somehow those ancient lips had smiled with all the freshness and charm of a young girl. Then she heard the broken voice saying, "Wait for me."

And she watched Amelia withdraw to the room at the left, her hideous limp more pronounced than ever. Alone now with Hortensia, she glanced about the parlor. Her eyes fell on the huge, irregular stain which, like the map of an isthmus uniting two worlds on the wall, went from the ceiling to the floor. Upon the wallpaper which at one time had been pink and gray, the water had left its mark in order to immortalize in the parlor the memory of the storm. And it was in that same year of the hurricane of *San Felipe* that she learned of the other catastrophe. On that occasion the old notary came right to the point: the estate at Toa Alta had been sold at public auction in order to cover unpaid taxes. Since then, misery had been like the continual turning of a slow but implacable whirlwind which dragged on and on for years, for decades, up to the time when the revolutionaries attacked La Fortaleza and the cancer was discov-

el pecho de Hortensia. Y ya no era posible tener conciencia del hambre porque el torbellino había detenido su girar de *tempo* lento ante la avasallante destrucción de las células (y el huir de la sangre, y el dolor hondo que roía sin gritos). Pero sangre y dolor petrificáronse en el pecho sin células y la sonrisa se puso fría en los labios de Hortensia. Y ayer su cuerpo no tenía aún la rigidez postrera (ella lo sabía porque acababa de lavar el cadáver) cuando al zaguán llegaron los extraños con sus ademanes amplios y sus angostas sonrisas defuncionarios probos: el Gobierno había decidido que la casa (la de la Calle del Cristo, la de los soles truncos) se convirtiese en hostería de lujo para los turistas, y los banqueros, y los oficiales de la armada aquella que bombardeó a San Juan. No fue preciso fingirse loca porque en esta ocasión estaba enloquecida. Y sus largas uñas con olor a muerta claváronse en el rostro que tenía más próximo (hasta que saltó la sangre, y desaparecieron las sonrisas). Y después sus puños golpearon despiadadamente, con la misma furia con que habían combatido la vida; golpeando así, !así!, contra la miseria, y los hombres, y el mundo, y el tiempo, y la muerte, y el hambre, y los años, y la sangre, y de nuevo la vida, y el portalón de ausubo que los otros habían logrado cerrar en su precipitada huida. Y en la pared de la sala, la enorme mancha del tiempo dibujaba el mapa de dos mundos unidos por un istmo. Y era preciso destruir el istmo.

Emilia salió de la habitación y vio a Inés de pie, inmóvil, con la vista fija en la pared de enfrente. Avanzó penosamente y fue a depositar el pequeño cofre de sándalo a los pies del féretro. *Mi corazón a tus pies, Hortensia.* Luego volvióse hacia Inés y quedó se en actitud de espera. La vio apartar los ojos de la pared y dejarlos resbalar por su rostro hasta fijarlos por un instante en el cofre de sándalo, y luego alejarse hacia la consola y tomar una bolsa de seda negra que ella no había observado sobre el mármol rosa, y regresar junto a Hortensia. Estaban ambas ante el féretro abierto e Inés derramó el contenido de la bolsa negra sobre la falda de Hortensia. Emilia observó con asombro aquellos ricos objetos que había creído devorados por el tiempo, o por el hambre (en fin, por la miseria y el tiempo).

Inés tomó la sortija de brillantes y trabajosamente pudo colocarla en el anular izquierdo de Hortensia. Luego colocó la de perlas en el dedo de Emilia. La ajorca de oro y rubíes fue a ador-

ered in Hortensia's breast. No longer was it possible to be aware of hunger because the whirlwind had stopped its slow-tempo spinning before the devastating destruction of the cells (and the fleeing of the blood, and the deep pain that gnawed silently away). But blood and pain were petrified in the cell-less breast and the smile became cold on Hortensia's lips. Yesterday her body still had not attained that final rigidity (she knew because she had just bathed the corpse) when the strangers came to the door with their broad gestures and their narrow smiles of stalwart functionaries; the Government had decided that the house (the house on Cristo Street, the house of the truncated suns) should be converted into a luxury hotel for tourists, bankers, and officers of the fleet which bombarded San Juan. It was not necessary to feign insanity, for this time she was truly enraged. And her long nails smelling of death dug deep into the nearest face (until blood came forth and the smiles disappeared). Then her fists beat mercilessly, with the same fury with which they had fought against life; beating thus, thus!, against misery, and men, and the world, and time and death, and hunger, and the years, and the blood, and life, and the great wooden door that the others had managed to close in their precipitous flight. And on the parlor wall, the enormous stain of time had drawn the map of two worlds joined by an isthmus. It was necessary to destroy the isthmus.

Amelia came out of the other room and saw Inés standing motionless, her gaze fixed on the opposite wall. She advanced painfully and went to place the small redwood coffer at the foot of the bier. *My heart at thy feet, Hortensia.* Then she turned toward Inés and waited. She saw her look from the wall to her face and then for an instant at the redwood coffer, then go to the pier table, take a black silk purse that she had not noticed on the pink marble, and return to Hortensia. They were both standing before the open casket and Inés emptied the contents of the black purse upon Hortensia's skirt. Amelia viewed with astonishment those rich objects that she had thought devoured by time or by hunger (in short, by misery and time).

Inés took the diamond ring and with some difficulty was able to place it on Hortensia's left hand. Then she placed the pearl ring on Amelia's finger. With the gold and ruby bracelet she

nar la muñeca de Hortensia. Con la diadema de zafiros y brillantes en su mano, se detuvo indecisa. Echó una ojeada a la cabeza postrada, ceñida de azahares, y con gesto decidido volvióse y ciñó la diadema de mamá Eugenia en la frente de Emilia. Tomó al fin la última prenda (el ancho anillo de oro de papá Bukhart) y, colocándolo en su propio dedo anular, salió presurosa de la estancia; sus pasos haciendo crujir la casa en ruinas.

El leve resplandor del cirio arrancaba luces fantásticas a los brillantes en el dedo de Hortensia. Y Emilia vio pasar como una sombra a Inés, por el fondo, con un quinqué en la mano. El olor a tiempo y a polvo que caracterizaba a la sala empezó a desvanecerse ante el olor penetrante a petróleo. De pronto, a los rubíes de la ajorca se les coaguló la sangre. Porque la sala toda se había puesto rojo. Y Emilia vio a Inés acercarse de nuevo y detenerse junto a Hortensia. Y encontró la figura erguida de su hermana tan horriblemente hermosa sobre el trasfondo de llamas, que con gesto espontáneo apartó la diadema de sus propias sienes y ciñó con ella la frente marchita de Inés. Luego fue a sentarse en el sillón de Viena y se puso a observar la maravilla azul de los zafiros sobre las crenchas desteñidas, que ahora adquirían tonalidades de sangre, porque el fuego era un círculo purificador alrededor de ellas.

Y estaban allí, reunidas como siempre en la gran sala; las tres puertas de dos hojas sobre el balcón, cerradas como siempre; los tres soles truncos emitiendo al mundo exterior por vez primera la extraordinaria belleza de una luz propia, mientras se consumía lo feo y horrible que una vez fuera hermoso y lo que siempre fuera horrible y feo, por igual.

adorned Hortensia's wrist. She hesitated a moment, holding the sapphire and diamond tiara in her hand. She glanced at the prostrate head garlanded with orange blossoms and, with a determined gesture, turned and placed Mama Eugenia's tiara on Amelia's brow. Finally she took the last item (Papa Bukhart's wide gold ring) and placing it on her own finger, hurriedly left the room, her steps causing the old house to creak.

The faint glow from the candle evoked fantastic lights from the diamonds on Hortensia's finger. And Amelia saw Inés pass like a shadow with an oil lamp in her hand. The characteristic odor of time and dust began to fade before the penetrating smell of kerosene. Suddenly the blood coagulated in the rubies of the bracelet, for the entire parlor had turned red. Amelia saw Inés approach once more and stop beside Hortensia. And she found her sister's erect figure so hideously beautiful against the background of flames, that with a spontaneous gesture she removed the tiara from her own temples and girded Inés' withered brow with it. Then, sitting down in the old Viennese rocking chair, she watched the marvelous blue from the sapphires play upon the faded hair, which now acquired tones of blood, since the fire was a purifying circle around them.

They were there, together as usual in the big parlor; the three double doors to the balcony shut as always; the three truncated suns emitting for the first time to the outside world the extraordinary beauty of a light of their own, while that which was ugly and horrible but had once been beautiful and that which had always been horrible and ugly were being equally consumed.

—tr. Charles Pilditch

CAMPEONES

Pedro Juan Soto

EL taco hizo un último vaivén sobre el paño verde, picó al mingo y lo restalló contra la bola quince. Las manos rollizas, cetrinas, permanecieron quietas hasta que la bola hizo clop en la tronera y luego alzaron el taco hasta situarlo diagonalmente frente al rostro ácnido y fatuo: el rizito envaselinado estaba ordenadamente caído sobre la frente, la oreja atrapillaba el cigarrillo, la mirada era oblicua y burlona, y la pelusilla del bigote había sido acentuada a lápiz.

—¿Quiubo, men?—dijo la voz aguda—. Ese sí fue un tiro de campión, ¿eh?

Se echó a reír entonces. Su cuerpo chaparro, grasiento, se volvió una mota alegremente tembluzca dentro de los ceñidos mahones y la camiseta sudada.

Contemplaba a Gavilán—los ojos demasiado vivos no parecían tan vivos ya, la barba de tres días pretendía enmarañar el malhumor del rostro y no lo lograba, el cigarrillo cenizoso mantenía cerrados los labios detrás de los cuales nadaban las palabrotas—y disfrutaba de la hazaña perpetrada. Le había ganado dos mesas corridas. Cierto que Gavilán había estado seis meses en la cárcel, pero eso no importaba ahora. Lo que importaba era que había perdido dos mesas con él, a quien estas victorias colocaban en una posición privilegiada. Lo ponían sobre los demás, sobre los mejores jugadores del barrio y sobre los que le echaban en cara la inferioridad de sus dieciséis años—su "nenura"—en aquel ambiente. Nadie podría ahora despojarle de su lugar en Harlem. Era *el nuevo,* el sucesor de Gavilán y los demás individuos respetables. Era igual . . . No. Superior, por

THE CHAMP

Pedro Juan Soto

THE cue made a last swing over the green felt, hit the cue ball and cracked it against the fifteen ball. The stubby, yellowish hands remained motionless until the ball went "clop" into the pocket and then raised the cue until it was diagonally in front of the acned, fatuous countenance: the tight little vaselined curl fell tidily over the forehead, the ear clipped a cigarette, the glance was oblique and mocking, and the mustache's scarce fuzz had been accentuated with pencil.

"Wha' happen, man?" said the sharp voice. "That was a champ shot, hey?"

Then he started to laugh. His squat, greasy body became a cheerfully quaking blob inside the tight jeans and the sweaty T-shirt.

He contemplated Gavilán—the eyes, too wise, didn't look so wise now; the three-day beard tried to camouflage the face's ill temper, but didn't make it; the long-ashed cigarette kept the lips shut tight, obscene words wading in back of them—and enjoyed the feat he had perpetrated. He had beaten him in two straight games. Gavilán had been six months in jail, sure, but that didn't matter now. What mattered was that he had lost two games with him, whom these victories placed in a privileged position. They placed him above the others, over the best players in the neighborhood and over the ones who belittled him for being nothing but a sixteen-year-old, nothing but a "baby." Now nobody could cut him out of his spot in Harlem. He was the *new one,* the successor to Gavilán and other individuals worthy of respect. He was the same as . . . no. He was better, on account of

su juventud: tenía más tiempo y oportunidades para sobrepasar todas las hazañas de ellos.

Tenía ganas de salir a la calle y gritar: "¡Le gané dos mesas corridas a Gavilán! ¡Digan ahora! ¡Anden y digan ahora!" No lo hizo. Tan sólo entizó su taco y se dijo que no valía la pena. Hacía sol afuera, pero era sábado y los vecinos andarían por el mercado a esta hora de la mañana. No tendría más público que chiquillos mocosos y abuelas desinteresadas. Además, cierta humildad era buena característica de campeones.

Recogió la peseta que Gavilán tiraba sobre el paño y cambió una sonrisa ufana con el coime y los tres espectadores.

—Cobra lo tuyo—dijo al coime, deseando que algún espectador se moviera hacia las otras mesas para regar la noticia, para comentar cómo él—Puruco, aquel chiquillo demasiado gordo, el de la cara barrosa y la voz cómica—había puesto en ridículo al gran Gavilán. Pero al parecer, estos tres esperaban otra prueba.

Guardó sus quince centavos y dijo a Gavilán, que se secaba su demasiado sudor de la cara:

—¿Vamos pa la otra?

—Vamoh—dijo Gavilán, cogiendo de la taquera otro taco para entizarlo meticulosamente.

El coime desenganchó el triángulo e hizo la piña de la próxima tanda.

Rompió Puruco, dedicándose en seguida a silbar y a pasearse alrededor de la mesa elásticamente, casi en la punta de las tenis.

Gavilán se acercó al mingo con su pesadez característica y lo centró, pero no picó todavía. Simplemente alzó la cabeza peludísima, dejando el cuerpo inclinado sobre el taco y el paño, para decir:

—Oye, déjame el pitito.

—Okey, men—dijo Puruco, y batuteó su taco hasta que oyó el tacazo de Gavilán y volvieron a correr y a chasquear las bolas. Ninguna se entroneró.

—Ay, bendito—rió Puruco—. Si lo tengo muerto a ehte hombre.

Picó hacia la uno, que se fue y dejó a la dos enfilada hacia la tronera izquierda. También la dos se fue. El no podía dejar de

his youth: he had more time and opportunities to surpass all their feats.

He felt like running out into the street and shouting, "I won two straight games from Gavilán! Speak out now! C'mon, say something now!" He didn't do it. He only chalked his cue and told himself it wasn't worth the trouble. It was sunny out, but it was Saturday and the neighbors would be at the market place at this hour of the morning. He would have no more audience than snot-nosed kids and disinterested grannies. Anyway, a little humility suited champs well.

He picked up the quarter Gavilán threw on the felt and exchanged a conceited smile with the scorekeeper and the three spectators.

"Collect yours," he told the scorekeeper, hoping that some spectator would move to the other pool tables to spread the news, to comment how he—Puruco, the too-fat kid with the pimply face and the comic voice—had made a fool of the great Gavilán. It seemed, however, that they were waiting for another show.

He put away his fifteen cents and said to Gavilán, who was wiping his sweaty face, "Play another?"

"Let's" Gavilán said, taking from the rack another cue that he would chalk meticulously.

The scorer took down the triangular rack and shaped up the balls for the next round.

Puruco broke, and immediately began to whistle and pace around the table with a springy walk, almost on the tips of his sneakers.

Gavilán came up to the cue ball with his characteristic heaviness, and centered it, but didn't hit it yet. He simply raised his very shaggy head, his body still bent over the cue and the felt, and said, "Hey, quit the whistle."

"Okay, man," Puruco said, and twirled his cue until he heard Gavilán's shot and the balls went running around and clashed again. None of them went home.

"*Ay, bendito,*" Puruco laughed. "Got this man like dead."

He hit number one, which went in and left number two lined up for the left pocket. Number two also dropped in. He could not

sonreír hacia uno y otro rincón del salón. Parecía invitar a las arañas, a las moscas, a los boliteros dispersos entre la concurrencia de las demás mesas, a presenciar esto.

Estudió cuidadosamente la posición de cada bola. Quería ganar esta otra mesa también, aprovechar la reciente lectura del libro de Willie Hoppe y las prácticas de todos aquellos meses en que había recibido la burla de sus contrincantes. El año pasado no era más que una chata; ahora comenzaba la verdadera vida, la de campeón. Derrotado Gavilán, derrotaría a Mamerto y al Bimbo . . . "¡Abranle paso a Puruco!" dirían los conocedores. Y él impresionaría a los dueños de billares, se haría de buenas conexiones. Sería guardaespaldas de algunos y amigo íntimo de otros. Tendría cigarrillos y cerveza gratis. Y mujeres, no chiquillas estúpidas que andaban siempre con miedo y que no iban más allá de algún apretujón en el cine. De ahí, a la fama: el macho del barrio, el individuo indispensable para cualquier asunto—la bolita, el tráfico de narcóticos, la hembra de Riverside Drive de paseo por el barrio, la pelea de esta pandilla con la otra para resolver "cosas de hombres."

Con un pujido pifió la tres y maldijo. Gavilán estaba detrás de él cuando se dio vuelta.

—¡Cuidado con echarme fufú!—dijo encrespándose.

Y Gavilán:

—Ay, deja eso.

—No, no me vengah con eso, men. A cuenta que estáh perdiendo.

Gavilán no respondió. Centró al mingo a través del humo que le arrugaba las facciones y lo disparó para entronrear dos bolas en bandas contrarias.

—¿Lo ve?—dijo Puruco, y cruzó los dedos para salvaguardarse.

—¡Cállate la boca!

Gavilán tiró a banda, tratando de meter la cinco, pero falló. Puruco estudió la posición de su bola y se decidió por la tronera más lejana pero más segura. Mientras centraba, se dio cuenta de que tendría que descruzar los dedos. Miró a Gavilán con suspicacia y cruzó las dos piernas para picar. Falló el tiro.

Cuando alzó la vista, Gavilán sonreía y se chupaba la encía superior para escupir su piorrea. Ya no dudó de que era víctima de un hechizo.

stop smiling toward the corners of the parlor. He seemed to invite the spiders, the flies, and the numbers bookies dispersed among the bystanders at the other pool tables, to take a look at this.

He carefully studied the position of each ball. He wanted to win this other set, too, to take advantage of his recent reading of Willie Hoppe's book, and all that month-after-month practicing, when he had been the butt of his opponents. Last year he was just a little pisspot; now the real life was beginning for him, the life of a champ. Once he beat Gavilán, he would lick Mamerto and Bimbo . . .

"Make way for Puruco!" the cool men would say. And he would make it with the owners of the pool parlors, gather good connections. He'd be bodyguard to some, and buddy-buddy to others. Cigarettes and beer for free, he would have. And women, not the scared, stupid chicks who went no further than some squeezing at the movies. From there, right into fame: big man in the neighborhood, the one and only guy for any job—the numbers, the narco racket, the broad from Riverside Drive slumming in the neighborhood, this gang's rumble with that one to settle "manly things."

With a grunt, he missed the three ball and cursed. Gavilán was right behind him when he turned.

"Watch out puttin' foofoo on me!" he said, ruffling up.

And Gavilán:

"Ah, stop that."

"No. Don't give me that, man, just 'cause yuh losin'?"

Gavilán did not answer. He centered the cue ball through the smoke which wrinkled his features, and pocketed two balls in opposite sides.

"See?" Puruco said, and he crossed his fingers to protect himself.

"Shaddup yuh mouth!"

Gavilán tried to ricochet the five in, but failed. Puruco studied the position of his ball and settled for the farthest but surest pocket. While aiming, he realized that he would have to uncross his fingers. He looked at Gavilán suspiciously and crossed his legs to shoot. He missed.

When he looked up, Gavilán was smiling and sucking his upper gums to spit his pyorrhea. Now he had no doubt that he was the victim of a spell.

—No relaje, men. Juega limpio.

Gavilán lo miró extrañado, pisando el cigarrillo distraídamente.

—¿Qué te pasa a ti?

—No—dijo Puruco—, que no sigah con ese bilongo.

—¡Adió!—rió Gavilán—. Si éhte cree en brujoh.

Llevó el taco atrás de su cintura, amagó una vez, y entroneró fácilmente. Volvió a entronerar en la próxima. Y en la otra. Puruco se puso nervioso. O Gavilán estaba recobrando su destreza, o aquel bilongo le empujaba el taco. Si no sacaba más ventaja, Gavilán ganaría esta mesa.

Entizó su taco, tocó madera tres veces, y aguardó turno. Gavilán falló su quinto tiro. Entonces Puruco midió distancia. Picó, metiendo la ocho. Hizo una combinación para entronerar la once con la nueve. La nueve se fue luego. Caramboleó la doce a la tronera y falló luego la diez. Gavilán también la falló. Por fin logró Puruco meterla, pero para la trece casi rasga el paño. Sumó mentalmente. No le faltaban más que ocho tantos, de manera que podía calmarse.

Pasó el cigarrillo de la oreja a los labios. Cuando lo encendía de espaldas a la mesa para que el abanico no apagara el fósforo, vio la sonrisa socarrona del coime. Se volteó rápidamente y cogió a Gavilán *in fraganti:* los pies levantados del piso mientras el cuerpo se ladeaba sobre la banda para hacer fácil el tiro. Antes de que pudiera hablar, Gavilán había entronerado la bola.

—¡Oye, men!

—¿Qué pasa?—dijo Gavilán tranquilamente, ojeando el otro tiro.

—¡No me vengah con eso, chico! Así no me ganah.

Gavilán arqueó una ceja para mirarlo, y aguzó el hocico mordiendo el interior de la boca.

—¿Qué te duele?—dijo.

—No, que así no—abrió los brazos Puruco, casi dándole al coime con el taco. Tiró el cigarrillo violentamente y dijo a los espectadores—: Uhtedeh lo han vihto, ¿veldá?

—¿Vihto qué?—dijo, inmutable, Gavilán.

—Na, la puercá esa—chillaba Puruco—. ¿Tú te creh que yo soy bobo?

—Adióh, cará—rió Gavilán—. No me pregunteh a mí, porque a lo mejol te lo digo.

"No foolin', man. Play it clean." Gavilán gazed at him with surprise, stepping on the cigarette distractedly.

"What's the matter?"

"No," Puruco said. "Don't you go on with that *bilongo!*"

"Hey!" Gavilán laughed. "This one t'inks a lot about witches."

He put the cue behind his back, feinted once, and pocketed the ball easily. He pocketed again in the next shot, and in the next. Puruco began to get nervous. Either Gavilán was recovering his ability, or else that voodoo spell was pushing his cue. If he didn't get to raise his score, Gavilán would win this set.

Chalking his cue, he touched wood three times and awaited his turn. Gavilán missed his fifth shot. Then Puruco eyed the distance. He hit, putting in the eight. He pulled a combination shot to pocket the eleven with the nine. The nine went home later. He caromed the twelve in, and then missed the ten. Gavilán also missed it. Finally Puruco managed to send it in, but for ball thirteen he almost ripped the felt. He added the score in his head. About eight more to call it quits—he could relax a little.

The cigarette went from behind his ear to his lips. When he lit it, turning his back to the table so that the fan would not blow out the match, he saw the sly smile of the scorekeeper. He turned around rapidly and caught Gavilán right in the act: feet lifted off the floor, body leaning against the table rim to make an easy shot. Before he could speak, Gavilán had pocketed the ball.

"Hey, man!"

"Wha' happen?" Gavilán said calmly, eyeing the next shot.

"Don't you pull that on me, boy! You can't beat me that way."

Gavilán raised an eyebrow at him, and bit the inside of his mouth while making a snout.

"Wha's hurtin' you?" he said.

"No, like that no!" Puruco jerked his arms open and almost hit the scorekeeper with his cue. He threw the cigarette down violently and said to the onlookers, "You seen it, right?"

"See wha'?" said Gavilán, unmoved.

"Nothin', that dirty play," squealed Puruco. "T'ink I'm stupid?"

"Aw, man," Gavilán laughed. "Don't you go askin' me, maybe I tell you."

Puruco dio con el taco sobre una banda de la mesa.

—A mí me tieneh que jugar limpio. No te conformah con hacerme cábala primero, sino que dehpuéh te meteh hacer trampa.

—¿Quién hizo trampa?—dijo Gavilán. Dejó el taco sobre la mesa y se acercó sonriendo a Puruco—. ¿Tú diceh que yo soy tramposo?

—No—dijo Puruco, cambiando de tono, aniñando la voz, vacilando sobre sus pies—. Pero eh qui así no se debe jugar, men. Si ti han vihto.

Gavilán se volvió hacia los otros.

—¿Yo he hecho trampa?

Sólo el coime sacudió la cabeza. Los demás no dijeron nada, cambiaron la vista.

—Pero si ehtabah encaramao en la mesa, men—dijo Puruco.

Gavilán le empuñó la camiseta como sin querer, desnudándole la espalda fofa cuando lo atrajo hacia él.

—A mí nadie me llama tramposo.

En todas las otras mesas se había detenido el juego. Los demás observaban desde lejos. No se oía más que el zumbido del abanico y de las moscas, y la gritería de los chiquillos en la calle.

—¿Tú te creeh qui un pilemielda como tú me va llamar a mí tramposo?—dijo Gavilán, forzando sobre el pecho de Puruco el puño que desgarraba la camiseta—. Te dejo ganar doh mesitah pa que tengas de qué echártelah, y ya te creeh rey. Echa p'allá, infelih—dijo entre dientes—. Cuando crehcas noh vemo.

El empujón lanzó a Puruco contra la pared de yeso, donde su espalda se estrelló de plano. El estampido llenó de huecos el silencio. Alguien rió, jijeando. Alguien dijo: "Fanfarrón que es."

—Y lárgate di aquí anteh que te meta tremenda patá—dijo Gavilán.

—Okey, men—tartajeó Puruco, dejando caer el taco.

Salió sin atreverse a alzar la vista, oyendo de nuevo tacazos en las mesas, risitas. En la calle tuvo ganas de llorar, pero se resistió. Eso era de mujercitas. No le dolía el golpe recibido; más le dolía lo otro: aquel "cuando crehcas noh vemo." El era un hombre ya. Si le golpeaban, si lo mataban, que lo hicieran olvidándose de sus dieciséis años. Era un hombre ya. Podía hacer daño, mucho daño, y también podía sobrevivir a él.

Puruco struck the table rim with the cue.

"With me you gotta play fair. You ain't satisfied with puttin' a spell on me first, but after you put me on with cheatin'."

"Who cheatin'?" Gavilán said. He left the cue on the table and, smiling, moved closer to Puruco. "You say I'm cheatin'?"

"No," Puruco said, changing his tone, babying his voice, wavering on his feet. "But that's no way to play, man. They seen you."

Gavilán turned to the others.

"I been cheatin'?"

Only the scorekeeper shook his head. The others said nothing and looked away.

"But like he's lyin' on the table, man," Puruco said.

Gavilán clutched the T-shirt as if by chance, baring the pudgy back as he pulled him over.

"Me, nobody call me a cheatin' man."

The playing had stopped at all the other pool tables. The rest of the people watched from a distance. Nothing was heard but the buzz of the fan and the flies, and the screaming of children in the street.

"You t'ink a pile of crap like you gonna call me a cheater?" Gavilán said, forcing his fist against Puruco's chest, ripping the shirt. "I let you win two tables so you have somethin' to put on, and now you t'ink you king. Get outta here, jerk," he said between his teeth. "When you grow up we'll see ya."

The push threw Puruco against the plaster wall, where his back smashed flat. The crash filled the silence with holes. Somebody laughed, tittering. Somebody said: "He a bragger."

"An' get outta here before I kick you for good," Gavilán said.

" 'Kay man," Puruco stammered, dropping the cue.

Out he went without daring to raise his eyes, hearing cues clicking again on the tables, and some giggles. On the street, he felt like crying, but held it in. That was for sissies. The blow didn't hurt; that other thing—"When you grow up we'll see ya"—hurt more. He was a full-grown man. If they beat him, if they killed him, let them do it paying no mind at all to his being a sixteen-year-old. He was a man already. He could do a lot of damage, plenty of damage, and he could also survive it.

Cruzó a la otra acera pateando furiosamente una lata de cerveza, las manos pellizcando, desde dentro de los bolsillos, su cuerpo clavado a la cruz de la adolescencia.

Le había dejado ganar dos mesas, decía Gavilán. Embuste. Sabía que las perdería todas con él, de ahora en adelante, con el nuevo campeón. Por eso la brujería, por eso la trampa, por eso el golpe. Ah, pero aquellos tres individuos regarían la noticia de la caída de Gavilán. Después Mamerto y el Bimbo. Nadie podía detenerlo ahora. El barrio, el mundo entero, iba a ser suyo.

Cuando el aro del barril se le enredó entre las piernas, lo pateó a un lado. Le dio un manotazo al chiquillo que venía a recogerlo.

—Cuidao, men, que te parto un ojo—dijo iracundo.

Y siguió andando, sin preocuparse de la madre que le maldecía y corría hacia el chiquillo lloroso. Con los labios apretados, respiraba hondo. A su paso, veía caer serpentinas y llover vítores de las ventanas desiertas y cerradas.

Era un campeón. Iba alerta sólo al daño.

He crossed over to the other sidewalk, furiously kicked a beer can, his hands, from inside the pockets, pinching his body nailed to the cross of adolescence.

Two sets he had let him win, Gavilán said. Dirty lie. He knew he would lose every one of them to him, from now on, to the new champ. He had pulled the voodoo stuff on account of that, on account of that the cheating, the blow on account of that. Oh, but those three other men would spread the news of Gavilán's fall. After that, Mamerto and Bimbo. Nobody could stop him now. The neighborhood, the whole world, would be his.

When the barrel hoop got trapped between his legs, he kicked it aside. He gave a slap to the kid who came to pick it up.

"Careful, man, or I knock yuh eye out," he growled.

And he went on walking, unconcerned with the mother who cursed him and ran toward the tearful kid. Lips held tight, he inhaled deeply. At his passing, he could see confetti falling and cheers pouring from the closed and deserted windows.

He was a champ. He was on the lookout only for harm.

—tr. Pedro Juan Soto

LOS INOCENTES

Pedro Juan Soto

treparme frente al sol en aquella nube con las palomas sin caballos sin mujeres y no oler cuando queman los cacharros en el solar sin gente que me haga burla

Desde la ventana, vistiendo el traje hecho y vendido para contener a un hombre que no era él, veía las palomas revolotear en el alero de enfrente.

o con puertas y ventanas siempre abiertas tener alas

Comenzaba a agitar las manos y a hacer ruido como las palomas cuando oyó la voz a sus espaldas.

—Nene, nene.

La mujer acartonada estaba sentada a la mesa (debajo estaba la maleta de tapas frágiles, con una cuerda alrededor por única llave), y le observaba con sus ojos vivos, derrumbada en la silla como una gata hambrienta y abandonada.

—Pan—dijo él.

Dándole un leve empujón a la mesa, la mujer retiró la silla y fue a la alacena. Sacó el trozo de pan que estaba al descubierto sobre las cajas de arroz y se lo llevó al hombre, que seguía manoteando y haciendo ruido.

ser paloma

—No hagah ruido, Pipe.

El desmoronó el trozo de pan sobre el alféizar, sin hacer caso.

—No hagah ruido, nene.

Los hombres que jugaban dominó bajo el toldo de la bodega ya miraban hacia arriba.

THE INNOCENTS

Pedro Juan Soto

to climb up to the sun on that cloud with the pigeons without horses without women and not to have to smell the junk burning in the lot with no one to make fun of me

Dressed in a suit that had been made and sold to contain some other man, he could see from the window the pigeons fluttering about the eaves of the house opposite.

or with doors and windows always open to have wings

He began to flap his hands and coo like the pigeons when he heard a voice behind him.

"Baby, baby."

The woman, dried up by age, was seated at the table, underneath which stood the flimsy suitcase, a rope its only lock; she looked at him with her bright eyes, spread out over the chair like a hungry, abandoned cat.

"Bread," he said.

Her hands on the table, the woman pushed back her chair and went to the cupboard. She took out some bread that was lying unwrapped upon boxes of rice and gave it to the man, who was still gesticulating and mouthing sounds.

to be a pigeon

"Stop your noise, Pipe."

He crumbled the piece of bread on the windowsill, paying no attention to her.

"Stop your noise, baby."

Some men playing dominoes under the awning of the grocery store stared up at them.

El dejó de sacudir la lengua.

sin gente que me haga burla

—A pasiar a la plaza—dijo.

—Sí, Holtensia viene ya pa sacalte a pasiar.

—A la plaza.

—No, a la plaza no. Se la llevaron. Voló.

El hizo pucheros. Atendió de nuevo al revoloteo de las palomas.

no hay plaza

—No, no fueron lah palomah—dijo ella—. Fue el malo, el diablo.

—Ah.

—Hay que pedirle a Papadioh que traiga la plaza.

—Papadioh—dijo él mirando hacia fuera—, trai la plaza y el río . . .

—No, no. Sin abrir la boca—dijo ella—. Arrodíllate y háblale a Papadioh sin abrir la boca.

El se arrodilló frente al alféizar y enlazó las manos y miró por encima de las azoteas.

yo quiero ser paloma

Ella miró hacia abajo: al ocio de los hombres en la mañana del sábado y al ajetreo de las mujeres en la ida o la vuelta del mercado.

Lenta, pesarosa, pero erguida, como si balanceara un bulto en la cabeza, echó a andar hacia la habitación donde la otra, delante del espejo, se quitaba los ganchos del pelo y los amontonaba sobre el tocador.

—No te lo lleveh hoy, Holtensia.

La otra miró de reojo.

—No empieceh otra veh, mamá. No le va pasal na. Lo cuidan bien y no noh cuehta.

Saliendo de los ganchos, el cabello se hacía una mota negra sobre las orejas.

—Pero si yo lo sé cuidal. Eh mi hijo. ¿Quién mejol que yo?

Hortensia estudió en el espejo la figura magra y menuda.

—Tú ehtáh vieja, mamá.

Una mano descarnada se alzó en el espejo.

—Todavía no ehtoy muerta. Todavía puedo velar por él.

—No eh eso.

He left off moving his tongue from side to side in his mouth.

with no one to make fun of me

"Walk in the square," he said.

"All right, Hortensia is coming now to take you for a walk."

"In the square."

"No, not in the square. They took it away. It flew away."

He pouted. His attention shifted again to the fluttering pigeons.

no more square

"It wasn't the pigeons," she said. "It was the evil one, the devil."

"Oh."

"Must ask Papa God to bring back the square."

"Papa God," he said, gazing upward, "bring back the square and the river . . ."

"No, no. Without opening your mouth," she said. "Kneel down and talk to Papa God without opening your mouth."

He knelt by the windowsill, joined his hands and stared out over the flat roofs.

I want to be a pigeon

She looked down at the men's Saturday morning idleness and the bustle of the women going to and from market.

Slowly, heavily, but erect, as if balancing a bundle on her head, she went into the room where, in front of the mirror, her daughter was removing hairpins from her hair and piling them on the dresser.

"Don't take him today, Hortensia."

The younger woman glanced at her out of the corner of her eye.

"Don't start that again, Mama. Nothing'll happen to him. They'll take good care of him and it won't cost us a cent."

Freed of its pins, her hair formed a black mass about her ears.

"But I know how to take care of him. He's my son. Who knows better than I?"

Hortensia, in the mirror, studied the small, lean figure.

"You're old, Mama."

In the mirror, one fleshless hand was raised.

"I'm not dead yet. I can still look after him."

"That's not the point."

Los bucles seguían apelmazados a pesar de que ella trataba de aflojárselos con el peine.

—Pipe'h inocente—dijo la madre, haciendo de las palabras agua para un mar de lástima—. Eh un nene.

Hortensia echó el peine a un lado. Sacó un lápiz del bolso que mantenía abierto sobre el tocador y comenzó a ennegrecer las cejas escasas.

—Eso no se cura—dijo al espejo—. Tú lo sabeh. Por eso lo mejor . . .

—En Puerto Rico no hubiera pasao ehto.

—En Puerto Rico era dihtinto—dijo Hortensia, hablando por encima del hombro—. Lo conocía la gente. Podía salir porque lo conocía la gente. Pero en Niu Yol la gente no se ocupa y uno no conoce al vecino. La vida eh dura. Yo me paso los añoh cose que cose y todavía sin casalme.

Buscando el lápiz labial, vio en el espejo cómo se descomponía el rostro de la madre.

—Pero no eh por eso tampoco. El ehtá mejol atendío allá.

—Eso diceh tú—dijo la madre.

Hortensia tiró los lápices y el peine dentro del bolso y lo cerró. Se dio vuelta: blusa porosa, labios grasientos, cejas tiznadas, bucles apelmazados.

—Dehpuéh di un año aquí, merecemoh algo mejor.

—El no tiene la culpa de lo que noh pase a nosotrah.

—Pero si se queda aquí, la va tenel. Fíjate.

Se abalanzó sobre la madre para cogerle un brazo y alzarle la manga que no pasaba del codo. Sobre los ligamentos caídos había una mancha morada.

—Ti ha levantao ya la mano y yo en la factoría no estoy tranquila pensando qué'htará pasando contigo y con él. Y si ya pasao ehto . . .

—Fue sin querel—dijo la madre, bajando la manga y mirando al piso al mismo tiempo que torcía el brazo para que Hortensia la soltara.

—¿Sin querel y te tenía una mano en el cuello? Si no agarro la botella, sabe Dioh. Aquí no hay un hombre que li haga frente y yo m'ehtoy acabando, mamá, y tú le tieneh miedo.

—Eh un nene—dijo la madre con su voz mansa, ahuyentando el cuerpo como un caracol.

The curls remained stubbornly tight, in spite of her efforts to loosen them with a comb.

"Pipe is innocent," the mother said, her words drawn from a sea of pity. "He's a baby."

Hortensia threw down the comb. She took a pencil from the purse that lay open on the dresser and began to darken her scanty eyebrows.

"There's no cure for that," she said to the mirror. "You know it. So the best thing . . ."

"In Puerto Rico this wouldn't have happened."

"In Puerto Rico things were different," said Hortensia over her shoulder. "People knew him. He could go out because people knew him. But in New York people can't be bothered and they don't know their neighbors. Life is hard. The years go by while I sew my life away and I'm still not married."

As she looked for her lipstick, she saw in the mirror her mother's despondent face.

"But that's not the reason either. He'll be better taken care of there."

"That's what you say," her mother replied.

Hortensia tossed eyebrow pencil, lipstick, and comb into her purse and snapped it shut. She turned around—a thin blouse, greasy lips, blackened eyebrows, tight curls.

"After a year here, we deserve something better."

"He's not to blame for what happens to us."

"But if he stays here he will be. Take it from me."

She darted to her mother, grasped her arm, and pushed up her sleeve to the elbow. On the thin corded flesh was a purple bruise.

"He's already raised a hand to you, and I'm never easy in my mind at the factory thinking what might be happening to you and to him. And if this has already happened . . ."

"He didn't mean to," the mother said, pulling down her sleeve and staring at the floor, at the same time twisting her arm to make Hortensia let go.

"He didn't mean to when he had you by the neck? If I hadn't grabbed the bottle, God knows what would have happened. There's no man here to stand up to him, and I'm worn out, Mama, and you're scared to death of him."

"He's a baby," the mother said in her gentle voice, withdrawing into herself like a snail.

Hortensia entornaba los ojos.

—No vengah con eso. Yo soy joven y tengo la vida por delante y él no. Tú también ehtáh cansá y si él se fuera podríah vivil mejor los añoh que te quedan y tú lo sabeh pero no ti atreveh a decirlo porque creeh que'h malo pero yo lo digo por ti *tú ehtáh cansá* y por eso filmahte loh papeleh porque sabeh que'n ese sitio lo atienden máh bien y tú entonceh podráh sentalte a ver la gente pasar por la calle y cuando te dé la gana puedeh pararte y salir a pasiar como elloh pero prefiereh creer que'h un crimen y que *yo* soy la criminal pa tú quedar como madre sufrida y *hah sido una madre sufrida* eso no se te puede quital pero tieneh que pensar en ti y en mí. Que si el caballo lo tumbó a loh diez añoh . . .

La madre salía a pasos rápidos, como empujada, como si la habitación misma la soplara fuera, mientras Hortensia decía:

— . . . y los otroh veinte los ha vivío así tumbao . . .

Y se volvía para verla salir, sin ir tras ella, tirándose sobre el tocador donde ahora sentía que sus puños martillaban un compás para su casi grito.

— . . . nosotroh loh hemoh vivío con él.

Y veía en el espejo el histérico dibujo de carnaval que era su rostro.

y no hay gallos y no hay perros y no hay campanas y no hay viento del río y no hay timbre de cine y el sol no entra aquí y no me gusta

—Ya—dijo la madre inclinándose para barrer con las manos las migajas del alféizar. La muchachería azotaba y perseguía una pelota de goma en la calle.

y la frialdad duerme se sienta camina con uno aquí dentro y no me gusta

—Ya, nene, ya. Di amén.

—Amén.

Lo ayudó a incorporarse y le puso el sombrero con la mano, viendo que ya Hortensia, seria y con los ojos irritados, venía hacia ellos.

—Vamoh, Pipe. Dali un beso a mamá.

Puso el bolso en la mesa y se dobló para recoger la maleta. La

Hortensia half-closed her eyes.

"Don't give me that. I'm young and I have my life before me, but he hasn't. You are worn out and if he went away you could live out the rest of your days in peace and you know it but you don't dare admit it because you think it's wrong but I'll say it for you *you're worn out* and that's why you signed the papers because you know they'll take better care of him in that place and then you can sit down and watch the people go by in the street and whenever you take the notion you can get up and go out and walk around like the rest but you'd rather think it's a crime and I'm the criminal so you can go on being the long-suffering mother and *you have been a long-suffering mother* no one can take that away from you but you've got to think of yourself and of me. What if the horse knocked him down when he was ten years old . . ."

The mother walked rapidly away, as if she were being pushed, as if the room itself were blowing her out, while Hortensia went on, ". . . and for the other twenty he's lived knocked down like that . . ."

And she turned to watch her mother go, not following, leaning her weight on the dresser upon which her fists beat out a rhythm for what was almost a scream: ". . . we've had to live all those years with him."

And in the mirror she could see the hysterical carnival mask that was her face.

and there's no roosters and there's no dogs and there's no bell and there's no wind off the river and there's no buzzer from the movie house and the sun doesn't come in here and I don't like it

"All right," the mother said, bending over to brush the crumbs off the windowsill. Below in the street, the boys were hitting a rubber ball and chasing it.

and the cold sleeps sits walks with you in here and I don't like it

"All right, baby, all right. Say amen."

"Amen."

She helped him to his feet and put his hat in his hand, for she saw that Hortensia was coming toward them, serious, her eyes red.

"Let's go, Pipe. Give Mama a kiss."

She put her purse on the table and bent over to pick up the

madre se abalanzó al cuello de él—las manos como tenazas—y besó el rostro de avellana chamuscada y pasó los dedos sobre la piel que había afeitado esta mañana.

—Vamoh—dijo Hortensia cargando bolso y maleta.

El se deshizo de los brazos de la madre y caminó hacia la puerta meciendo la mano que llevaba el sombrero.

—Nene, ponte'l sombrero—dijo la madre, y parpadeó para que él no viera las lágrimas.

Dándose vuelta, él alzó y dejó encima del cabello envaselinado aquello que por lo chico parecía un juguete, aquello que quería compensar el desperdicio de tela en el traje.

—No, que lo deje aquí—dijo Hortensia.

Pipe hizo pucheros. La madre tenía los ojos fijos en Hortensia y la mandíbula le temblaba.

—Ehtá bien—dijo Hortensia—, llévalo en la mano.

El volvió a caminar hacia la puerta y la madre lo siguió, encogiéndose un poco ahora y conteniendo los brazos que querían estirarse hacia él.

Hortensia la detuvo.

—Mamá, lo van a cuidal.

—Que no lo mal . . .

—No. Hay médicoh. Y tú . . . cada do semanah. Yo te llevo.

Ambas se esforzaban por mantener firme la voz.

—Recuéhtate, mamá.

—Dile que se quede . . . no haga ruido y que coma de to.

—Sí.

Hortensia abrió la puerta y miró fuera para ver si Pipe se había detenido en el rellano. El se entretenía escupiendo sobre la baranda de la escalera y viendo caer la saliva.

—Yo vengo temprano, mamá.

La madre estaba junto a la silla que ya sobraba, intentando ver al hijo a través del cuerpo que bloqueaba la entrada.

—Recuéhtate, mamá.

La madre no respondió. Con las manos enlazadas enfrente, estuvo rígida hasta que el pecho y los hombros se convulsionaron y comenzó a salir el llanto hiposo y delicado.

Hortensia tiró la puerta y bajó con Pipe a toda prisa. Y ante la inmensa claridad de un mediodía de junio, quiso huracanes y eclipses y nevadas.

suitcase. The mother threw herself around his neck—her hands like pincers—and kissed his burned hazelnut of a face, running her fingers over the skin she had shaved that morning.

"Let's go," Hortensia said, picking up purse and suitcase.

He pulled away from his mother's arms and walked toward the door, swinging the hand that carried his hat.

"Baby, put your hat on," his mother said, and blinked lest he see her tears.

Turning, he placed on his vaseline-coated hair that which on account of its smallness looked like a toy trying to compensate for the waste of cloth in the suit.

"No, he better leave it here," Hortensia said.

Pipe pouted. The mother kept her eyes fixed on Hortensia, her jaw trembling.

"All right," Hortensia said, "carry it in your hand."

Again he walked toward the door, the mother following, barely restraining herself from reaching out to him.

Hortensia barred the way. "Mama, they'll take care of him."

"Don't let them mistreat . . ."

"No. There are doctors. And you . . . every two weeks. I'll take you."

They were both making an effort to keep their voices steady.

"Go lay down, Mama."

"Tell him to stay . . . not to make any noise and to eat everything."

"Yes."

Hortensia opened the door and looked out to see if Pipe had waited on the landing. He was amusing himself by spitting over the stair rail and watching his saliva fall.

"I'll be back early, Mama."

The mother stood by the chair that was now one too many, trying to catch a glimpse of her son through the body that blocked the doorway.

"Go lay down, Mama."

Not answering, her hands clasped, she stayed rigid till chest and shoulders were shaken by a spasm, and, hiccuping, she began softly to weep.

Slamming the door, Hortensia ran downstairs with Pipe as fast as she could. Faced with the immense clarity of a June midday, she longed for hurricanes, eclipses, blizzards.

—tr. Barbara Howes with the author

EL JOSCO

Abelardo Díaz Alfaro

SOMBRA imborrable del Josco sobre la loma que domina el valle del Toa. La cabeza erguida, las aspas filosas estoqueando el capote en sangre de un atardecer luminoso. Aindiado, moreno, la carrillada en sombras, el andar lento y rítmico. La baba gelatinosa le caía de los belfos negros y gomosos, dejando en el verde enjoyado estela plateada de caracol. Era hosco por el color y por su carácter reconcentrado, huraño, fobioso, de peleador incansable. Cuando sobre el lomo negro del cerro Farallón las estrellas clavaban sus banderillas de luz, lo veía descender la loma, majestuoso, doblar la recia cerviz, resoplar su aliento de toro macho sobre la tierra virgen y tirar un mugido largo y potente para las rejoyas del San Lorenzo.

—Toro macho, padrote como ése, denguno; no nació pa yugo—me decía el jincho Marcelo, quien una noche negra y hosca le parteó a la luz temblona de un jacho. Lo había criado y lo quería como a un hijo. Su único hijo.

Hombre solitario, hecho a la reyerta de la alborada, veía en aquel toro la encarnación de algo de su hombría, de su descontento, de su espíritu recio y primitivo. Y toro y hombre se fundían en un mismo paisaje y en un mismo dolor.

No había toro de las fincas lindantes que cruzase la guardarraya, que el Josco no le grabase en rojo sobre el costado, de una cornada certera, su rúbrica de toro padrote.

JOSCO*

Abelardo Díaz Alfaro

Josco's eternal shadow, cast upon the mountainside overlooking the Toa valley. Head erect, rapier-tipped horns stabbing the blood-tinged cape of a luminous sunset. Savage, dark brown, the fleshy jowls in shadows, his gait slow and rhythmic. The gelatinous slaver fell from the black, rubbery lips, leaving foamy silver snails on the jewel-green grass. He was sullen in color and in manner—self-centered, hostile, a tireless fighter. When the stars nailed their small pennants of light above the black ridge of the Farallón range, I would watch him descend the mountainside majestically, bend his thick neck, blow his virile bull's breath on the virgin soil and send a long, powerful bellow toward the low lands near the River.

"All bull, a lusty sire like that, not another like him; wasn't born for the yoke," pale Marcelo used to tell me. One black, sullen night he had midwifed Josco's birth by the feeble light of a torch. He had reared him and loved him like a son. His only son.

A solitary man, a veteran witness to the break of dawn, he saw in the bull the incarnation of something of his own manhood, of his own discontent, of his own obstinate, primitive spirit. And bull and man fused together into the same landscape and the same sorrows.

Any bull in the neighboring farms who crossed the boundary lines into his territory earned a bloody brand on its flank, a sure horn thrust, Josco's rubric of siredom.

*A dialectic form of *hosco:* sullen, arrogant.

Cuando el cuerno plateado de la luna rasgaba el telón en sombras de la noche, oí al tío Leopo decir al Jincho:

—Marcelo, mañana me traes el toro americano que le compré a los Velilla para padrote; lo quiero para el cruce; hay que mejorar la crianza.

Y vi al Jincho luchar en su mente estrecha, recia y primitiva con una idea demasiado sangrante, demasiado dolorosa para ser realidad. Y tras una corta pausa musitó débilmente; como si la voz se le quebrase en suspiros:

—Don Leopo, ¿y qué jacemos con el Josco?

—Pues lo enyugaremos para arrastre de caña, la zafra se mete fuerte este año, y ese toro es duro y resistente.

—Usté dispense, don Leopo, pero ese toro es padrote de nación, es alebrestao, no sirve pa yugo.

Y descendió la escalera de caracol y por la enlunada veredita se hundió en el mar de sombras del cañaveral. Sangrante, como si le hubieran clavado un estoque en mitad del corazón.

Al otro día por el portalón blanco que une los caminos de las fincas lindantes, vi al Jincho traer atado a una soga un enorme toro blanco. Los cuernos cortos, la poderosa testa mapeada en sepia. La dilatada y espaciosa nariz taladrada por una argolla de hierro. El Jincho venía como empujado, lentamente, como con ganas de nunca llegar, por la veredita de los guayabales.

Y de súbito se oyó un mugido potente y agudo por las mayas de la colindancia de los Cocos, que hizo retumbar las rejoyas del San Lorenzo y los riscos del Farallón. Un relámpago cárdeno de alegría iluminó la faz macilenta del Jincho.

Era el grito de guerra del Josco, el reto para jugarse en puñales de cuernos la supremacía del padronazgo. Empezó a mover la testa en forma pendular. Tiró furiosas cornadas al suelo, trayéndose en el filo de las astas tierra y pasto. Alucinado, lanzó cabezadas frontales al aire, como luchando con una sombra.

El Jincho en la loma, junto a la casa, aguantó al toro blanco. El Josco ensayó un tranco ligero, hasta penetrar en la veredita. Se detuvo un momento. Remolineó ágil y comenzó a estoquear los pequeños guayabos que bordean la veredita. La testa coronada se le enguirnaldó de ramas, flores silvestres y bejucales. Venía lento, taimado, con un bramar repetido y monotono. Alargaba la cabeza, y el bramar culminaba en un mugido

When the silver horn of the moon was tearing the shadowy curtain of night, I heard Uncle Leopo tell Marcelo:

"Tomorrow bring me the American bull I bought from Velillas for breeding; I want to start using him; we've got to improve the breed."

And I saw Marcelo struggling in his strong, primitive mind with an idea much too wounding, much too painful, to be true. And after a short pause he mumbled weakly, as if his voice were splintered into sighs:

"*Don* Leopo, and what do we do with Josco?"

"We'll yoke him up to haul cane. The crop's heavy this year and that bull is strong, can take a lot of hard work."

"Your pardon, *don* Leopo, but that bull was born a sire, he's wild, he can't be yoked." And he descended the winding steps, walked along the moonlit pathway and was lost in the sea of shadows of the cane field. Wounded, as though they had thrust a sword through the center of his heart.

The next day I saw Marcelo walk through the big white gate that opened from the road to the adjacent farms, leading a huge white bull by a rope. Short-horned, a powerful head with sepia spots. His broad, dilated nostrils pierced by an iron ring. Pale Marcelo walked along the path by the guava trees reluctantly, slowly, as though he never wanted to get there.

And suddenly a powerful, piercing bellow came from the *maya* hedges that formed the boundary lines of the Cocos' sector, echoing and reechoing from the steep banks of the San Lorenzo River and the cliffs of the Farallón. A red lightning flash of joy brightened Marcelo's lean face.

It was Josco's war cry, his challenge to match horns for the leadership of the herd. He began to sway his head like a pendulum. He thrust furiously at the earth, bearing aloft clods of earth and grass on the sharp-pointed horns. Frenzied, he made frontal attacks at the air, as though fighting against a shadow.

Marcelo, on the slope next to the house, yanked the white bull to a stop. Josco moved with a quick stride, until he got to the path. He stopped for a moment. He milled about rapidly, and began to prod the small guava trees that bordered the path. His crowned head became festooned with branches, wild flowers and twigs. He came on slowly, craftily, with a monotonous, repeated lowing. He stretched up his head and the lowing ended with a

largo y de clarinada. Raspó la tierra con las bifurcadas pezuñas hasta levantar al cielo polvaredas de oro. Avanzó un poco. Luego quedó inmóvil, hierático, tenso. En los belfos negros y gomosos la baba se le espumaba en burbujas de plata. Así permaneció un rato. Dobló la cerviz, el hocico pegado al ras del suelo, resoplando violentamente, como husmeando una huella misteriosa.

En la vieja casona la gente se fué asomando al balcón. Los agregados salían de sus bohíos. Los chiquillos de vientres abultados perforaban el aire con sus chillidos:

—El Josco pelea con el americano de los Velilla.

En el redondel de los cerros circunvecinos las voces se hicieron ecos.

Los chiquillos azuzaban al Josco. —Dale, Josco, que tú le puedes.

El Josco seguía avanzando, la cabeza baja, el andar lento y grave. Y el Jincho no pudo contenerse y soltó el toro blanco. Este se cuadró receloso, empezó a escarbar la tierra con las anchas pezuñas y lanzó un bronco mugido.

—Jey . . . Jey . . . Oiseee . . . Josco—gritaba la peonada.

—Palante, mi Josco—vibró el Jincho.

Y se oyó el seco y violento chocar del las cornamentas. Acreció el grito ensordecedor de la peonada.—Dale, jey . . . Josco.

Las cabezas pegadas, los ojos negros y refulgentes inyectados de sangre, los belfos dilatados, las pezuñas firmemente adheridas a la tierra, las patas traseras abiertas, los rabos leoninos erguidos, la trabazón rebullente de los músculos ondulando sobre las carnes macisas.

Colisión de fuerzas que por lo potentes se inmovilizaban. Ninguno cejaba; parecían como estampados en la fiesta de colores del paisaje.

La baba se espesaba. Los belfos ardorosos resonaban como fuelles.

Separaron súbitamente las cornamentas y empezaron a tirarse cornadas ladeadas, tratando de herirse en las frentes. Los cuernos sonaban como repiquetear de castañuelas. Y volvieron a unir las testas florecidas de puñales.

Un agregado exclamó:—El blanco es más grande y tiene más arrobas.

Y el Jincho con rabia le ripostó:—Pero el Josco tiene más maña y más cría.

long, clarion bellow. He scraped the earth with his cleft hoofs and raised clouds of golden dust. He advanced a little. Then he stood immobile, hieratic, tense. On his black rubbery lips the slaver foamed in silvery bubbles. He remained like that for a while. He bent his neck, nose level with the ground, snorting violently, as though he were sniffing a mysterious footprint.

The people crowded onto the porch of the huge old farmhouse. The tenants came from their shacks. The swollen-bellied children cut the air with their shrill cries:

"Josco's going to fight the *americano* from Velilla."

In the surrounding hillside, others echoed them.

The children egged Josco on. "Give it to him, Josco, you can do it."

Josco continued to advance, head lowered, his pace slow and serious. Pale Marcelo could not control himself and let go of the white bull. He squared off distrustfully, began to paw the dirt with his broad hoofs and uttered a harsh bellow.

"Hey, hey! Yaaah, Josco!" the peons shouted.

"Go on, my Josco!" yelled Marcelo.

And the violent, hard crash of horns sounded. The deafening screams of the peons increased. "Give it to him! Hey, Josco!"

Heads tight together, black eyes bloodshot and glaring, lips dilated, forehoofs firmly planted on the ground, hindhoofs widespread, leonine tails erect, firmly knit muscles undulating upon solid flesh.

A collision of forces whose very strength immobilized each other. Neither gave way; they seemed to be engraved on the festive-colored landscape.

The slaver thickened. The fiery lips resounded like bellows.

Suddenly they pulled their horns apart and began to dart at each other with sidewise blows, each trying to stab the other in the face. The clash of horns sounded like castanets. The dagger-blossomed heads came together once more.

A tenant shouted: "The white one is bigger and weighs more!"

And Marcelo angrily snapped back: "But Josco is smarter and has better blood."

El toro blanco, haciendo un supremo esfuerzo, se retiró un poco y avanzó egregio, imprimiéndole a la escultura imponente de su cuerpo toda la fuerza de sus arrobas. Y se vió al Josco recular arrollado por aquella avalancha incontenible.

—Aguante mi Josco—gritaba desesperado el Jincho. —No juya; usté eh de raza.

El Josco hincaba las patas traseras en la tierra buscando un apoyo para resistir, pero el blanco lo arrastraba. Dobló los corvejones tratando de detener el empuje, se irguió nuevamente y "rebuleó" rápido hacia atrás amortiguando la embestida del blanco.

—Lo ve; es mah grande—añadió con pena un agregado.

—Pero no juye—le escupió el Jincho.

Y las patas traseras del Josco toparon con una eminencia en el terreno, la cual le servió de sostén. Afirmado, sesgó a un lado, zafando el cuerpo a la embestida del blanco, que se perdió en el vacío. A éste faltó el equilibrio, y el Josco, aprovechándose del desbalance del contrario, volteó rápido y le asestó una cornada certera, trazándole en rojo sobre el albo costado una grieta de sangre. El blanco lanzó un bufido quejumbroso, huyendo despavorido entre la algarabía jubilosa del peonaje. El Jincho vibrante de emoción gritaba a voz en cuello:

—Toro jaiba, toro mañoso, toro de cría.

Y el Josco alargó el cuerpo estilizado, levantó la testa triunfal, las astas filosas doradas de sol, apuñaleando el mantón azul de un cielo sin nubes.

El blanco siempre se quedó de padrote. Orondo se paseaba por el cercao de las vacas.

Al Josco trataron de uncirlo al yugo con un buey viejo para que lo amaestrara, pero se revolvió violento poniendo en peligro la vida del peonaje. Andaba mohino, huraño, y se le escuchaba bramar quejoso, como agobiado por una pena inconmensurable.

Tranqueaba hacia el cercao de los bueyes de arrastres, de cogotes pelados y de pastar apacibles. Levantando la cabeza sobre la alambrada, dejaba escapar un triste mugido. Se veía buey rabisero, buey soroco, buey manco, buey toruno, buey castrao.

Aquel atardecer lo contemplé al trasluz de un crepúsculo tinto en sangre de toros, sobre la loma verdeante que domina el valle del Toa. No tenía la arrogancia de antes, no levantaba al

The white bull, with a supreme effort, retreated a bit and advanced egregiously, putting all the power of his weight behind his impressively sculptured body. And Josco backed up, swept away by that uncontrollable avalanche.

"Hold it, my Josco!" shouted Marcelo desperately. "Don't run! You're a thoroughbred."

Josco's hindhoofs dug into the ground, searching for support, but the white bull pushed him along. He bent his haunches trying to ward off the impact, straightened up again and whirled rapidly backwards, lessening the white one's charge.

"See? He's bigger," a peon said sorrowfully.

"But Josco doesn't run away," Marcelo spit at him.

And Josco's hindhoofs bumped into a mound which gave him support. Firm on his feet now, he swung his body to one side, clear of the white bull's charge, which continued into empty space. Taking advantage of his opponent's loss of balance, Josco turned rapidly and ripped him, tracing a deep bloody gash along the snowy flank. The white bull gave a snort of pain and fled in fright amidst the jubilant uproar of the peons. Pale Marcelo cried out excitedly:

"Sly bull, smart bull, thoroughbred!"

And Josco stretched his fine body and raised the triumphant head with its sharp horns golden in the sun, puncturing the blue mantle of the cloudless sky.

The white bull stayed on for breeding purposes anyway. Pompously he would parade the corrals where the cows were kept.

They tried to put Josco to the yoke with an old ox to train him, but he turned violent, threatening the lives of the peons. He wandered alone, hostile, and bellowed mournfully, as though stricken by an immeasurable sorrow.

He would stride over to the enclosure of the bald-headed, slow-gaited work oxen. Raising his head over the barbed-wire fence, he would low sadly. He would watch the frayed-tail oxen, the lame oxen, the one-horned oxen, the bad-tempered oxen, the castrated bulls.

That afternoon I saw him by the light of a sunset stained with the blood of bulls, on the verdant mountainside overlooking the Toa valley. He no longer looked arrogant, his crowned head

cielo airosamente la testa coronada; lo veía desfalleciente, como estrujado por una inmensa congoja. Babeó un rato, alargó la cabeza y suspendió un débil mugido, descendió la loma y su sombra se fundió en el misterio de una noche sin estrellas.

A eso de la media noche me pareció escuchar un mugir dolorido. El sueño se hizo sobre mis párpados.

Al otro día el Josco no aparecía. Se le buscó por todas las lindancias. No podía haberse pasado a las otras fincas, porque no había boquetes en los mayales, ni en las alambradas de las guardarrayas. El Jincho iba y venía desesperado. El tío Leopo apuntó:

—Tal vez se fué por el camino del Farallón a las malojillas del río. El Jincho hacia allí se encaminó. Regresó decepcionado. Luego se dirigió hacia una rejoya entre árboles en la colindancia de los Cocos, donde el Josco solía sestear. Lo vimos levantar la manos y con la voz transida de angustia gritó:

—Don Leopo, aquí está el Josco. Corrimos presurosos hacia donde el Jincho estaba, la cabeza baja, los ojos turbios de lágrimas. Señaló hacia un declive entre raíces, bejucales y flores silvestres. Y vimos al Josco inerte, las patas traseras abiertas y rígidas; la cabeza sepultada bajo el peso del cuerpo musculoso.

Y el Jincho con la voz temblorosa y llena de reconvenciones exclamó:

—Mi pobre Josco, se esnucó de rabia. Don Leopo se lo dije. Ese toro era padrote de nación; no nació pa yugo.

was no longer reared defiantly against the sky; he looked worn out, as though stricken by a great anguish. He drooled a little, stretched his head forward and let out a weak bellow, descended the hill and his shadow blended into the depths of the starless night.

About midnight I thought I heard a painful bellow. Sleep overcame me.

The next day Josco could not be found. They looked all around for him. He could not have gone to any of the neighboring farms, for there were no openings among the *maya* hedges nor in the barbed-wire fences. Pale Marcelo walked around frantically. Uncle Leopo suggested, "Perhaps he followed the Farallón path down to the grass along the river." Marcelo journeyed there. He came back disappointed. Later he went toward a hollow among the trees on the Cocos' boundary line, where Josco used to sleep after eating. We saw him throw up his arms and, in a voice choked with anguish, cry out: "*Don* Leopo, here's Josco." We ran anxiously to where he waited, head bent, eyes blinded by tears. He pointed in the direction of a slope covered with roots, wild flowers and reeds. And there we saw the inert form of Josco, hindlegs spread wide apart and stiff, head buried beneath the weight of the brawny body.

And Marcelo, in a trembling, recriminating voice, exclaimed:

"My poor Josco broke his neck in rage. *Don* Leopo, I told you so. That bull was a sire from birth; he wasn't born for the yoke."

—tr. C. Virginia Matters

PEYO MERCÉ ENSEÑA INGLÉS

Abelardo Díaz Alfaro

A la comay Margó Arce, de Peyo Mercé

TRAS el comentado episodio de la introdución de Santa Claus en la Cuchilla se recrudeció la animosidad prevaleciente entre Peyo Mercé y el supervisor Rogelio Escalera. Este, mediante carta virulenta y en términos drásticos, ordenaba al viejo maestro que redoblase sus esfuerzos y enseñase a todo trance inglés: "so pena de tener que apelar a recursos nada gratos para él; pero saludables para la buena marcha de la educación progresista." Ese obligado final de las cartas del supervisor se lo tenía bien sabido, y con un mohín de desprecio tiró a un lado la infausta misiva. Lo inusitado del caso era que con ella le llegaban también unos libros extraños de portadas enlucidas y paisajes a colorines, donde mostraban sus rostros unos niños bien comidos y mejor vestidos.

Peyo agarró uno de los libros. En letras negras leíase: *Primer*. Meditó un rato y rascándose la oreja masculló: *Primer,* eso debe derivarse de primero y por ende con ese libro debo iniciar mi nuevo via crucis. Otra jeringa más. ¡Y que Peyo Mercé enseñando inglés en inglés! Quiera que no voy a tener que adaptarme; en ello me van las habichuelas. Será estilo Cuchilla. ¿Si yo no lo masco bien, cómo lo voy a hacer digerir a mis discípulos? Mister Escalera quiere inglés, y lo tendrá del que guste. Y hojeó rápidamente las olorosas páginas del recién editado libro.

De las reflexiones lo fué sacando la algarabía de los niños campesinos que penetraban en el vetusto salón. Los mamelucos de tirillas manchosas de plátano, las melenas lacias y tostadas,

PEYO MERCÉ: ENGLISH TEACHER

Abelardo Díaz Alfaro

AFTER the story about Santa Claus' debut in the *barrio* of La Cuchilla made the rounds, the animosity between Peyo Mercé and Rogelio Escalera, the school supervisor, grew worse. Escalera ordered the old teacher, by means of a virulent and drastic letter, to emphasize at once the teaching of English, or else he would be forced to resort to methods that were not to his taste, "but that would prove healthful for the development of progressive education." That oft-repeated letter-ending of the supervisor, Peyo already knew by heart; scornfully, he threw aside the wretched message. The unusual thing about the whole matter was that, along with the letter, he received some books with white-plastered covers and glaring landscapes adorned with well-fed, neatly dressed children.

Peyo grabbed one of the books. It read *Primer,* in black letters. He thought for a while and then, scratching an ear, said to himself, "*Primer* must come from '*primero,*' which means that with this book I must start my new trip to the Calvary. One more headache. Peyo Mercé to teach English in English! And I'll have to—my job depends on it. Cuchilla style, it will be. If I myself don't chew it right, how am I going to make the kids digest it? But Mr. Escalera wants English and English it will be." He then went quickly through the book pages, which smelled brand-new.

The children's gabble, as they entered the shabby schoolroom, began to pull him out of his pondering. Funny-looking skirts and pants held by cloth-suspenders which had been tar-

los piecesitos apelotonados del rojo barro de los trillos y en caras marchitas el brillo tenue de los ojos de hambre.

La indignación que le produjera la carta del supervisor se fué disipando a medida que se llenaba el salón de aquellos sus hijos. Los quería por ser de su misma laya y porque le presentía un destino oscuro como noche de cerrazón. Buenos días, don Peyo, proferían y con ligera inclinación de cabeza se adelantaban hacia sus bancos-mesas. A Peyo no le gustaba que le llamaran mister: "Yo he sido batatero de la Cuchilla, y a honra lo llevo. Eso de míster me sabe a kresto, a chuingo y otras guazaberías que ahora nos venden. Estoy manchao del plátano y tengo la vuelta del motojo."

Se asomó a la mal recortada ventanita en el rústico tabique como para cobrar aliento. Sobre el verde plomizo de los cerros veteados de cimbreantes tabacales, unas nubes blancas hinchaban sus velas luminosas de sol. En la llamarada roja de unos bucayos los mozambiques quemaban sus alas negras. Y sintió que le invadía un desgano, una flojedad de ánimo, que le impelía más bien a encauzar su clase al estudio de la tierra, la tierra fecunda que frutecía en reguero de luces en coágulo de rubíes. Le estaba penoso el retornar a la labor cotidiana, en pleno día soleado. Y doloroso el tener que enseñar una cosa tan árida como un inglés de *Primer*.

Con pasos lentos se dirigió al frente del salón. En los labios partidos se insinuaba la risa precursora del desplante. Un pensamiento amargo borró la risa y surcó la frente de arrugas. Hojeó de nuevo el intruso libro. No encontraba en él nada que despertara el interés de sus discípulos, nada que se adaptara al medio ambiente. Con júbilo descubrió una lámina donde un crestado gallo lucía su frondoso rabo. El orondo gallo enfilaba sus largas y curvas espuelas en las cuales muy bien podía dormir su noche un isabelino. "Ya está, mis muchachos tendrán hoy gallo en inglés." Y un poco más animado se decidió a enfrentarse serenamente a su clase.

—Well, children—, wi are goin to talk in inglis today—Y mientras estas palabras, salpicadas de hipos sofocantes salían de su boca, paseaba la mirada arisca sobre los rostros atónitos de los niños. Y como para que no se le fuera la "rachita" inquirió con voz atiplada—¿understán?—

nished by plantain, hair straight and faded, tiny feet covered by the red clay of the rural trails, and the soft glow of hungry eyes on withered faces.

The indignation that the supervisor's letter had stirred up in him diminished as all his children began to fill the room. He loved them because they were his own kind and because for each of them he envisioned a destiny as dark as the night becomes just before a storm. Good morning, *Don* Peyo, they said, and with a light movement of the head approached the benches nailed to tabletops. Peyo did not like to be addressed as *mister*. "I'm a hick from La Cuchilla and I feel honored to be so. That *mister* thing tastes to me just like Kresto and 'chewing-gaw' and the other stuff they sell us now. I bear within me the stain of the plantain and can turn whichever way, just like the bushleaf."

He looked out the lopsided window as if to collect his breath. Over the grayish-green of the hills spotted by the swaying tobacco groves, white clouds raised their swollen sunlit sails. Against the red blaze of some shade trees, crackles burnt their black wings. And he felt a lack of interest, a weakening of the will, come over him, driving his attention rather to a class study of the land—the fertile land that yielded so much light, so many ruby-colored clots. To return to everyday chores on such a sunny day was something that he could not help but lament. And painful it was to have to teach as dry a thing as *Primer English*.

He walked slowly to the front of the class. His cracked lips hinted at the laughter that would damn it all. A bitter thought put away the laughter from his thoughts and wrinkled his forehead. Once again he turned the pages of the meddlesome book. There was not a single thing in it that could arouse his students' interest, nothing that related to the environment. He joyfully came upon a print of a bigcrest rooster that displayed its luxuriant tail. The proud rooster had long, bent spurs in which an Isabela game-cock could well spend the night. "That's it; today the kids will have rooster in English." In better spirits now, Peyo decided to face his class most calmly.

"Well, children . . . We are goin' to talk in Englis' toooday." While these gaspingly bespattered words came out of his mouth, his eyes went fleetingly over the astonished faces of his children. And in order to make the best of his approach, he asked in a high pitch, *"Under-es-stan'?"*

El silencio absoluto fué la respuesta a su interrogación. Y a Peyo le dieron ganas de reprender a la clase, ¿pero cómo se iba a arreglar para hacerlo en inglés? Y volvió a asomarse a la ventanita para cobrar ánimo. Una calandria surcaba la plenitud azulina—pétalo negro en el viento—. Y sintió más su miseria. Ansias de liberarse.

Aprovechó el momento para ensayar la pronunciación de la palabra que iba a enseñar. Y haciendo una grotesca mueca seguida de un sonido semejante al que se produce al estornudar, mascullό—cock— —cock— —cock—Y hastiado increpó: "Idioma del diablo."

Y se decidió a intentar un método que se apartaba algo de lo aconsejado en las latosas pláticas pedagógicas de los eruditos en la materia.

Reinó el silencio en el salón. Peyo era querido y respetado por sus discípulos. ¡Costa tan inexplicable para Rogelio Escalera! Peyo desconocía los últimos estudios sobre la personalidad del maestro y más sobre la psicología del niño. No le gustaba concurrir a las "amañadas clases modelo," cosa esta en la cual se fijaba mucho el supervisor.

Un chorro de luz clara penetraba por la ventanita moteando en rojo los rostros pálidos y cabrilleando inquieta en las sueltas cabelleras.

—Bueno, muchachos, vamos a rejentiar hoy un poco en inglés, apuras. Y mientras las palabras brotaban trabajosas pensó echar a voleo su discursito alusivo a las bienandanzas de lo que iba a poner en práctica. Pero la sinceridad era su defecto capital como maestro.

Sentía que se le formaba un taco en la garganta, y con los dedos convulsos se aflojaba el nudo de la desteñida corbata para librarse de la opresión. Maldijo en lo más remoto del subconsciente unas cuantas cosas, entre ellas al supervisor que lo quería hacer nadar en aguas donde el que no es buen pez se ahoga. Y con resignación musitó: "A fuete y a puya cualquier yegua vieja camina." Y la frase jíbara cobró en su mente toda su dolorosa realidad.

Y Peyo rebuscó en su magín todos los "devices" que se aconsejaban en los libros versados en la enseñanza del inglés. La mente de Peyo estaba entenebrecida como noche de barrunto. "Un atajo, un atrecho, una maña, que me saquen al camino,"

Complete silence was the answer they gave him. And Peyo felt like reprimanding them, but—how could he manage that in English? He moved over again to the window in search of courage. A lark cut through the bluish expanse—a black petal in the wind. And he felt loaded with misery. With a deep longing for freedom.

He availed himself of the moment to rehearse the pronunciation of the word he would be teaching next. And with a wry face followed by a sort of sneezing sound, he muttered, "*Cock . . . Cock . . . Cock . . .*" And scolded, "Language of the devil."

He decided to try out a method that was not exactly what the tedious pedagogical lectures of the experts advised.

Silence came over the classroom. Peyo was loved and respected by his students. That was something that Rogelio Escalera could not understand! Peyo did not know anything about the latest studies conducted on the teacher's personality traits and even less about child psychology. He did not like to attend the "fixed model classes," something that the supervisor took very much to heart.

A spurt of light came through the small window, red-spotting the wan faces and white-capping the loose, long hair.

"Well, children, today we're going to gad about in English for a while—straight English." His words coming out laboriously, he was inclined to give out with a little speech concerning the goodness of what he was about to deal with. But his main fault as a teacher was sincerity.

Feeling a lump in his throat, he loosened the knot of his faded tie with nervous fingers. Out in the farthest corner of his mind, he cursed a few things—among them, the supervisor who wanted him to swim in deep-sea waters where only the best fish can keep alive. With full resignation, he said to himself, "You can spike and lash any old mare into making a move." And the *jíbaro* saying acquired in his own mind all of its painful reality.

Peyo tried to think about the "devices" suggested in the books that had to do with the teaching of English. His mind, however, was as gloomy as a night that threatened stormy weather. "A shortcut, a footpath, a trick—anything that can lead me out to

clamó. Y remeciéndose la atribulada cabeza entre los toscos dedos, ante el asombro de los alelados discípulos, dejó caer estas palabras: "¡Qué paraíso sería esto, sino fuera por el supervisor y sus mojigangas!" Y convencido de que baldíos serían sus esfuerzos para conducir su clase en inglés, como otras veces se agenció un medio propio, "un corte," como él los denominaba. Y optó por hacer una mixtura, un mejurje, un injerto. "Y que saliera pato o gallareta."

Levantó el libro sobre las cabezas de sus discípulos. Y con el índice manchoso de tabaco mostró la lámina en que se extasiaba el soberbio gallo.—Miren, this is a cock. Repitan. Y los muchachos empezaron a corear la palabra en forma inarmónica: cock, cock, cock. Y Peyo, los nervios excitados, la cabeza congestionada, gritó desaforadamente:—¡So, más despacio; ya estos condenados me han formado la gallera aquí mismo. Se apagaron las desentonadas voces. Peyo se ahogaba del calor. Se alejó otra vez hacia la ventanita. El sudor empapaba su coloreada camisa. Le hacía falta aire, mucho aire. Y se detuvo un momento, las manos agarradas como garfios al marco desnivelado de la ventana.

Inconscientemente fijó la mirada en el chorro de la quebrada vecina—una lágrima fresca en la tosca peña. Y envidió al hijo de la Petra que sumergía la sucia cara en las aguas perladas de sol.

Hastiado se decidió a salir lo más pronto posible del lío en que se había metido. Y con pasos nerviosos se dirigió al frente de la clase: —Ya ustedes saben, cock es gallo en inglés, en americano. Y volvió a señalar con el dedo manchoso de tabaco al vistoso gallo. —Esto en inglés es cock, cock es gallo. Vamos a ir poco a poco, que así se doma un potro, si no se desboca. —¿Qué es esto en inglés, Telco? Y éste, que estaba como pasmado mirando aquel gallo extraño, con timidez respondió: "Ese es gallo pava." Y el vetusto salón se etremeció con el cascabeleo de las risas infantiles. Peyo disimulando la gracia que le producían aquellas palabras, frunció el entrecejo, por el aquel de no perder la fuerza moral, y con sorna ripostó: —Ya lo sabía, éste se cuela en la gallera de don Cipria. ¡Y que gallo pava! Este es un gallo doméstico, un gallo respetable, no un gallo "mondao" como esos de pelea.

Y volvió a inquirir: "¿Qué es esto en inglés?" Y los niños entonaron la monótona cantinela: "Cock, cock, cock." Y Peyo se

the road," he implored. And shaking his distressed head with rough fingers, while his students stared with surprise, he said, "What paradise this would be if it were not for the supervisor and his nonsense."

Convinced that his efforts to conduct the class in English would prove futile, he again resorted to a method all his own, "a cut-through" as he called it. He would mix it, concoct it, graft it. And whatever would come out of it, duck or widgeon, would be all right.

He raised the book over the head of his students. With a tobacco-stained finger, he pointed at the illustration of the superb rooster.

"Look, *this is a cock.* Repeat that."

And the students sang way out of tune, *"Cock, cock, cock."*

Peyo, all excited, head stuffed up, shouted, "Whoa! Easy. These brats are setting up a cockpit right here!" The dissonant voices died down. Peyo was stifling. Once again he walked to the window. Sweat soaked his many-colored shirt. He needed air, a lot of air. And he held himself there for a while, hands stuck like hooks on the slanted window-frame.

He stared unconsciously at the neighboring stream—a fresh tear sliding through the rocks. And he envied Petra's son, who was dunking his face in the sunlit water.

Disgusted, he decided to get out of the mess he had gotten into. And nervously he walked back to the front of the room.

"All right, *cock* is rooster in English, in American." Again he pointed the tobacco-stained finger at the luxurious rooster. "This is *cock* in English, *cock* is rooster. Now let's go easy, 'cause that's the way to tame a stallion. Otherwise, he runs wild. What's this in English, Teclo?"

Teclo, who had been staring at the strange rooster, answered timidly, "That's a turkey game-cock." And the children's laughter made the shabby room rattle. Peyo frowned, pretending not to be moved by the funny remark, and said maliciously, "I knew it, he walks on the sly into *Don* Cipria's cockpit. Turkey gamecock, indeed! Child, this is a tame rooster, a respectable rooster, not one of those shaved ones that fight around."

And again he asked, "What's this in English?" And the students went into the monotonous sing-song, *"Cock, cock, cock."*

sintió bastante complacido, Había salido ileso de aquella cruenta pelea. Repartió algunos libros e hizo que los abrieran en la página en que se "istoriaba" el fachendoso gallo. "Vamos a leer un poco en inglés." Los muchachos miraban con sorpresa la página y a duras penas podían contener los bufidos de risa.

Se le demudó el rostro. Un calofrío le atravesó el cuerpo. Hasta pensó presentar la renuncia con carácter irrevocable al supervisor. "Ahora sí que se le entorchó a la puerca el rabo." Ya a tropezones, gagueando, la lengua pesada y un sabor a maya en los labios, leyó: "This is the cock, the cock says coocadoodledoo." Y Peyo se dijo para su capote. "O ese gallo tiene pepita, o es que los americanos no oyen bien." Aquello era lo último. Pero pensó en el pan nuestro de cada día.

"Lean conmigo: The cock says coocadoodledoo." Y las voces templaban en el viento mañanero. —Está bien . . .
—Tellito, ¿cómo es que canta el gallo en inglés?
—No sé, don Peyo.
—Pero, mira, muchacho, si lo acabas de leer . . .
—No, gimió Tellito, mirando la lámina.
—Mira, canuto, el gallo dice coocadoodledoo.

Y Tellito, como excusándose, dijo: Don Peyo, ese será el cantió del manilo americano, pero el girito de casa jace cocoroco clarito.

Peyo olvidó todo su dolor y soltó una estrepitosa carcajada, que fué acompañada de las risas frescas de los niños.

Asustado por la algazara, el camagüey de don Cipria batió las tornasoladas alas y tejió en la seda azul del cielo su cocoroco límpido y metálico.

And Peyo felt pretty good. Out of that bloody encounter, he had emerged unharmed. He distributed some books and ordered the students to turn to the page that told all about that bragging rooster. "Let's read a little in English." The children looked surprised at the page and could hardly hold back the roars of laughter.

Peyo's face changed colors. A chill ran through his body. He even thought of handing the supervisor his most definite resignation. "The pig's tail is curling for sure now." And by fits and starts, stuttering, with a heavy tongue and lips tasting of thorny *maya* leaves, he read, *"This is the cock. The cock says cock-a-doodle-do."* He then told himself, "Either that rooster has distemper or else Americans don't hear too good." That was really the last straw. But he gave a moment's thought to his everyday bread.

"Read with me. *The cock says cock-a-doodle-do.*" The voices shimmered on the morning wind. "That's good."

"Now, Tellito, how does the rooster sing in English?"

"I don't know, *Don* Peyo."

"But you just read it, boy."

"No," Tellito whimpered, looking at the print.

"Look, you dumb-bell, the rooster says *cock-a-doodle-do.*"

And Tellito, as though apologizing, said, "*Don* Peyo, that American Manila rooster may go like that, but the black and white one we got home goes caw-caw-raw-caw."

Peyo forgot all his pain and let out a boisterous laugh that was accompanied by the children's own titter.

Alarmed by the noise, *Don* Cipria's own *camagüey* cock shook his iridescent wings and wove into the sky's blue silk his own clean, metallic caw-caw-raw-caw.

—tr. Pedro Juan Soto

EN EL FONDO DEL CAÑO HAY UN NEGRITO

José Luis González

A René Depestre

La primera vez que el negrito Melodía vio al otro negrito en el fondo del caño fue en la mañana del tercer o cuarto día después de la mudanza, cuando llegó gateando hasta la única puerta de la nueva vivienda y se asomó para mirar hacia la quieta superficie del agua allá abajo.

Entonces el padre, que acababa de despertar sobre el montón de sacos vacíos extendidos en el piso, junto a la mujer semidesnuda que aún dormía, le gritó:

—¡Mire . . . eche p'adentro! ¡Diantre 'e muchacho desinquieto!

Y Melodía, que no había aprendido a entender las palabras, pero sí a obedecer los gritos, gateó otra vez hacia adentro y se quedó silencioso en un rincón, chupándose un dedito porque tenía hambre.

El hombre se incorporó sobre los codos. Miró a la mujer que dormía a su lado y la sacudió flojamente por un brazo. La mujer despertó sobresaltada, mirando al hombre con ojos de susto. El hombre rió. Todas las mañanas era igual: la mujer salía del sueño con aquella expresión de susto que a él le provocaba un regocijo sin maldad. La primera vez que vio aquella expresión en el rostro de su mujer no fue en ocasión de un despertar, sino la noche que se acostaron juntos por primera vez. Quizá por eso a él le hacía gracia verla despabilarse así todas las mañanas.

THERE'S A LITTLE COLORED BOY IN THE BOTTOM OF THE WATER

José Luis González

To René Depestre

THE first time the little baby Melodía saw the other little colored boy at the bottom of the water was early in the morning, the third or fourth day after they had moved, when he crawled to the door of the new house, leaned over and looked down at the still surface below.

His father, who had just awakened on the pile of empty sacks stretched on the floor, next to the half-naked and still-sleeping woman, shouted at the boy:

"Hey! . . . git youself down an' inside! Restless li'l' baastad!"

And Melodía, who had not yet learned to understand words, but understood shouting, crawled inside again and stayed quiet in a corner sucking one small finger, for he was hungry.

The man raised himself on his elbows. He looked at the woman who slept beside him and shook her lazily by one arm. The woman woke up startled, looking at the man with fear in her eyes. The man laughed. Every morning it was the same: the woman woke up with that frightened face which made him want to laugh, but without malice. The first time he'd seen that frightened face on the woman was the night they had lain together for the first time. Perhaps this was why it seemed attractive to him to see her come up out of sleep like that every morning.

El hombre se sentó sobre los sacos vacíos.

—Bueno—se dirigió entonces a la mujer—. Cuela el café.

Ella tardó un poco en contestar:

—Ya no queda.

—¿Ah?

—No queda. Se acabó ayer.

El empezó a decir: "¿Y por qué no compraste más?" pero se interrumpió cuando vio que en el rostro de su mujer comenzaba a dibujarse aquella otra expresión, aquella mueca que a él no le causaba regocijo y que ella sólo hacía cuando él le dirigía preguntas como la que acababa de truncar ahora. La primera vez que vio aquella expresión en el rostro de su mujer fue la noche que regresó a la casa borracho y deseoso de ella pero la borrachera no lo dejó hacer nada. Tal vez por eso al hombre no le hacía gracia aquella mueca.

—¿Conque se acabó ayer?

—Ajá.

La mujer se puso de pie y empezó a meterse el vestido por la cabeza. El hombre, todavía sentado sobre los sacos vacíos, derrotó su mirada y la fijó durante un rato en los agujeros de su camiseta.

Melodía, cansado ya de la insipidez del dedo, se decidió a llorar. El hombre lo miró y le preguntó a la mujer:

—¿Tampoco hay na pal nene?

—Sí. Conseguí unas hojitas de guanábana y le gua hacer un guarapillo horita.

—¿Cuántos días va que no toma leche?

—¿Leche?—la mujer puso un poco de asombro inconsciente en la voz—. No me acuerdo.

El hombre se levantó y se puso los pantalones. Después se allegó a la puerta y miró hacia afuera. Le dijo a la mujer:

—La marea ta alta. Hoy hay que dir en bote.

Luego miró hacia arriba, hacia el puente y la carretera. Automóviles, guaguas y camiones pasaban en un desfile interminable. El hombre observó cómo desde casi todos los vehículos alguien miraba con extrañeza hacia la casucha enclavada en medio de aquel brazo de mar: el "caño" sobre cuyas márgenes pantanosas había ido creciendo hacía años el arrabal. Ese alguien por lo general empezaba a mirar la casucha cuando el

The man sat upright on the empty sacks.
"Good," he said to her then. "Make the coffee."

"There's none left."
"Oh?"
"No, there's none left. It ran out yesterday."
The man started to ask: "Why didn't you buy more?" but stopped himself when he saw that the woman was beginning to make that other face, a face that did not please him, the one she put on only when he asked questions like that. The first time he had seen that particular look on the woman's face was the night he'd come home drunk, wanting her, and got on top of her, but the drunkenness kept him from doing anything. Perhaps for that reason it did not please him to see that face on the woman.

"Mean to say we ran out yesterday?"
"Mmhm."
The woman got to her feet and began putting her dress on over her head. The man, still seated on the empty sacks, shifted his glance and looked at the holes in his undershirt for a while.

Melodía, already bored by the uninteresting taste of his finger, decided to cry. The man looked at him and asked the woman:
"There's nuthin' for the kid either?"
"Yes . . . I got some guanábana leaves. Goin' to make him some broth in a little bit."
"How many days he go he don't have milk?"
"Milk?" the woman asked, and there was a little unconscious fear in her voice. "I don't recall."
The man stood up and put on his trousers. He went to the door and looked out. He said to the woman:
"Tide's high. Have to go in the boat today."
Then he glanced upward to the bridge and the highway. Automobiles, buses, and trucks passed in an endless file. And the man smiled, noticing that from almost every vehicle someone looked with surprise at the hut sitting in the center of that arm of the sea: the *caño,* on whose quaggy edges the slum had been growing for years. Whoever they were, they began to stare at the hut, generally when they came to the middle of the bridge, then

automóvil, la guagua o el camión llegaba a la mitad del puente, y después seguía mirando, volviendo gradualmente la cabeza hasta que el automóvil, la guagua o el camión tomaba la curva allá adelante y se perdía de vista. El hombre se llevó una mano desafiante a la entrepierna y masculló:

—¡Pendejos!

Poco después se metió en el bote y remó hasta la orilla. De la popa del bote a la puerta de la casa había una soga larga que permitía a quien quedara en la casa atraer nuevamente el bote hasta la puerta. De la casa a la orilla había también un puentecito de tablas, que se cubría con la marea alta.

Ya en tierra, el hombre caminó hacia la carretera. Se sintió mejor cuando el ruido de los automóviles ahogó el llanto del negrito en la casucha.

La segunda vez que el negrito Melodía vio al otro negrito en el fondo del caño fue poco después del mediodía, cuando volvió a gatear hasta la puerta y se asomó hacia abajo. Esta vez el negrito en el fondo del caño le regaló una sonrisa a Melodía. Melodía había sonreído primero y tomó la sonrisa del otro negrito como una respuesta a la suya. Entonces hizo así con la manita, y desde el fondo del caño el otro negrito también hizo así con su manita. La madre lo llamó entonces porque el segundo guarapillo de hojas de guanábana ya estaba listo.

Dos mujeres, de las afortunadas que vivían en tierra firme, sobre el fango endurecido de las márgenes del caño, comentaban:

—Hay que velo. Si me lo bieran contao, biera dicho que era embuste.

—La necesidá, doña. A mí misma, quién me lo biera dicho, que yo diba llegar aquí. Yo que tenía hasta mi tierrita . . .

—Pues nosotros juimos de los primeros. Casi no bía gente y uno cogía la parte más sequecita, ¿ve? Pero los que llegan ahora, fíjese, tienen que tirarse al agua, como quien dice. Pero, bueno . . . y esa gente, ¿de onde diantre haberán salío?

—A mí me dijieron que por ai por Isla Verde tan orbanisando y han sacao un montón de negros arrimaos. A lo mejor son desos.

kept on looking, turning their heads slowly until whatever vehicle it was took the curve there up ahead.

The man put his hand to his groin, gestured defiantly, and muttered: "Shitheads!"

In a little while he got into the boat and rowed to shore. From the boat's stern a long mooring line was made fast to the door of the house, so that whoever stayed in the house could draw the boat back to the door again. Between the house and the shore there was also a small bridge, which now, at high tide, was covered.

Once ashore, the man walked up to the highway. He felt better when the traffic noise drowned out the crying of the small Negro boy in the hut.

The second time little Melodía saw the other little colored boy at the bottom of the water was a little after midday, when he crawled to the door of the hut again and leaned out and looked down below. This time, the little boy at the bottom of the water favored Melodía with a smile. Melodía had smiled first and now he took the other's smile as an answer to his own. Then he went like that with his little hand, and from the bottom of the water the other little boy waved back. At that moment his mother called him, because the second broth of guanábana leaves was finally ready.

Two women, two of the lucky ones who lived on dry land, on the hardened mud alongside the inlet, were swapping opinions:

"You have to see it to believe it. If they'd told me about it, I'd have said it was a lie."

"It's necessity, lady. Even me, for instance, I even had my little bit of land . . . Who'd've said I'd have to end up here?"

"Well, we were one of the firsts, there were almost no people here then and you grabbed the driest spot, see? But those who are coming now, well, they're stuck, they have to throw themselves into the water, like they say. But still . . . those people, where the devil could they have come from?"

"I was told that over there, by Isla Verde, they're building new homes and have got rid of a whole heap of Negro riffraff. They're probably part of that."

—¡Bendito! . . . ¿Y usté se ha fijao en el negrito qué mono? La mujer vino ayer a ver si yo tenía unas hojitas de algo pa hacerle un guarapillo, y yo le di unas poquitas de guanábana que me quedaban.

—¡Ay, Virgen, bendito . . . !

Al atardecer, el hombre estaba cansado. Le dolía la espalda; pero venía palpando las monedas en el fondo del bolsillo, haciéndolas sonar, adivinando con el tacto cuál era un vellón, cuál de diez, cuál una peseta. Bueno, hoy había habido suerte. El blanco que pasó por el muelle a recoger su mercancía de Nueva York. Y el compañero de trabajo que le prestó su carretón toda la tarde porque tuvo que salir corriendo a buscar a la comadrona para su mujer, que estaba echando un pobre más al mundo. Sí, señor. Se va tirando. Mañana será otro día.

Entró en un colmado y compró café y arroz y habichuelas y unas latitas de leche evaporada. Pensó en Melodía y apresuró el paso. Se había venido a pie desde San Juan para ahorrarse los cinco centavos del pasaje.

La tercera vez que el negrito Melodía vio al otro negrito en el fondo del caño fue al atardecer, poco antes de que el padre regresara. Esta vez Melodía venía sonriendo antes de asomarse, y le asombró que el otro también se estuviera sonriendo allá abajo. Volvió a hacer así con la manita y el otro volvió a contestar. Entonces Melodía sintió un súbito entusiasmo y un amor indecible por el otro negrito. Y se fue a buscarlo.

"By all the saints . . . ! And have you seen what a cute little colored boy they have? The woman came over yesterday to see if I had some leaves of anything to make a drink, and I gave her a few guanábana leaves I had left over."

"Ai, holy Virgin . . . !"

At sunset the man was tired. His back hurt. But he walked along feeling the coins at the bottom of his pocket, making them tinkle against one another, guessing from the touch which was a nickel, which a dime, which a quarter. Fine . . . today he'd had luck: the white man who'd driven by the dock to pick up his merchandise from New York. Then the worker who'd lent him his cart for the whole afternoon because he had to go chasing to find a midwife for his woman, who was dropping one more poor wretch into the world. *Sí, señor*. I'll get it going. Tomorrow's another day.

The man slipped into a grocery store and bought coffee and rice and kidney beans and some small tins of evaporated milk. He thought of Melodía and quickened his pace. He had come from San Juan on foot so as not to spend the five cents for the bus.

The third time that little Melodía saw the other little colored boy at the bottom of the water was at sunset, a little before his father came home. This time Melodía started smiling before he peered over, and was surprised to see that the other little boy had also been smiling down below. Again he waved his small hand and again the other one answered him. Then Melodía felt a sudden warmth and an inexpressible love for the other little colored boy.

And he went to look for him.

—tr. Lysander Kemp

LA NOCHE QUE VOLVIMOS A SER GENTE

José Luis González

A Juan Sáez Burgos

¿QUE si me acuerdo? Se acuerda el Barrio entero si quieres que te diga la verdad, porque eso no se le va a olvidar ni a Trompoloco, que ya no es capaz de decir ni dónde enterraron a su mamá hace quince días. Lo que pasa es que yo te lo puedo contar mejor que nadie por esa casualidad que tú todavía no sabes. Pero antes vamos a pedir unas cervezas bien frías porque con esta calor del diablo quién quita que hasta me falle la memoria.

Ahora sí, salud y pesetas. Y fuerza donde tú sabes. Bueno, pues de eso ya van cuatro años y si quieres te digo hasta los meses y los días porque para acordarme no tengo más que mirarle la cara al barrigón ése que tú viste ahí en la casa cuando fuiste a procurarme esta mañana. Sí, el mayorcito, que se llama igual que yo pero que si hubiera nacido mujercita hubiéramos tenido que ponerle Estrella o Luz María o algo así. O hasta Milagros, mira, porque aquello fue . . . Pero si sigo así voy a contarte el cuento al revés, o sea desde el final y no por el principio, así que mejor sigo por donde iba.

Bueno, pues la fecha no te la digo porque ya tú la sabes y lo que te interesa es otra cosa. Entonces resulta que ese día le había dicho yo al foreman, que era un judío buena persona y ya sabía su poquito de español, que me diera un overtime porque me iban a hacer falta los chavos para el parto de mi mujer, que ya estaba en el último mes y no paraba de sacar cuentas. Que si lo del canastillo, que si lo de la comadrona . . . Ah, porque ella estaba empeñada en dar a luz en la casa y no en la clínica donde los doctores y las norsas no hablan español y además sale más caro.

THE NIGHT WE BECAME PEOPLE AGAIN

José Luis González

To Juan Sáez Burgos

DO I remember? The whole Barrio remembers, if you want to know the truth; even Crazytop won't forget, and he couldn't even tell you where they buried his mother fifteen days later. I can tell you about it better than anybody because of a coincidence you don't know about. But first let's have a couple of nice cold beers, because this damn heat is even affecting my memory.

Ah, now, *salud y pesetas* . . . and plenty of strength you know where. Well, it's been four years already; I can even tell you how many months and days, because to remember all I've got to do is take a look at the chubby little fellow you saw at home when you came to get me this morning. Yeah, the oldest one, who's named after me, but if he'd been born a girl we would have had to call her Estrella, or Luz María, or something like that. Or even Milagros, because that was really . . . but if I keep on like this I'll tell you the whole thing backwards.*

Well, I won't mention the date, because you already know that. Turns out, that day I had told the foreman, a Jewish fellow, nice guy, knows a bit of Spanish, that I wanted some overtime, because I would need the dough for my wife's pregnancy, she was in her final months, and there were plenty of things to get. The crib, the midwife . . . ah, because she wanted to give birth at home, not in the clinic, because the doctors and the *norsas* don't speak Spanish, and anyways it's more expensive.

*The literal translations of the girls' names are Star (Estrella), Light (Luz), Miracles (Milagros).

Entonces a las cuatro acabé mi primer turno y bajé al come-y-vete ése del italiano que está ahí enfrente de la factoría. Cuestión de echarme algo a la barriga hasta que llegara a casa y la mujer me recalentara la comida, ¿ves? Bueno, pues me metí un par de hot dogs con una cerveza mientras le tiraba un vistazo al periódico hispano que había comprado por la mañana, y en eso, cuando estaba leyendo lo de un latino que había hecho tasajo a su corteja porque se la estaba pegando con un chino, en eso, mira, yo no sé si tú crees en esas cosas, pero como que me entró un presentimiento. O sea que sentí que esa noche iba a pasar algo grande, algo que yo no podía decir lo que iba a ser. Yo digo que uno tiene que creer porque tú me dirás qué tenía que ver lo del latino y el chino y la corteja con eso que yo empecé a sentir. A sentir, tú sabes, porque no fue que lo pensara, que eso es distinto. Bueno, pues acabé de mirar el periódico y volví rápido a la factoría para empezar el overtime.

Entonces el otro foreman, porque el primero ya se había ido, me dice: ¿Qué, te piensas hacer millonario para poner un casino en Puerto Rico? Así, relajando, tú sabes, y vengo yo y le digo, también vacilando: No, si el casino ya lo tengo. Ahora lo que quiero poner es una fábrica. Y me dice: ¿Una fábrica de qué? Y le digo: Una fábrica de humo. Y entonces me pregunta: ¿Ah, si? ¿Y qué vas a hacer con el humo? Y yo bien serio, con una cara de palo que había que ver: ¡Adiós! . . . ¿y qué voy a hacer? ¡Enlatarlo! Un vacilón, tú sabes, porque ese foreman era todavía más buena persona que el otro. Pero porque le conviene, desde luego: así nos pone de buen humor y nos saca el jugo en el trabajo. Él se cree que yo no lo sé, pero cualquier día se lo digo para que vea que uno no es tan ignorante como parece. Porque esta gente aquí a veces se imagina que uno viene de la última sínsora y confunde el papel de lija con el papel de inodoro, sobre todo cuando uno es trigueñito y con la morusa tirando a caracolillo.

Pero, bueno, eso es noticia vieja y lo que tengo que contarte es otra cosa. Ahora, que la condenada calor sigue y la cerveza ya se nos acabó. La misma marca, ¿no? Okay. Pues como te iba diciendo, después que el foreman me quiso vacilar y yo lo dejé con las ganas, pegamos a trabajar en serio. Porque eso sí, aquí la guachafita y el trabajo no son compadres. Time is money, ya tú sabes. Pegaron a llegarme radios por el assembly line y yo a meterles los tubos: chan, chan. Sí, yo lo que hacía entonces era

So at four o'clock I finished my first shift and went down to the Italian's snack bar in front of the factory. Wanted to put something into my belly, until I got home and my wife reheated the supper, you see. Well, I gulped down a couple of hot dogs with a beer while I flipped through the Spanish paper I'd bought that morning, and while I'm reading about this Latino who had cut up his girlfriend because she'd been running around with a Chinaman, I don't know if you believe in those things, but like I had a funny feeling. I felt that something big was going to happen that night. I think a person has to believe, because you might ask what's the thing about the Latino and his girlfriend and the Chinaman got to do with what I began to feel. Feel, you see, because I wasn't thinking it, which is different. Well, I stopped reading the paper and hurried back to the factory to start my overtime.

Then the other foreman, the first one had already left, he says to me, "Say, do you plan to become a millionaire and open a casino in Puerto Rico?" He's just fooling around, and then I tell him, still fooling, "No, I've already got a casino. Now I wanna open a factory." And he says, "What kinda factory?" And I tell him, "A smoke factory." So he says, "Ah, really? And what are you gonna do with the smoke?" And me, real serious, deadpan, I say, "Do with it? I'm gonna can it!" Just fooling around, y'know, because that foreman was an even nicer guy than the first. That's because it's to his benefit. He puts us in a good mood and gets us to work that much harder. He thinks I don't know, but any day now I'm going to tell him that I'm not as dumb as he might think. These people think that you come from the sticks and don't know the difference between sandpaper and toilet paper, especially if you're a bit dark-skinned, and your hair is kind of kinky.

Well, anyway, that's old news, and I've got something else to tell you. That damn heat . . . and our glasses are empty. Same brand, right? Okay. Well, as I was saying, after the foreman started joking around, we got down to some serious work. Because around here goofing and work don't mix. Time is money, you know. Radios started coming at me along the assembly line and I started sticking tubes into them, bam, bam. Yeah, that was my job then, putting tubes in. Two for every radio, one in

poner los tubos. Dos a cada radio, uno en cada mano: chan, chan. Al principio, cuando no estaba impuesto, a veces se me pasaba un radio y entonces, ¡muchacho!, tenía que correrle detrás y al mismo tiempo echarle el ojo al que venía seguido, y creía que me iba a volver loco. Cuando salía del trabajo sentía como que llevaba un baile de San Vito en todo el cuerpo. A mí me está que por eso en este país hay tanto borracho y tanto vicioso. Sí, chico, porque cuando tú quedas así lo que te pide el cuerpo es un juanetazo de lo que sea, que por lo general es ron o algo así, y ahí se va acostumbrando uno. Yo digo que por eso las mujeres se defienden mejor en el trabajo de factoría, porque ellas se entretienen con el chismorreo y la habladuría y el comentario, ¿ves?, y no se imponen a la bebida.

Bueno, pues ya tenía yo un rato metiendo tubos y pensando boberías cuando en eso viene el foreman y me dice: Oye, ahí te buscan. Yo le digo: ¿A quién, a mí? Pues claro, me dice, aquí no hay dos con el mismo nombre. Entonces pusieron a otro en mi lugar para no parar el trabajo y ahí voy yo a ver quién era el que me buscaba. Y era Trompoloco, que no me dice ni qué hubo sino que me espeta: Oye, que te vayas para tu casa que tu mujer se está pariendo. Sí, hombre, así de sopetón. Y es que el pobre Trompoloco se cayó del coy allá en Puerto Rico cuando era chiquito y según decía su mamá, que en paz descanse, cayó de cabeza y parece que del golpe se le ablandaron los sesos. Tuvo un tiempo, cuando yo lo conocí aquí en el Barrio, que de repente se ponía a dar vueltas como loco y no paraba hasta que se mareaba y se caía al suelo. De ahí le vino el apodo. Eso sí, nadie abusa de él porque su mamá era muy buena persona, medium espiritista ella, tú sabes, y ayudaba a mucha gente y no cobraba. Uno le dejaba lo que podía, ¿ves?, y si no podía no le dejaba nada. Entonces hay mucha gente que se ocupa de que Trompoloco no pase necesidades. Porque él siempre fue huérfano de padre y no tuvo hermanos, así que como quien dice está solo en el mundo.

Bueno, pues llega Trompoloco y me dice eso y yo digo: Ay, mi madre, ¿y ahora qué hago? El foreman, que estaba pendiente de lo que pasaba porque esa gente nunca le pierde ojo a uno en el trabajo, viene y me pregunta: ¿Cuál es el trouble? Y yo le digo: Que vienen a buscarme porque mi mujer se está pariendo. Y entonces el foreman me dice: Bueno, ¿y qué tú estás esperando? Porque déjame decirte que ese foreman también era judío y para los judíos la familia siempre es lo primero. En eso no son como

each hand, bam, bam. At first, when I was new at it, a radio would pass me right by and—oh, boy!—I had to run after it and also keep an eye on the next radio coming up; thought I would go crazy. When I left work, I felt like my whole body had St. Vitus dance. That's why I think there's so much drinking and vice in this country. Yeah, because after all that, you feel like having a shot of rum, or something, and you start getting into the habit. I think that's why women get along better in factory work, because they entertain themselves with gossip and tongue-wagging, you see, and they don't need to drink. Well, I was working along, sticking tubes into radios, and thinking silly thoughts, when the foreman comes up and says, "Say, someone's looking for you." "Who, me?" I say. "Yeah," he tells me, "you're the only one here with that name." So they got someone to take my place, because they can't stop the line, and I go to see who was looking for me. It was Crazytop. Doesn't even say hello. He spits it right out. "Hey, go home, your wife's having a baby." Just like that. You see, poor Crazytop fell out of his crib in Puerto Rico when he was little, and according to his mother, may she rest in peace, he fell on his head, and it seems that the blow softened up his brains. There was a time, when I met him here in the Barrio, that he would suddenly start spinning around, like a nut, and wouldn't stop until he was dizzy, and fell to the floor. That's where his nickname comes from. Now, nobody makes fun of him, because his mother was a good person, a spiritualist medium, you know, and she helped lots of people without charge. You gave her whatever you could, you see. And if you were broke, you didn't give her anything. So there are lots of people who kind of look after Crazytop. Because he was always an orphan on his father's side, and he had no brothers or sisters, so as they say, he's all alone in the world.

Well, Crazytop comes along and says that to me, and I say, "*Ay, mi madre,* what'll I do now?" The foreman, who was keeping an eye on us, because those people never take their eyes off you at work, comes over and asks, "What's the trouble?" And I tell him, "They came to get me because my wife is giving birth." And the foreman says, "Well, what are you waiting for?" Let me tell you, that foreman was Jewish, too, and for the Jews the family is always number one. In that sense they're not like the rest

los demás americanos, que entre hijos y padres y entre hermanos se insultan y hasta se dan por cualquier cosa. Yo no sé si será por la clase de vida que la gente lleva en este país. Siempre corriendo detrás del dólar, como los perros ésos del canódromo que ponen a correr detrás de un conejo de trapo. ¿Tú los has visto? Acaban echando el bofe y nunca alcanzan al conejo. Eso sí, les dan comida y los cuidan para que vuelvan a correr al otro día, que es lo mismo que hacen con la gente, si miras bien la cosa. Así que en este país todos venimos a ser como perros de carrera.

Bueno, pues cuando el foreman me dijo que qué yo estaba esperando, le digo: Nada, ponerme el coat y agarrar el subway antes de que mi hijo vaya a llegar y no me encuentre en casa. Contento que estaba yo ya, ¿sabes?, porque iba a ser mi primer hijo y tú sabes cómo es eso. Y me dice el foreman: No se te vaya a olvidar ponchar la tarjeta para que cobres la media hora que llevas trabajando, que de ahora palante es cuando te van a hacer falta los chavos. Y le digo: Cómo no, y agarro el coat y poncho la tarjeta y le digo a Trompoloco, que estaba parado allí mirando las máquinas como eslembao: ¡Avanza, Trompo, que vamos a llegar tarde! Y bajamos las escaleras corriendo para no esperar el ascensor y llegamos a la acera, que estaba bien crowded porque a esa hora todavía había gente saliendo del trabajo. Y digo yo: ¡Maldita sea, y que tocarme la hora del rush! Y Trompoloco que no quería correr: Espérate, hombre, espérate, que yo quiero comprar un dulce. Bueno, es que Trompoloco es así ¿ves?, como un nene. El sirve para hacer un mandado, si es algo sencillo, o para lavar unas escaleras en un building o cualquier cosa que no haya que pensar. Pero si es cuestión de usar la calculadora, entonces búscate a otro. Así que vengo y le digo: No, Trompo, qué dulce ni qué carajo. Eso lo compras allá en el Barrio cuando lleguemos. Y él: No, no, en el Barrio no hay de los que yo quiero. Esos nada más se consiguen en Brooklyn. Y le digo: Ay, tú estás loco, y en seguida me arrepiento porque eso es lo único que no se le puede decir a Trompoloco. Y se para ahí en la acera, más serio que un chavo de queso, y me dice: No, no, loco no. Y le digo: No, hombre, si yo no dije loco, yo dije bobo. Lo que pasa es que tú oíste mal. ¡Avanza, que el dulce te lo llevo yo mañana! Y me dice: ¿Seguro que tú no me dijiste loco? Y yo: ¡Seguro, hombre! Y él: ¿Y mañana me llevas dos dulces? Mira, loco y todo lo que tú quieras, pero bien que sabe aprovecharse. Y a mí casi me entra la risa y le digo: Claro, chico, te llevo hasta tres si quieres. Y entonces

of the Americans, who between fathers and brothers and sons insult each other, even hit each other, for the slightest reason. I don't know if it's because of the kind of life people lead in this country. Always running after the dollar, like dogs at the track, after a rag rabbit. Have you seen that? They wear their lungs out and never catch the rabbit. Oh yeah, they feed them and care for them, so they'll run again another day, which is the same thing they do with people, if you really look at the way things are. In this country we're all like racing dogs.

Well, when the foreman asked me what was I waiting for, I told him, "Nothing, just to put on my coat and grab a subway before my son arrives and doesn't find me in the house." I was really happy, you see, because this was going to be my first child, and you know what that's like. And the foreman says, "Don't forget to punch out, so that you get credit for the half-hour you worked; from now on, you're going to really need money." And I tell him, "That's right," and grabbed my coat, punched my card, and I tell Crazytop, who was standing there, looking open-mouthed at all the machines, "Let's go, Crazytop, we'll be late!" And we ran down the stairs rather than wait for the elevator, and we got to the sidewalk, which was plenty crowded, because everyone was going home from work. "Damn it," I said, "I would have to get mixed up in the rush hour!" But Crazytop didn't want to run. "Wait a minute, man, wait a minute, I wanna buy a candy." Crazytop is like that, you see, just like a baby. He's good for running errands, if it's something simple, or for washing floors in a building, or anything that doesn't need thinking. But if it's a question of using the old calculator, look for someone else. So I tell him, "No, Top, the hell with candy. Buy it in the Barrio, when we get there." "No, no," he says, "they don't have the kind I want in the Barrio. You can only get them in Brooklyn." And I say to him, "*Ay*, you're crazy," and right away I'm sorry, because that's the one thing you can't say to Crazytop. He stops right there on the sidewalk, looking sadder than a penny's worth of cheese, and says to me, "No, no, not crazy." I tell him, "No, man, I didn't say crazy. I said silly. You didn't hear me right. C'mon! I'll get you the candy tomorrow!" And he says, "You sure you didn't call me crazy?" "Sure I am, man!" "And you'll get me the candy tomorrow?" He may be crazy, but he's pretty shrewd, too. I'm almost laughing, and I say, "Sure, I'll even get you three candies if you want." So he

vuelve a poner buena cara y me dice: Está bien, vámonos, pero tres dulces, acuérdate, ¿ah? Y yo, caminando para la entrada del subway con Trompoloco detrás: Sí, hombre, tres. Después me dices de cuáles son.

Y bajamos casi corriendo las escaleras y entramos en la estación con aquel mar de gente que tú sabes cómo es eso. Yo pendiente de que Trompoloco no se fuera a quedar atrás porque con el apeñuscamiento y los arrempujones a lo mejor le entraba miedo y quién iba a responder por él. Cuando viene el tren expreso lo agarro por un brazo y le digo: Prepárate y echa palante tú también, que si no nos quedamos afuera. Y él me dice: No te ocupes, y cuando se abre la puerta y salen los que iban a bajar, nos metemos de frente y quedamos prensados entre aquel montón de gente que no podíamos ni mover los brazos. Bueno, mejor, porque así no había que agarrarse de los tubos. Trompoloco iba un poco azorado porque yo creo que era la primera vez que viajaba en subway a esa hora, pero como me tenía a mí al lado no había problema, y así seguimos hasta Columbus Circle y allí cambiamos de línea porque teníamos que bajarnos en la 110 y Quinta para llegar a casa, ¿ves?, y ahí volvimos a quedar como sardinas en lata.

Entonces yo iba contando los minutos, pensando si ya mi hijo habría nacido y cómo estaría mi mujer. Y de repente se me ocurre: Bueno, y yo tan seguro de que va a ser macho y a lo mejor me sale una chancleta. Tú sabes que uno siempre quiere que el primero sea hombre. Y la verdad es que eso es un egoísmo de nosotros, porque a la mamá le conviene más que la mayor sea mujer para que después la ayude con el trabajo de la casa y la crianza de los hermanitos. Bueno, pues en eso iba yo pensando y sintiéndome ya muy padre de familia, te das cuenta, cuando . . . ¡fuácata, ahí fue! Que se va la luz y el tren empieza a perder impulso hasta que se queda parado en la mismita mitad del túnel entre dos estaciones. Bueno, la verdad es que de momento no se asustó nadie. Tú sabes que eso de que las luces se apaguen en el subway no es nada del otro mundo: en seguida vuelven a prenderse y la gente ni pestañea. Y eso de que el tren se pare un ratito antes de llegar a una estación tampoco es raro. Así que de momento no se asustó nadie. Prendieron las luces de emergencia y todo el mundo lo más tranquilo. Pero empezó a pasar el tiempo y el tren no se movía. Y yo pensando: Coño, qué mala suerte, ahora que tenía que llegar pronto. Pero todavía creyendo que

smiles and says, "All right, let's go, but three candies, all right?" And I'm walking towards the subway entrance with Crazytop behind me. "Sure, man, three. You tell me later which kind."

We practically ran down the stairs and found the station packed with people, you know how it gets. And I was worried about Crazytop falling behind, because with all the pushing and shoving he might get scared. When the express train pulls in, I grab him by the arm and say: "Get ready to push, or we'll be left behind." And he tells me not to worry, and when the door opened and a few people got out, we pushed in and wound up so squeezed that we couldn't even move our arms. Just as well, that way we didn't have to hold on. Crazytop looked a bit scared, because I think it was the first time he'd been on the subway at rush hour, but since I was next to him there was no problem. So we got to Columbus Circle and changed trains, because we had to go to 110th and Fifth to get home, you see, and again we were just like sardines in a can.

I was counting the minutes, wondering if my son had already been born, and how my wife was. Suddenly it occurs to me: here I am so sure it'll be a boy, and what if it winds up being a girl? You know how a fellow wants a son at first. Truth is, it's selfishness on our part, because it's better for the mother if the eldest is a girl, so she can help with the housework and raising the little ones. Well, I'm thinking about all those things, and feeling very much like a father, you see, when . . ., wham! The lights go out and the train starts to lose power, and stops right in the middle of the tunnel, between stations. Nobody got frightened right away. Lights going out in the subway isn't such a rare thing, you know: they usually come right back on, and people don't even blink. And the train stopping for a bit isn't so strange, either. They put on the emergency lights, and everyone seemed fine. But time went by, and the train didn't move. And I'm thinking, "Shit, what luck, just when I'm in a hurry." But I'm still believing it was just a question of a few minutes, you see, and about three minutes go by, and this lady next to me starts to cough. An American lady, a bit on the old side. I looked at her and saw that she was coughing, but not very hard. I thought to myself: that's

sería cuestión de un ratito, ¿ves? Y así pasaron como tres minutos más y entonces una señora empezó a toser. Una señora americana ella, medio viejita, que estaba cerca de mí. Yo la miré y vi que estaba tosiendo como sin ganas, y pensé: Eso no es catarro, eso es miedo. Y pasó otro minuto y el tren seguía parado y entonces la señora le dijo a un muchacho que tenía al lado, un muchacho alto y rubio él, tofete, con cara como de irlandés, le dijo la señora: Oiga, joven, ¿a usted esto no le está raro? Y él le dijo: No, no se preocupe, eso no es nada. Pero la señora como que no quedó conforme y siguió con su tosesita y entonces otros pasajeros empezaron a tratar de mirar por las ventanillas, pero como no podían moverse bien y con la oscuridad que había allá afuera, pues no veían nada. Te lo digo porque yo también traté de mirar y lo único que saqué fue un dolor de cuello que me duró un buen rato.

Bueno, pues siguió pasando el tiempo y a mí empezó a darme un calambre en una pierna y ahí fue donde me entró el nerviosismo. No, no por el calambre, sino porque pensé que ya no iba a llegar a tiempo a casa. Y decía yo para entre mí: No, aquí tiene que haber pasado algo, ya es demasiado de mucho el tiempo que tenemos aquí parados. Y como no tenía nada que hacer, puse a funcionar el coco y entonces fue que se me occurrió lo del suicidio. Bueno, era lo más lógico, ¿por qué no? Tú sabes que aquí hay muchísima gente que ya no se quieren para nada y entonces van y se trepan al Empire State y pegan el salto desde allá arriba y creo que cuando llegan a la calle y están muertos por el tiempo que tardan en caer. Bueno, yo no sé, eso es lo que me han dicho. Y hay otros que se le tiran por delante al subway y quedan que hay que recogerlos con pala. Ah, no, eso sí, a los que brincan desde el Empire State me imagino que habrá que recogerlos con secante. No, pero en serio, porque con esas cosas no se debe relajar, a mí se me ocurrió que lo que había pasado era que alguien se le había tirado debajo al tren que iba delante de nosotros, y hasta pensé: Bueno, pues que en paz descanse pero ya me chavó a mí, porque ahora sí que voy a llegar tarde. Ya mi mujer debe estar pensando que Trompoloco se perdió en el camino o que yo ando borracho por ahí y no me importa lo que está pasando en casa. Porque no es que yo sea muy bebelón, pero de vez en cuando, tú me entiendes . . . Bueno, y ya que estamos hablando de eso, si quieres cambiamos de marca, pero que estén bien frías a ver si se nos acaba de quitar la calor.

no cold, she's scared. Another minute went by and the train wasn't moving and the lady says to a young fellow next to her—tall, blond, tough-looking, with like an Irish face—she says, "Young man, doesn't this seem a bit odd?" And he says, "No, don't worry, it's nothing." But the lady didn't seem satisfied with that, and she kept on with her little cough, and other passengers tried to look out the windows, but they could barely move, and anyway it was so dark you couldn't see anything. I tried to look, too, but all I got out of it was a stiff neck, which lasted quite a while.

Well, time went by and I started getting a cramp in my leg, and that's when I started feeling nervous. Not because of the cramp, but I thought I'd never get home on time. I said to myself, "Something must've happened; we've been stuck here too long." Since I had nothing else to do I started my head working, and that's when I thought about suicide. It seemed logical, right? You know that there are lot of people here who don't give a damn about themselves and they climb up the Empire State Building and jump, and by the time they reach the street they're already dead from the fall. I don't know, but that's what I've heard. And there are others who jump in front of subway cars, and you have to pick up what's left with a shovel. The ones who jump from the Empire State, I guess you'd need tissue paper to pick them up. No, but seriously, because a person shouldn't joke about such things, I figured someone had thrown himself in front of a train, and I thought: "Well, may he rest in peace, but he really screwed me up, because now I'll be late." By now, my wife must be thinking that Crazytop got lost, or that I'm drunk and don't care about what's happening at home. It's not that I'm a lush, but once in a while, you understand . . . Well, now that we're on that subject, if you want to change brands, but make sure they're plenty cold.

¡Aaajá! Entonces . . . ¿por dónde iba yo? Ah sí, estaba pensando en eso del suicidio y qué sé yo, cuando de repente—¡ran!—vienen y se abren las puertas del tren. Sí, hombre, sí, allí mismo en el túnel. Y como eso, a la verdad, era una cosa que yo nunca había visto, entonces pensé: Ahora sí que a la puerca se le entorchó el rabo. Y en seguida veo que allá abajo frente a la puerta estaban unos como inspectores o algo así porque tenían uniforme y traían unas linternas de ésas como faroles. Y nos dice uno de ellos: Take it easy que no hay peligro. Bajen despacio y sin empujar. Y ahí mismo la gente empezó a bajar y a preguntarle al mister aquél: ¿Qué es lo que pasa, qué es lo que pasa? Y él: Cuando estén todos acá abajo les voy a decir. Yo agarré a Trompoloco por el brazo y le dije: ¿Ya tú oíste? No hay peligro, pero no te vayas a apartar de mí. Y él me decía que sí con la cabeza, porque yo creo que del susto se le había ido hasta la voz. No decía nada, pero parecía que los macos se le iban a salir de la cara: los tenía como platillos y casi le brillaban en la oscuridad, como a los gatos.

Bueno, pues fuimos saliendo del tren hasta que no quedó nadie adentro. Entonces, cuando estuvimos todos alineados allá abajo, los inspectores empezaron a recorrer la fila que nosotros habíamos formado y nos fueron explicando, así por grupos, ¿ves?, que lo que pasaba era que había habido un blackout o sea que se había ido la luz en toda la ciudad y no se sabía cuándo iba a volver. Entonces la señora de la tosesita, que había quedado cerca de mí, le preguntó al inspector: Oiga, ¿y cuándo vamos a salir de aqui? Y él le dijo: Tenemos que esperar un poco porque hay otros trenes delante de nosotros y no podemos salir todos a la misma vez. Y ahí pegamos a esperar. Y yo pensando: Maldita sea mi suerte, mira que tener que pasar esto el día de hoy, cuando en eso siento que Trompoloco me jala la manga del coat y me dice bien bajito, como en secreto: Oye, oye, panita, me estoy meando. ¡Imagínate tú! Lo único que faltaba. Y le digo: Ay, Trompo, bendito, aguántate, ¿tú no ves que aquí eso es imposible? Y me dice: Pero es que hace rato que tengo ganas y ya no aguanto más. Entonces me pongo a pensar rápido porque aquello era una emergencia, ¿no?, y lo único que se me ocurre es ir a preguntarle al inspector qué se podía hacer. Le digo a Trompoloco: Bueno, espérame un momentito, pero no te vayas a mover de aquí. Y me salgo de la línea y voy y le digo al inspector: Listen, mister, my friend wanna take a leak, o sea que mi amigo

Ah! Where was I? Oh yeah, thinking about the suicide, when suddenly—bang!—they opened the doors. Right there in the tunnel. I'd never seen anything like that, and I thought to myself, there's gotta be trouble. Down below, in front of the door, I see a few inspectors, they're wearing uniforms, and carrying lanterns. One of them says, "Take it easy, there's no danger. Come down slowly, without pushing." Right away people start asking the mister: What's happened? What's happened? And he says, "When you're all down here, I'll tell you." I grabbed Crazytop by the arm and told him, "Did you hear? There's no danger, but don't get separated from me." He nodded. I think the fright had robbed him of his voice. He didn't say a thing, but it seemed that his eyeballs would pop right out of his head; they were shining in the dark, just like a cat's.

Well, we all got out of the train, and when we're all lined up the inspectors started walking along the line and explaining what happened. There had been a blackout in the entire city, and nobody knew when the lights would come back on. Then the lady with the little cough, who was still close to me, asked the inspector, "Say, when will we get out of here?" And he says, "We have to wait a bit, because there are other trains ahead of us, and we can't all get out at the same time." So we began to wait. And I'm thinking, "Dammit, this having to happen today," when I feel Crazytop pulling at my coat sleeve. He says to me real low, like in secret, "Say, buddy, I'm practically peeing in my pants." Imagine! That's all we needed. "*Ay*, Top," I say to him, "hold on. Can't you see it's impossible here?" And he says, "But I've had to go for a long time now, and I can't hold it in." So I start thinking fast, because this is an emergency, right? All I could think of was asking the inspector. "Wait right here," I say to Crazytop, "and don't move." I get out of line and walk up to the inspector. "Listen, mister, my friend wanna take a leak." And he says to me, "Goddamit to hell, can't he hold it in awhile?" I let him know that's just what I told my friend, to hold it in, but he says he can't. So he says, "Well, go ahead, but don't wander off too far." So I go back to Crazytop and tell him, "Come with me; let's see if we can find someplace there in back." We start walking,

quería cambiarle el agua al canario. Y me dice el inspector: Goddamit to hell, can't he hold it in a while? Y le digo que eso mismo le había dicho yo, que se aguantara, pero que ya no podía. Entonces me dice: Bueno, que lo haga donde pueda, pero que no se aleje mucho. Así que vuelvo donde Trompoloco y le digo: Vente conmigo por ahí atrás a ver si encontramos un lugarcito. Y pegamos a caminar, pero aquella hilera de gente no se acababa nunca. Ya habíamos caminado un trecho cuando vuelve a jalarme la manga y me dice: Ahora sí que ya no aguanto, brother. Entonces le digo: Pues mira, ponte detrás de mí pegadito a la pared, pero ten cuenta que no me vayas a mojar los zapatos. Y hazlo despacito, para que no se oiga. Y ni había acabado de hablar cuando oigo aquello que . . . bueno, ¿tú sabes cómo hacen eso los caballos? Pues con decirte que parecía que eran dos caballos en vez de uno. Si yo no sé cómo no se le había reventado la vejiga. No, una cosa terrible. Yo pensé: Ave María, éste me va a salpicar hasta el coat. Y mira que era de esos cortitos, que no llegan ni a la rodilla, porque a mí siempre me ha gustado estar a la moda, ¿verdad? Y entonces, claro, la gente que estaba por allí tuvo que darse cuenta y yo oí que empezaron a murmurar. Y pensé: Menos mal que está oscuro y no nos pueden ver la cara, porque si se dan cuenta que somos puertorriqueños . . . Ya tú sabes cómo es el asunto aquí. Yo pensando todo eso y Trompoloco que no acababa. ¡Cristiano, las cosas que le pasan a uno en este país! Después las cuentas y la gente no te las cree. Bueno, pues al fin Trompoloco acabó, o por lo menos eso creí yo porque ya no se oía aquel estrépito que estaba haciendo, pero pasaba el tiempo y no se movía. Y le digo: Oye, ¿ya tú acabaste? Y me dice: Sí. Y yo: Pues ya vámonos. Y entonces me sale con que: Espérate, que me estoy sacudiendo. Mira, ahí fue donde yo me encocoré. Le digo: Pero, muchacho, ¿eso es una manguera o qué? ¡Camina por ahí si no quieres que esta gente nos sacuda hasta los huesos después de esa inundación que tú has hecho aquí! Entonces como que comprendió la situación y me dijo: Está bien, está bien, vámonos.

Pues volvimos adonde estábamos antes y ahí nos quedamos esperando como media hora más. Yo oía a la gente alrededor de mí hablando en inglés, quejándose y diciendo que qué abuso, que parecía mentira, que si el alcalde, que si qué sé yo. Y de repente oigo por allá que alguien dice en español: Bueno, para estirar la

but that line of people never ended. We had already gone quite a distance when he pulls my sleeve again and says, "I really can't hold it anymore, brother." So I tell him, "Well, look, get behind me, right next to the wall, but be careful not to wet my shoes. And do it slow, so nobody hears." I hadn't even finished talking when I hear, you know how a horse sounds? Well, it was like two horses, not one. It's a wonder he hadn't ruptured his bladder. Oh, it was terrible. *"Ave María,"* I think to myself, "he's gonna splash my coat." And I was wearing just a short coat, didn't even reach my knees, because I like to be in style, right? Well, of course, the people nearby had to notice, and I hear them whispering. I think to myself, "Just as well it's dark, and they can't see our faces. If they notice that we're Puerto Ricans . . . " You know how things are here. I'm thinking, and Crazytop still isn't finished. *Cristiano!* The things that happen to a fellow in this country! And people don't believe you. Well, Crazytop finally finished, or at least I thought he did, because I didn't hear any more noise, but he still stood there. So I say, "Hey, did you finish?" He says, "Yes." "Well," I say, "let's go." Then he says, "Wait a minute. I'm shaking it." That's when I blew my top. I ask him, "What've you got there, a garden hose? Get going, or these people are going to shake even your bones after making such a flood here." I think he finally understood the situation, and he says, "Okay, all right, let's go."

So we go back to where we were, and we're waiting for about half an hour more. I hear people around me talking English, complaining, and griping about the mayor, and everything. And suddenly I hear someone over there, in Spanish, say, "Well, it's just as well to die here as up there. At least down here the gov-

pata lo mismo da aquí adentro que allá afuera, y mejor que sea aquí porque así el entierro tiene que pagarlo el gobierno. Sí, algún boricua que quería hacerse el gracioso. Yo miré así a ver si lo veía, para decirle que el entierro de él lo iba a pagar la sociedad protectora de animales, pero en aquella oscuridad no pude ver quién era. Y lo malo fue que el chistecito aquél me hizo su efecto, no te creas. Porque parado allí sin hacer nada y con la preocupación que traía yo y todo ese problema, ¿tú sabes lo que se me ocurrió a mí entonces? Imagínate, yo pensé que el inspector nos había dicho un embuste y que lo que pasaba era que ya había empezado la tercera guerra mundial. No, no te rías, yo te apuesto que yo no era el único que estaba pensando eso. Sí, hombre, con todo lo que se pasan diciendo los periódicos aquí, de que si los rusos y los chinos y hasta los marcianos en los platillos voladores . . . Pues claro, ¿y por qué tú te crees que en este país hay tanto loco? Si ahí en Bellevue ya ni caben y creo que van a tener que construir otro manicomio.

Bueno, pues en esa barbaridad estaba yo pensando cuando vienen los inspectores y nos dicen que ya nos tocaba el turno de salir a nosotros, pero caminando en fila y con calma. Entonces pegamos a caminar y al fin llegamos a la estación, que era la de la 96. Así que tú ves, no estábamos tan lejos de casa, pero tampoco tan cerca porque eran unas cuantas calles las que nos faltaban. Imagínate que eso nos hubiera pasado en la 28 o algo así. La cagazón, ¿no? Pero, bueno, la cosa es que llegamos a la estación y le digo a Trompoloco: Avanza y vamos a salir de aquí. Y subimos las escaleras con todo aquel montón de gente que parecía un hormiguero cuando tú le echas agua caliente, y al salir a la calle, ¡ay, bendito! No, no, tiniebla no, porque estaban las luces de los carros y eso, ¿verdad? Pero oscuridad sí porque ni en la calle ni en los edificios había una sola luz prendida. Y en eso pasó un tipo con un radio de esos portátiles, y como iba caminando en la misma dirección que yo, me le emparejé y me puse a oír lo que estaba diciendo el radio. Y era lo mismo que nos había dicho el inspector allá abajo en el túnel, así que ahí se me quitó la preocupación ésa de la guerra. Pero entonces me volvió la otra, la del parto de mi mujer y eso, ¿ves?, y le digo a Trompoloco: Bueno, paisa, ahora la cosa es en el carro de don Fernando, un ratito a pie y otro andando, así que a ver quién llega primero. Y me dice él: Te voy, te voy, riéndose, ¿sabes?, como que ya se la había pasado el susto.

ernment has to pay for the funeral." Yeah, some *boricua** trying to be funny. I tried to spot him, and tell him that his funeral was going to be paid for by the animal shelter, but it was too dark. His little joke affected me, believe it or not. Standing there, with all my worries, you know what I thought? Imagine, I thought, if the inspector was lying, and the Third World War had really started. No, don't laugh. I'll bet I wasn't the only one thinking it. With all the things you read in the papers, about Russians, and Chinese, and Martians in flying saucers. Why do you think there are so many nuts in this country? They don't even fit in Bellevue anymore, and I think they're going to have to build another insane asylum.

Well, just then, the inspectors come and tell us it's our turn to get out, but to stay in line and be calm. We start walking and finally reach the station, which was at 96th. We weren't too far from home, but not too close either. Imagine if we'd stopped at 28th, or something. Up shit creek, right? Well, we get to the station and I tell Crazytop, "Let's hurry." We climb the stairs with that crowd of people, it looked like when you throw hot water on an anthill, and when we reach the street, *ay bendito!* The cars had their lights on, but there wasn't a single light on in the street, or in the buildings. A guy comes by with one of those portable radios. Since I was walking in the same direction I got close to him and started listening. Just what the inspector had told us down in the tunnel, so I stopped worrying about the war. But then I got to thinking again about my wife, and I tell Crazytop, "Well, my friend, now we use a special kind of transportation: a little on foot, and another while walking, to see who gets there first." And he says, "Let's race, let's race," laughing, as though he'd gotten over his fright.

*"Boricua" is another word for "Puerto Rican."

Y pegamos a caminar bien ligero porque además estaba haciendo frío. Y cuando íbamos por la 103 o algo así, pienso yo: Bueno, y si no hay luz en casa, ¿cómo habrán hecho para el parto? A lo mejor tuvieron que llamar la ambulancia para llevarse a mi mujer a alguna clínica y ahora yo no voy a saber ni dónde está. Porque, oye, lo que es el día que uno se levanta de malas . . . Entonces con esa idea en la cabeza entré yo en la recta final que parecía un campeón: yo creo que no tardamos ni cinco minutos de la 103 a casa. Y ahí mismo entro y agarro por aquellas escaleras oscuras que no veía ni los escalones y . . . Ah, pero ahora va a empezar lo bueno, lo que tú quieres que yo te cuente porque tú no estabas en Nueva York ese día, ¿verdad? Okay. Pues entonces vamos a pedir otras cervecitas porque tengo el gaznate más seco que aquellos arenales de Salinas donde yo me crié.

Pues como te iba diciendo. Esa noche rompí el record mundial de tres pisos de escaleras en la oscuridad. Ya ni sabía si Trompoloco me venía siguiendo. Cuando llegué frente a la puerta del apartamento traía la llave en la mano y la metí en la cerradura al primer golpe, como si la estuviera viendo. Y entoces, cuando abrí la puerta, lo primero que vi fue que había cuatro velas prendidas en la sala y unas cuantas vecinas allí sentadas, lo más tranquilas y dándole a la sin hueso que aquello parecía la olimpiada del bembeteo. Ave María, y es que ése es el deporte favorito de las mujeres. Yo creo que el día que les prohíban eso se forma una revolución más grande que la de Fidel Castro. Pero eso sí, cuando me vieron entrar así de sopetón les pegué un susto que se quedaron mudas de repente. Cuantimás que yo ni siquiera dije buenas noches sino que ahí mismo empecé a preguntar: Oigan, ¿y quí ha pasado con mi mujer? ¿Dónde está? ¿Se la llevaron? Y entonces una de las señoras viene y me dice: No, hombre, no, ella está ahí adentro lo más bien. Aquí estábamos comentando que para ser el primer parto . . . Y en ese mismo momento oigo yo aquellos berridos que empezó a pegar mi hijo allá en el cuarto. Bueno, yo todavía no sabía si era hijo o hija, pero lo que sí te digo es que gritaba más que Daniel Santos en sus buenos tiempos. Y entonces le digo a la señora: Con permiso, doña, y me tiro para el cuarto y abro la puerta y lo primero que veo es aquel montón de velas prendidas que eso parecía un

We started walking real fast, because it was cold. When we reached 103rd, I wonder, "If there's no lights at home, how did they do the delivery? Maybe they had to call an ambulance to take her to some clinic, and I won't even know where she is." With that idea in my head, I looked like a champ in the stretch. I don't think it took us even five minutes from 103rd to home. I start running up the stairs, and they were in pitch darkness, couldn't even see the steps. Ah, but now the good part starts, because you weren't in New York that day, right? Okay. Well, let's get a couple more beers, because my throat is drier than the sand dunes of Salinas, where I grew up.

Well, as I was saying, that night I broke the world record for climbing three flights of stairs in the dark. I didn't even notice if Crazytop was behind me. When I reached the apartment door I grabbed my key and shoved it right into the lock on the first try, just as though I could see it. When I open the door the first thing I see are four candles lit in the parlor, and quite a few lady neighbors sitting there, looking plenty relaxed, and gossiping away. It looked like the Olympics for tongue-wagging. *Ave María,* that must be the ladies' favorite sport. I think that when the day comes that they abolish gossiping, there'll be a revolution bigger than Fidel Castro's. But as soon as they spotted me, they all turned quiet. I didn't even say good evening; right away I asked, "What's happened to my wife? Where is she? Did they take her away?" One of the ladies comes over and says, "No, she's in there, and she's fine. We were just saying that for a first pregnancy . . ." And just then I hear those squeals from my son there in the room. Well, I still didn't know if it was a boy or a girl, but I'll tell you, he was shouting more than Daniel Santos in his good times.* So I tell the lady, "Excuse me, *doña,*" and I rush into the room and the first thing I see is so many candles I thought it was a church altar. And the midwife there fussing with the pans, and rags, and things, and my woman in bed, nice and still, but with her eyes wide open. When she sees me, she says, her voice very slight, "*Ay,* my boy, how good that you got

*Daniel Santos is a Puerto Rican singer of popular music.

altar de iglesia. Y la comadrona allí trajinando con las palanganas y los trapos y esas cosas, y mi mujer en la cama quietecita, pero con los ojos bien abiertos. Y cuando me ve dice, así con la voz bien finita: Ay, mi hijo, qué bueno que ya llegaste. Yo ya estaba preocupada por ti. Fíjate, bendito, y que preocupada por mí, ella que era la que acababa de salir de ese brete del parto. Sí, hombre, las mujeres a veces tienen esas cosas. Yo creo que por eso es que les aguantamos sus boberías y las queremos tanto, ¿verdad? Entonces yo le iba a explicar el problema del subway y eso, cuando me dice la comadrona: Oiga, ese muchacho es la misma cara de usted. Venga a verlo, mire. Y era que estaba ahí en la cama al lado de mi mujer, pero como era tan chiquito casa ni se veía. Entonces me acerco y le miro la carita, que era lo único que se le podía ver porque ya lo tenían más envuelto que pastel de hoja. Y cuando yo estoy ahí mirándolo me dice mi mujer: ¿Verdad que salió a ti? Y le digo: Sí, se parece bastante. Pero yo pensando: No, hombre, ése no se parece a mí ni a nadie, si lo que parece es un ratón recién nacido. Pero es que así somos todos cuando llegamos al mundo, ¿no? Y me dice mi mujer: Pues salió machito, como tú lo querías. Y yo, por decir algo: Bueno, a ver si la próxima vez formamos la parejita. Yo tratando de que no se me notara ese orgullo y esa felicidad que yo estaba sintiendo, ¿ves? Y entonces dice la comadrona: Bueno, ¿y qué nombre le van a poner? Y dice mi mujer: Pues el mismo del papá, para que no se le vaya a olvidar que es suyo. Bromeando, tú sabes, pero con su pullita. Y yo le digo: Bueno, nena, si ése es tu gusto. . . Y en eso ya mi hijo se había callado y yo empiezo a oír como una música que venía de la parte de arriba del building, pero una música que no era de radio ni de disco, ¿ves?, sino como de un conjunto que estuviera allí mismo, porque a la misma vez que la música se oía una risería y una conversación de mucha gente. Y le digo a mi mujer: Adiós, ¿y por ahí hay bachata? Y me dice: Bueno, yo no sé, pero parece que sí porque hace rato que estamos oyendo eso. A lo mejor es un party de cumpleaños. Y digo yo: ¿Pero así, sin luz? Y entonces dice la comadrona: Bueno, a lo mejor hicieron igual que nosotros, que salimos a comprar velas. Y en eso oigo yo que Trompoloco me llama desde la sala: Oye, oye, ven acá. Sí, hombre, Trompoloco que había llegado después que yo y se había puesto a averiguar. Entonces salgo y le digo: ¿Qué pasa? Y me dice: Muchacho, que allá arriba en el rufo está chévere la cosa. Sí, en el rufo, o sea en la azotea. Y digo

here. I was worried about you." Imagine, she's worried about me, and she's been going through labor pains, and all that. Yeah, women are like that sometimes. I think that's why we put up with their foolishness and love them so much, right? Well, I was just going to tell her about the problem with the subway when the midwife says, "That little boy has got your identical face. Come see him, look." He was in the bed, right next to my woman, but since he was so tiny you could hardly see him. I go over and look at his little face, which is all you could see, since he was wrapped up more than a *pastel,** and when I'm looking at him, my woman says, "Doesn't he resemble you?" I say, "Yes, quite a bit." But I'm thinking to myself, "No, he doesn't look like me or anybody else. Looks like a newborn mouse." But we're all like that when we come into the world, right? And my woman says to me, "He's a little boy, just what you wanted." And I, just to say something, answered, "Well, let's see if next time we can make a nice match." I didn't want her to notice how proud I felt and how happy, you see? And the midwife asks, "Well, what are you going to name him?" My woman says, "The same as his papa, so he won't forget it's his." Just joking, you see, but with her little dig. And I say, "Well, baby, if it pleases you." My son had stopped crying by then, and I start to hear like the sound of music coming from the upper part of the building. But it wasn't from a radio or phonograph, you see. It was like a combo, right there, because I heard laughing and talking. Lots of people. And I ask my woman, "Is there a party?" And she says, "I don't know, but it seems so, because we've been hearing it for quite a while. Maybe it's a birthday party." And I say, "But without any light?" And then the midwife says, "Maybe they did the same as we did, went out and bought candles." Then I hear Crazytop calling to me from the parlor, "Hey, hey, c'mere." Crazytop had gone to check. "What's happening?" I asked him. *"Muchacho,"* he says, "thing's are really swell up there on the *rufo*." And I say, "Well, let's go see what's happening."

*A meat and vegetable pie wrapped in banana leaf.

yo: Bueno, pues vamos a ver qué es lo que pasa. Yo todavía sin imaginarme nada, ¿ves?

Entonces agarramos las escaleras y subimos y cuando salgo para afuera veo que allí estaba casi todo el building: doña Lula la viuda del primer piso, Cheo el de Aguadilla que había cerrado el cafetín cuando se fue la luz y se había metido en su casa, las muchachas del segundo que ni trabajan ni están en el welfare según las malas lenguas, don Leo el ministro pentecostés que tiene cuatro hijos aquí y siete en Puerto Rico, Pipo y los muchachos de doña Lula y uno de los de don Leo, que ésos eran los que habían formado el conjunto con una guitarra, un güiro, unas maracas y hasta unos timbales que no sé de dónde los sacaron porque nunca los había visto por allí. Sí, un cuarteto. Oye, ¡y sonaba! Cuando yo llegué estaban tocando "Preciosa" y el que cantaba era Pipo, que tú sabes que es independentista y cuando llegaba a aquella parte que dice: *Preciosa, preciosa te llaman los hijos de la libertad,* subía la voz que yo creo que lo oían hasta en Morovis. Y yo allí parado mirando a toda aquella gente y oyendo la canción, cuando viene y se me acerca una de las muchachas del segundo piso, una medio gordita ella que creo que se llama Mirta, y me dice: Oiga, qué bueno que subió. Véngase para acá para que se dé un palito. Ah, porque tenían sus botellas y unos vasitos de cartón allí encima de una silla, y yo no sé si eran de Bacardí o Don Q, porque desde donde yo estaba no se veía tanto, pero le digo en seguida a la muchacha: Bueno, si usted me lo ofrece yo acepto con mucho gusto. Y vamos y me sirve el ron y entonces le pregunto: Bueno, ¿y por qué es la fiesta, si se puede saber? Y en eso viene doña Lula, la viuda, y me dice: Adiós, ¿pero usted no se ha fijado? Y yo miro así como buscando por los lados, pero doña Lula me dice: No, hombre, cristiano, por ahí no. Mire para arriba. Y cuando yo levanto la cabeza y miro, me dice: ¿Qué está viendo? Y yo: Pues la luna. Y ella: ¿Y qué más? Y yo: Pues las estrellas. ¡Ave María, muchacho, y ahí fue donde yo caí en cuenta! Yo creo que doña Lula me lo vio en la cara porque ya no me dijo nada más. Me puso las dos manos en los hombros y se quedó mirando ella también, quietecita, como si yo estuviera dormido y ella no quisiera despertarme. Porque yo no sé si tú me lo vas a creer, pero aquello era como un sueño. Había salido una luna de este tamaño, mira, y amarilla amarilla como si estuviera hecha de oro, y el cielo estaba todito lleno de estrellas como si todos los cocuyos del mundo se hubieran subido hasta allá arriba

So we go up the stairs and onto the roof and I find almost the whole building there. *Doña* Lula, the widow from the first floor; Cheo, the guy from Aguadilla, who had closed down his coffee shop when the lights went out; the girls from the second floor, who neither worked nor collected welfare, according to the tongue-waggers; *don* Leo, the Pentecostal minister who has four children here and seven in Puerto Rico; Pipo and *doña* Lula's boys, and one of *don* Leo's had formed a combo with a guitar, a *güiro,* some maracas, and even some drums, I don't know where they got them because I'd never seen them before. Yeah, a quartet. Say, and they were really making quite a racket! When I got there, they were playing *"Preciosa,"* and the singer was Pipo, you know he's an *independentista,* and when he got to the part where it says, "*Preciosa, preciosa,* you're called by the sons of liberty," he raised his voice so much I think they heard him in Morovis. And I'm standing there looking at all those people, and listening to the song, when one of the girls from the second floor comes over, a little heavyset, I think her name is Mirta, and she says to me, "Say, how good it is that you're here. Come over and have a little shot." Ah, they had bottles and paper cups atop a chair, and I don't know if it was Bacardi or Don Q, because it was dark, but right away I tell her, "Well, if you're offering, I accept with great pleasure." She serves me the rum and I ask, "Say, can you tell me what the party's all about?" And *doña* Lula, the widow, comes over and says, "Haven't you noticed?" I look all around, but *doña* Lula says, "No, no, not there. Look *up*." And when I raise my eyes she says, "What do you see?" "Well, the moon." "And what else?" "Well, the stars."

Ave María, muchacho! That's when I realized! I think *doña* Lula saw it in my face, because she didn't say a thing more. She put her two hands on my shoulders and stood there looking, too, nice and still, as though I were asleep, and she didn't want to wake me. Because I don't know if you're going to believe me, but it was like a dream. The moon was this big, and yellow, yellow, as though it were made of gold, and the whole sky was full of stars, as though all the fireflies in the world had gone up there to rest in that immensity. Just like in Puerto Rico, 'most any night of the year. But it had been so long since I'd seen the sky, because of the glow of millions of electric bulbs that are turned on

y después se hubieran quedado a descansar en aquella inmensidad. Igual que en Puerto Rico cualquier noche del año, pero era que después de tanto tiempo sin poder ver el cielo, por ese resplandor de los millones de luces eléctricas que se prenden aquí todas las noches, ya se nos había olvidado que las estrellas existían. Y entonces, cuando llevábamos yo no sé cuánto tiempo contemplando aquel milagro, oigo a doña Lula que me dice: Bueno, y parece que no somos los únicos que estamos celebrando. Y era verdad. Yo no podría decirte en cuántas azoteas del Barrio se hizo fiesta aquella noche, pero seguro que fue en unas cuantas, porque cuando el conjunto de nosotros dejaba de tocar, oíamos clarita la música que llegaba de otros sitios. Entonces yo pensé muchas cosas. Pensé en mi hijo que acababa de nacer y en lo que iba a ser su vida aquí, pensé en Puerto Rico y en los viejos y en todo lo que demos allá nada más que por necesidad, pensé tantas cosas que algunas ya se me han olvidado, porque tú sabes que la mente es como una pizarra y el tiempo como un borrador que le pasa por encima cada vez que se nos llena. Pero de lo que sí me voy a acordar siempre es de lo que le dije yo entonces a doña Lula, que es lo que te voy a decir ahora para acabar de contarte lo que tú querías saber. Y es que, según mi pobre manera de entender las cosas, aquélla fue la noche que volvimos a ser gente.

here every night, and we had already forgotten that the stars existed. When we stood there contemplating that miracle for I don't know how long, I hear *doña* Lula say, "It seems we're not the only ones celebrating." It was true. I can't tell you on how many rooftops in the Barrio there were parties that night, but there were quite a few, because when our combo stopped playing, we could hear music from other places, nice and clear. Then I thought of so many things. I thought of my newborn son, and what his life would be like here; I thought of Puerto Rico and my folks, and everything that we left behind, just out of need; I thought of so many things that I've already forgotten some of them, because you know that your mind is like a blackboard, and time is like an eraser that sweeps across it when it's full. But what I'll always remember is what I said then to *doña* Lula, which is what I want to tell you now, to finish my story. And that is, according to my poor way of understanding things, that was the night we became people again.

—tr. Kal Wagenheim

SOL NEGRO

Emilio Díaz Valcárcel

EL negro Bernabé Quirindongo sentía que la sangre hervía en sus venas cuando escuchaba un son. Sentado a la puerta de su rancho, alrededor del cual se amontonaban las otras casuchas de la diminuta colonia negra del pueblo, pasaba horas y horas buscándoles sentido a los ruidos. En la orilla del solar se apretaba la docena de caras negras de los vecinos más próximos, los ojos encandilados, las manos sarmentosas golpeando sobre las rodillas para estimular a Bernabé Quirindongo, cuyos dedos tamborileaban sobre el tabique, sobre el soberado, inútilmente: ningún sonido rico, capaz de igualarse a los que resonaban en su cabeza. Luciana Quiles venía observando al muchacho desde bien pequeño, asomada a la ventana de su rancho; desde un principio intuyó el ritmo que lo torturaba; el negrito era tamborilero de nacimiento.

Mamá Romualda, sofocada detrás del hornillo, abanicando las brasas con un carón mantecoso, se angustiaba pensando en las sonoras frustraciones de su negro. Vendía fritangas que hasta las niñas más dulces y rubias del pueblo comían relamiéndose. En un cacharro, metía moneda tras moneda. El negro Bernabé Quirindongo, negro inútil para la gente, quería un cuero donde descargar su ritmo; molestaba a su mamá, exigiendo para sus dedos ansiosos los parches maravillosos de un bongó. *Pa cupá,* movía sus labios, *pa cupá,* pero el tabique, o el soberado o la lata de basuras, bajo sus yemas milagrosas, producían un ruido decepcionante. Las caras negras, apretadas en la orilla del solar, sonaban las palmas. La vecina Luciana

BLACK SUN

Emilio Díaz Valcárcel

Black Bernabé Quirindongo felt the blood boil in his veins whenever he heard his kind of music. Seated at the door of his wooden shack, surrounded by the other closely packed together huts of the tiny Negro colony of the town, he would spend hours and hours searching for meaning to the sounds. At the edge of the plot of land a dozen black faces crowded around, eyes burning, hands like knotted vines pounding against their knees, to help out Bernabé Quirindongo, whose fingers beat futilely against the flimsy wall partition, against the floor; not once was there a rich, full sound like the one ringing in his head. Luciana Quiles, leaning out from the window of her shack, had been watching the boy since he was very small; from the beginning she understood the rhythm which tortured him; the little black boy had been born a drummer.

Mama Romualda, sweltering over her little stove, fanning the flames with a greasy piece of cardboard, grew sad thinking about her black son's harmonic frustrations. She sold chitterlings which even the daintiest and blondest little girls of the town licked their lips over. In an old tin can she would drop the coins, one by one. Black Bernabé Quirindongo, black good-for-nothing to the people, wanted a hide on which to unload his rhythm; he pestered his mama demanding the marvelous skin of a bongo for his fingers.

Pa-coo-*pah,* moved his lips, pa-coo-*pah,* but the wooden wall, or the floorboards, or the garbage can produced only a disappointing noise under his miraculous fingertips. The black faces,

Quiles, de setenta años, nieta de esclavos, presa de un vértigo que estremecía su cuerpo huesudo, dirigía el grupo con trémula voz de cencerro.

En los sordos atardeceres los cocoteros se volvían sombras metálicas sobre el monte, enrojecía el horizonte y el alma de Bernabé Quirindongo se llenaba de una ruidosa paz sólo expresable con el repique lento de unos cueros. En las mañanas el sol maduraba en las puntas de los pinos, clavaba cuchillos de luz dentro del rancho y Bernabé Quirindongo (*"pa cupá,"* se estremecían sus labios) lo hubiera descrito con un allegro tamborero. Los truenos quemaban el silencio encima de las cumbreras, espantaban la paz de los blancos, rodaban hasta apagarse en las breñales del otro lado del río y Bernabé Quirindongo, mejor que nadie, hubiese copiado su misterio sonoro con sólo hacer trepidar sus dedos amorcillados. Pero Bernabé Quirindongo, negro inútil que golpeaba el aire en busca de un bongó impalpable, se tenía que vaciar por los labios.

—Pa cupá—murmuraba.

Cuando Bernabé Quirindongo fue recluido en el hospitalillo a causa de la hernia, su mamá Romualda Quirindongo se emborrachó y empezó a mendigar con los ojos arrasados de lágrimas. De cada peso recaudado se bebía medio. Fue un espectáculo del que gozaron hasta los blancos más refinados. La negra recorría las calles con su bata descolorida, dando traspiés, y sus enormes senos se bamboleaban como borrachos; suplicaba, gemía, mendigaba. Luego, a solas, contaba el dinero recogido.

En realidad, nunca se supo si el negro estuvo o no curándose la hernia. Lo cierto es que una mañana, después de los lamentos y de la recaudación de su mamá, apareció en la puerta del rancho con un bongó nuevo. La misma Luciana Quiles, que sabía de esas cosas, le arrancó la etiqueta del precio. Bernabé atacaba los parches y sus belfos seguían la cadencia y emitían sonidos de bongó golpeado: "rroc cotó, ta cupá." Sus ojos, agarrados a la lejanía, parecían encenderse. Su zarabanda no molestaba a nadie: el último marido de su mamá, el hombre colorado que apareció una mañana tirado en los pajonales de la antigua vaquería, se había marchado hacia el centro de la Isla, maldiciendo la costa. Bernabé nuna conoció a su padre. Luciana Quiles sospechaba de un santomeño que arribó, veinte años atrás, cuando la di-

huddled together at the edge of the lot, beat their palms together. Neighbor Luciana Quiles, seventy years old, granddaughter of slaves, caught up by a dizziness that shook her bony body, led the group with her cattle bell of a voice.

In the silent late afternoons the coconut groves atop the little rise turned into metallic shadows, the horizon burned red and Bernabé Quirindongo's soul was filled with a noisy peace, expressible only through the slow roll of the skins. In the mornings the sun ripened on the tips of the pines, nailing daggers of light within the shack and Bernabé Quirindongo (pa-coo-*pah,* his lips moved) would have described it all with a joyous drum roll. Thunder volleys burned the silence above the shack, scared away the peace of the whites, rolled on until quenched in the brambles on the other side of the river and Bernabé Quirindongo, better than anyone else, could have reproduced their sonorous mystery by vibrating his sausage-like fingers. But Bernabé Quirindongo, black good-for-nothing, who beat the air in search of a non-existent bongo, had to pour out his soul through his lips.

"Pa-coo-*pah,*" he murmured.

When Bernabé Quirindongo was sent to the little town hospital because of a hernia, his mama Romualda Quirindongo got drunk and began to beg, her eyes swimming in tears. Of each dollar collected, she drank half. It was a sight that amused even the most refined whites. The black woman went up and down the streets, staggering along in her faded rags, and her enormous breasts wobbled as if they, too, were drunk; she pleaded, whined, begged. Later, alone, she counted the money.

Actually, it was never known whether or not the Negro was being cured of a hernia. The truth is that one morning, after all his mama's pleas and collecting, he appeared at the door of the shack with a new bongo. Luciana Quiles herself, who understood about such things, yanked off the price tag. Bernabé attacked the skins and his thick lips followed the cadence and emitted sounds of a bongo being beaten: "r-roc ko-*to,* ta-coo-*pah*." His eyes, fixed in a faraway gaze, seemed to be aflame. His noise bothered no one: his mama's last husband, the red-skinned man who appeared one morning stretched out in the tall grass of the abandoned dairy farm, had left for the center of the island, cursing the coast.

Bernabé had never known his father. Luciana Quiles was

minuta colonia constaba sólo de media docena de cobertizos desportillados, a trabajar en la construcción del puente. Para los efectos, Romualda era papá y mamá del muchacho. El día de Reyes pasado, mientras Bernabé afinaba su instrumento y las caras negras comenzaban a apretujarse asombradas en la orilla del solar, Romualda le regaló un cortauñas.

—Eso e pa que no rompa lo cuero—le dijo. La vieja Luciana Quiles la abrazó. Coc coró pacú, dijo el bongó en tan memorable fecha.

Romualda tuvo muchas discusiones con la gente. Su hijo no era ningún idiota, simplemente le había salido músico; que miraran a ver si en todo el pueblo había alguien, fíjense bien, alguien que tuviese la armonía que tenía él. Los mozalbetes le rodeaban con güiros y maracas, intentando un ritmo. Bernabé Quirindongo no se dignaba mirarlos y sus ojos, encandilados, miraban por sobre los hombros. Cuando sus dedos golpeaban, ni la vecina Luciana Quiles, ni siquiera su misma mamá, merecían una mirada suya. Era todo concentración. Todo oídos. Bastaba gritarle una palabra al azar para que los cueros dejaran escapar su consonancia junto a los labios murmuradores. ¡Ramón!: rrocotó bembón. Cuando los relámpagos hendían el horizonte sobre los guayabales, permanecía inmóvil, el oído preparado, hasta que le llegaba el sordo rugir del trueno. Sus dedos cobraban entonces vida. Las caras negras corrían bajo la lluvia a oír la maravilla. Boróm bóm, y sus ojos se extraviaban por un instante mientras el oído mágico registraba la ruidosa cadencia.

—Ese e un negro santo—decía la vecina Luciana Quiles—. Va a morí po los oído.

Romualda se sentía orgullosa de su muchacho y lo estimulaba. Pasaba su mano mantecosa sobre la cabeza inclinada de su hijo. Había como una ancestral venganza en aquellas tocatas. Su negro la estaba redimiendo de algo que no comprendía. Se sentía liviana, ágil; algún peso indescriptible la abandonaba siempre que escuchaba el resonar en la puerta de su rancho.

Una mañana, sin que Bernabé Quirindongo la viera, llegó la más clara de las hijas. Tenía el pelo sedoso y los ojos amarillos. Mariana traía a un mulatito de seis meses en los brazos y le dijo bien claro, para que todo el vecindario lo oyera: el bebé, concebido en uno de los arrabales de San Juan, no habría quien se lo arrebatase. Hizo saber su nombre: Milton, Milton Quirindongo,

suspicious of a Jamaican who landed, twenty years back, when the tiny colony had only half a dozen tumbledown hovels, to work on the bridges. For all purposes, Romualda was the boy's papa and mama. Last Three Kings' Day, while Bernabé was tuning his instrument and the admiring black faces began to crowd together outside the plot, Romualda gave him a nail clipper.

"This is so you don't break the skin," she told him. Old Luciana Quiles hugged her. Coc, ko-*ro,* pa-*coo* said the bongo on that memorable date.

Romualda had many arguments with the people. Her son was no idiot, he had simply turned out to be a musician; let them look around all over town for anyone—anyone, mind you!—who could match his harmony. The young boys gathered around him with *güiros* and maracas, trying to pick up a rhythm. Bernabé Quirindongo didn't even look at them, and his eyes, glowing, stared over their shoulders. When his fingers were drumming, not even his own mama nor the neighbor Luciana Quiles merited a glance. He was complete concentration. All ears. A casually shouted word was enough to set the skins to releasing their harmonies together with the murmuring lips. Ramón! R-roco-*to* bem-*bon.* When lightning tore up the horizon above the guava bushes, he would wait motionless, ear ready, until the deafening roar of the thunder reached him. His fingers then came to life. The black faces ran through the rain to listen to the miracle. Bo-*roam boam,* and his eyes turned loose for a moment while his magical hearing registered the noisy cadence.

"Thass a black saint," neighbor Luciana Quiles would say. "He gonna die through the ears."

Romualda felt proud of her boy and encouraged him. She passed her greasy hand over her son's bent head. There was a somewhat ancestral vengeance in those drumbeats. Her black boy was redeeming her from something she couldn't understand. She felt light, agile; some indefinable weight dropped from her whenever she listened to the percussion in the doorway of her shack.

One morning, without Bernabé Quirindongo's seeing her, the lightest of the daughters arrived. She had silky hair and yellow eyes. Mariana brought a six-month-old mulatto in her arms and stated it very clearly, so all the neighborhood could hear: the baby, born in one of San Juan's slums, would not be taken away from her by anyone. She let them know his name:

y se quedó mirando a la gente por si alguien decía algo. Lo criaría aunque no tuviese padre. Para él las mejores mantas del mundo, las miradas tiernas, el mejor biberón, el lecho más blando, las mejores migajas. Bernabé no se dignó mirar a su sobrino, ocupado como estaba. La negra Romualda, de pronto, entusiasmada por el color lechoso de su nieto, dio un viraje sentimental. Sentía que se le ablandaban las rodillas cuando el nieto emitía un berrido. Vendía de prisa sus chicharrones, descuidaba la sazón de las fritangas, olvidaba dar el vuelto a los clientes. La imagen de su último marido desapareció como una ardilla en un matorral. Nadie más existía para ella. Y Bernabé Quirindongo, con su cara impertérrita, los ojos llameantes, les buscaba sentido a los ruidos. El bebé lloraba: guá, pa cupá. "Se me cayó la sartén," decía su mamá. "Ten ten terén," contestaba moviendo sus labios morados y resquebrajados por el silencio. Las caras negras apretadas en la orilla del solar, los ojos y los dientes blancos, las manos agitadas, rodeaban su cadencia. Luciana Quiles se estremecía, en trance; un meneo atávico hacía temblar su piel apergaminada. "¡Bernabé!" Merecumbé. Los sonidos saltaban enloquecidos. "¡Mariana!" Barám barambana.

Mariana trabajaba por las tardes. Acudía a fregar los trastes a casa del hombre más rico del pueblo. De allá traía pedacitos de pollo, golosinas envueltas en papel de periódico para su mulatito. Romualda permanecía en el quiosco, acalorada tras el hornillo, soplando las brasas. Sus ojos venosos se volvían dulces cuando contemplaba al nieto y ya no había palabras sonoras en la casa. No había palabras en la casa, pero el bongó era nuevo aunque tuviera manchas grasosas en el cuero.

Un día el sobrinito de Bernabé amaneció con fiebre. Corrió Luciana Quiles y su media docena de negros: traía un brebaje de yerbas. Llegó un hombre pálido, vestido de blanco, con un extraño collar de goma al cuello. El negro, en la puerta del rancho, esperaba con sus dedos puestos en los parches. Sólo el rumor indistinto del hombre pálido y de las mujeres en el cuarto.

—Doctor—suplicó una voz. Doctor, se repitió Bernabé, y por primera vez sintió la impotencia de no poder traducir la palabra en su instrumento.

—¿No se muere?—preguntó la misma voz. Rrrrrr resonaron

Milton, Milton Quirindongo, and she kept watching the people just in case anyone said something. She would raise him even though he had no father. For him, the best blankets in the world, the tenderest looks, the best bottles, the softest bed, the best scraps of food. Bernabé didn't even bother to look at his nephew, busy as he was. Black Romualda, enthused by the milky color of her grandson, changed the course of her affection. She felt her knees go soft when her grandson bawled. She sold her pork cracklings in a hurry, neglected the seasoning of her fried delicacies, forgot to give her customers the change. The memory of her husband disappeared like a mongoose into a bush. Nobody else existed for her.

And Bernabé Quirindongo, with his dauntless face, his eyes aflame, searched for the meaning to the sounds. The baby cried: gwa, pa coo-*pah.* "I've dropped the frying pan," his mama said. Tan, tan ta-*ran,* he answered, moving his lips, purple and cracked by silence. The black faces crowded about the plot, eyes and teeth white, hands restless, surrounding his cadence. Luciana Quiles quaked in a trance; an atavistic wriggling shook her parchment-like flesh. "Bernabé! . . ." Merecum-*bay.* The sounds leaped forth crazily. "Mariana!" Baram barambana.

Mariana worked in the afternoons. She went to wash dishes in the house of the richest man in town. From there she brought pieces of chicken, dainty tidbits wrapped in newspaper for her little mulatto. Romualda stayed in the kiosk, sweltering over the stove, blowing on the live coals. Her bloodshot eyes became tender when she looked at her grandson and now words no longer sounded in the house. There were no words in the house, but the bongo was new although grease had stained it almost blue.

One day Bernabé's little nephew woke up with a fever. Luciana Quiles and her half-dozen blacks came running: she brought a concoction of herbs. Then came a pale man, dressed in white and wearing a strange rubber necklace. The Negro, in the door of the shack, waited with his fingers ready on the skins. Only the indistinct murmur from the pale man and the women in the bedroom.

"Doctor," begged a voice. "Doctor," Bernabé repeated, and for the first time he felt helpless at not being able to translate the word on his instrument.

"He won't die?" asked the same voice. Rrrrrr, sounded the

los cueros inútilmente, sin vida. Sintió de pronto que una angustia sin nombre se precipitaba sobre él, cubriéndole.

Pasó algún tiempo tratando de atraer a los vecinos, ahora cansados de sus intentos. Luciana Quiles lo miraba con las cejas juntas, agoreramente. Los truenos lograban hacerle caer en una especie de trance: de ahí surgían sus mejores momentos. Pero la enfermedad del bebé preocupaba tanto a Mariana que, en un arrebato de desesperada cólera, rompió el cuero del bongó.

—Mientras él esté enfermo no se hace ningún ruido en esta casa—dijo, y hundió el tacón de su zapato en los parches, que al romperse produjeron un estampido disonante (pruó, pruá), hiriendo los oídos del negro.

Sin bongó, Bernabé Quirindongo se sintió acorralado por el silencio. Las tardes se hicieron espesas, insoportables. Las caras negras se volvieron y presentaron sus cogotes despreciativos. Sus dedos golpeaban sin éxito las paredes, la piedra que servía de escalón, sus rodillas, la banqueta. Romualda no quiso reponerle los cueros. Todo lo que ganaba lo gastaba en el nieto, que iba mejorando en los últimos días. Los vecinos acudían al rancho, pasaban por el lado de Bernabé, sin siquiera mirarle, y auscultaban, enternecidos, el color del mulatito. Bernabé se dio a la caza de nuevas superficies sonoras que sustituyeran su instrumento. Sus labios se movían desesperadamente: ta ta ta. Pero no era lo mismo. Había perdido ya dos buenas tronadas con largos relámpagos encendidos, así como cantidad de palabras a las que les hubiera encontrado su sinónimo rítmico. Una sensación confusa, inexpresable, se iba acumulando en su cabeza. Golpeaba lo que estuviese a su alcance: la jofaina, los cuartones desnudos; se trepaba en la banqueta y aporreaba ansioso la techumbre de lata, que sólo producía un túm túm desesperante. El respaldo de una silla le ofreció una posibilidad inmensa; se abalanzó sobre él, pero al percutir con sus dedos convulsos notó que el sonido salía opaco, derrotado, de tabla empobrecida por la polilla. Se tenía que conformar con una calidad inferior, mientras una serie de impulsos en desbandada le hacía mover los dedos sin cesar. Por momentos parecía golpear los cueros de un bongó invisible, y sus ojos permanecían clavados más allá de los pinos y las cercas de bambú. "Pa cupá," murmuraba; de sus axilas surgía un largo chorrito de sudor.

Por el pueblo se corrió la voz: comenzó como un murmullo

skins in vain, lifelessly. Suddenly he felt an indefinable anguish descend upon him, covering him.

He spent some time trying to attract the neighbors, already weary of his efforts. Luciana Quiles looked at him with a furrowed brow, a bad omen. Thunder made him fall into a sort of trance: from that came his best music. But the sickness of the baby had Mariana so worried that, in an outburst of hopeless rage, she broke the skin of the bongo.

"While he's sick, don't make any noise in this house," she said and pushed the sharp heel of her shoe through the skins, which, upon breaking, produced a dissonant noise (pru-*oh,* pru-*ah*), hurting the Negro's ears.

Without a bongo, Bernabé Quirindongo felt fenced in by the silence. The afternoons became heavy and insufferable. The black faces turned away, presenting only the disdainful backs of their heads. His fingers beat unsuccessfully on the walls, the stone that served as a doorstep, his knees, the stool. Romualda didn't want to replace the skins. Everything she earned she spent on her grandson, who was getting better as the days went by. The neighbors all came to the shack, passing Bernabé by without even looking at him, and peered tenderly at the color of the little mulatto. Bernabé spent his time hunting for new resonant surfaces that could take the place of his instrument. His lips moved in desperation: ta ta ta. But it was not the same. He had already lost two good thunder storms with long fiery lightning flashes, as well as a large number of words for which he could have found rhythmic synonyms. An inexpressible sensation of confusion began to mount up in his head. He beat upon whatever came within reach: a wash basin, the bare beams of the house; he would stand on the stool and anxiously pummel the tin roofing, which only gave forth a hopeless *toom toom.* The back of a chair offered him an immense possibility; he went at it, but as he beat it with his convulsive fingers he noted that the sound came out opaque, dissipated, from the termite-damaged wood. He had to content himself with an inferior quality, while a series of impulses in disordered flight made him move his fingers incessantly. At times he seemed to beat the skins of an invisible bongo, and his gaze remained fixed beyond the pines and the bamboo fences. Pa-coo-*pah,* he murmured; sweat streamed from his armpits.

A rumor swept the town: it began like a superstitious

supersticioso en la colonia negra, estalló al fin, y saltó de boca en boca por toda la municipalidad, llenando las ocho calles.

—Bernabé Quirindongo no toca más.
—Bernabé Quirindongo, negro inútil.
—Bernabé Quirindongo, negro loco que golpea el aire.
—Bernabé Quirindongo, viudo de un bongó.

Romualda permanecía ciega y sorda ante la necesidad de su hijo.

—No se pué hacé ruido—decía, llevándose el índice a los labios.

Mariana lo miraba cejijunta.

Así, Bernabé Quirindongo vivió aislado en un ominoso territorio de silencio. Asaltaban su memoria la infinidad de ruidos perdidos por falta de un cuero.

Una tarde, mirando al techo en busca de una tabla o algo apropiado para descargar su intolerable tensión, notó que el cielo se había puesto serio. Eran nubes oscuras, que por un momento parecieron escindirse en dos islas: un relámpago había azotado la atmósfera, sobre los largos cuellos de los pinos. El cielo parecía un inmenso cuero negro. Afinó el oído, ansiosamente. El trueno rodó por el valle, redondo, magnífico. Los dedos se agitaron. "Burúm, búm," articularon los labios. La lluvia flageló la tierra de pronto como un escupitajo monstruoso. Tic tic tiqui, palpitaron las gotas sobre la cumbrera de lata. Los pinos se inclinaron en una lánguida reverencia. Búm, barúm, le dijo con desparpajo un trueno. Un tacón puntiagudo, luminoso, rajó el cuero del cielo. Bernabé Quirindongo, negro inútil. "¡Bernabé!" le gritaron las voces que traía la lluvia. "Quirindongo," dejó escapar un trueno. "¡Bernabé Merecumbé!," gritó una ráfaga al barrer el seto.

Bernabé Quirindongo sintió que el ritmo maravilloso de la naturaleza lo encerraba en un monstruoso bongó. Sus dedos repicaron frenéticamente contra el tabique. Mariana no podría reprenderle: estaba trabajando en el pueblo. Mamá atendía el quiosco. Búm, se burló un trueno. Tic, tic, tiqui, se reclinó la lluvia a reírse contra el seto. Toc toc toc, golpeteaba gravemente una gota en un cacharro. "¿Dónde está tu cuero cuerón borombóm?" le preguntó una furiosa voz. Sin bongó, el negro Bernabé Quirindongo estaba perdido. Las voces le acosaban en la pequeña sala.

whisper in the Negro colony, broke out at last, and leapt from mouth to mouth through all the municipality, filling the eight streets.

"Bernabé Quirindongo isn't playing anymore."

"Bernabé Quirindongo, black good-for-nothing."

"Bernabé Quirindongo, crazy Negro beating the air."

"Bernabé Quirindongo, widower of a bongo."

Romualda was still blind and deaf to her son's need.

"Mustn't make no noise," she would say, putting her finger to her lips.

Mariana watched him, scowling.

So Bernabé Quirindongo lived isolated in an ominous territory of silence. An infinite number of noises, lost for lack of a skin, assaulted his memory.

One afternoon, looking at the roof in search of a board or something suitable to release his intolerable tension, he noticed that the sky had become stern. There were black clouds that for a moment seemed to split apart into two islands: a streak of lightning had lashed the air above the long necks of the pines. The sky was like an immense black skin. He tuned his ear, eagerly. The thunder rolled through the valley, full and round, magnificent. His fingers moved nervously. "Boo-*room boom,*" his lips articulated. The rain scourged the earth abruptly, like an enormous ejection of spittle. Tic-tic-ticky vibrated the drops on the tin. The pines bent in slow reverence. Boom, ba-*room,* a thunder clap said to him petulantly. A sharp-pointed heel, gleaming, slashed the skin of the sky. Bernabé Quirindongo, good-for-nothing. "Bernabé!" shouted the voices brought by the rain. "Quirindongo," let loose a thunderbolt. "Bernabé Merecumbé!" cried a gust of wind as it swept across the wall.

Bernabé Quirindongo felt that the marvelous rhythm of nature was enclosing him in a monstrous bongo. His fingers beat frenetically upon the partition-wall. Mariana could not scold him: she was working in the town. Mama was taking care of the kiosk. Boom, the thunder mocked. Tic-tic-ticky, laughed the rain, which leaned against the wall. Toc-toc-toc, said a drop which hammered solemnly into a tin can. "Where's your skin, your bongo bo-rom-*bom?*" a furious voice asked him. Without a bongo, black Bernabé Quirindongo was lost. The voices harassed him in the little living room.

Al abrirse de golpe, la ventana lanzó una carcajada. Toc, toc, búm, tic tiqui.

Se arrojó al soberado y machacó hasta que le dolieron las yemas. Pero sus dedos no lograron arrancar de las tablas el mundo de sonidos increíbles que martillaba en su cerebro. Búm, barúm, tiqui tic, toc cotó. Desde el cuarto la voz del bebé le llamó quedamente:

—Guée, Bernabé.

Sus gruesos labios se estremecieron: "Guée, merecumbé." Barúm, le retó el cielo. "Al negro Bernabé Cumbé Quirindongo Dongo le falta un cuero cuerón borombón," le susurraron al oído. Toc toc tiqui.

—¡Guée!—le volvió a llamar su sobrino.

La rama de un árbol daba palmadas en la espalda de la casa: tac, tac, tac. El viento silbaba su burla ante los dedos impotentes.

—Guée—llamó por tercera vez el bebé.

Bernabé Quirindongo fue hasta su sobrino y lo miró seriamente, circunspecto. El bebé se retorcía entre las mantas, esgrimiendo sus puñitos. Guée, merecumbé. "¿Dónde está tu cuero, negro inútil?" le dijeron al oído. Búm, barúm. La frente lisa, de cuero joven . . .

Ta cupá, sonaron los dedos prodigiosos en el cuero de la frente.

Búm, barúm, golpearon en el pecho.

Los truenos lo retaban, búm, barúm. "¡Ja!" rió la ventana.

El negro Bernabé Quirindongo sudaba arrancándole ritmo a su nuevo cuero. La tensión cedía: había descargado gran parte de su ritmo y sentía que tenía aún mucho más que expresar. Mientras siguieran las tronadas, las llamadas, mientras le susurraran palabras sonoras, tendría golpes maravillosos para ripostar. Ta cupá, búm.

Hasta que las uñas de Mariana se le prendieron desesperadamente y le lanzaron al piso. ¡Guap!, crujió sin la menor acústica el soberado. Los gritos de Mariana eran imposibles: ninguna calidad sonora había en ellos. Los rostros negros se apretaron a la entrada del rancho, con Luciana Quiles al frente,

The window, opening abruptly, let out a roar of laughter. Toc-toc-*boom*-tic-ticky.

He threw himself against the floor and pounded on it until his finger-tips hurt. But his fingers could not drag from the boards the world of unbelievable sounds that beat in his brain. *Boom,* ba-*room,* ticky-tic-toc, ko-*toh*. From the bedroom the baby's voice called him quietly.

"Waaaaaayyyyy, Bernabé."

His heavy lips trembled: "Waayyyy, merecoom-*bay*." Ba-*room,* challenged the sky. "Black Bernabé Cumbé Quirindongo Dongo doesn't have a rawskin bongo, borom-*bon,*" they whispered in his ear. Toc-toc-ticky.

"Waaaayyyyyy!" his nephew called again.

The branch of a tree slapped against the back of the house: tac, tac, tac. The wind whistled its mockery of the powerless fingers.

"Waaayyyyy," the baby called for a third time.

Bernabé Quirindongo went to his nephew and looked at him seriously, thoughtfully. The baby twisted among the blankets, shaking his little fists. "Waaayyyy, merecum-*bay*. Where's your skin, good-for-nothing!" they said in his ear. Boom ba-*room*. The smooth forehead, the young skin . . .

Ta coo-*pah,* sounded the gifted fingers on the skin of the forehead.

Boom, ba-*room,* they beat on the chest.

The thunder challenged him, *boom,* ba-*room*. "*Ha!*" laughed the window.

Black Bernabé Quirindongo was sweating, drawing out rhythm from his new skin. The tension was fading: he had unloaded a great part of his rhythm and felt there was still much more to be expressed. While the thunder continued to roll, calling him, while sonorous words hummed in his ear, he would have marvelous sounds with which to parry them. Ta coo-*pah, boom*.

Until Mariana's fingernails seized him furiously and threw him to the floor. Goo-*whop!* creaked the floor without the slightest acoustics. Mariana's shouts were terrible: there was no resonant quality in them. The black faces squeezed about the entrance of the shack, with Luciana Quiles at the fore, shaking

alzando los puños en medio de la centelleante penumbra, bajo la persistente lluvia; querían matar a Bernabé Quirindongo, negro inútil viudo de un bongó.

Mariana lo pateó fuera de ritmo.

Llegaron Romualda y un policía: tuc, tuc, sonó la macana con afortunado compás de clave en la cabeza del negro.

Mamá Romualda gritaba en forma desagradable, desafinada.

El policía agarró a Bernabé y se lo llevó bajo la lluvia.

Pa cúm barúm, le gritaba el cielo.

—Pa cupá, pa cupá—iba diciendo él.

her fists in the midst of the flashing half-light, beneath the persistent rain; they wanted to kill Bernabé Quirindongo, black good-for-nothing, bereft of his bongo.

Mariana kicked him unrhythmically.

Romualda and a policeman arrived: tuc, tuc, beat the nightstick on the Negro's head, with the fortunate timing of a pair of sticks in a dance band.

Mama Romualda was shouting very unpleasantly, way out of tune.

The policeman grabbed Bernabé and carried him off through the rain.

Pa-*coom,* ba-*room,* the sky shouted at him.

"Pa coo-*pah,* pa coo-*pah,*" he went off, saying.

—tr. C. Virginia Matters

LA MUERTE OBLIGATORIA

Emilio Díaz Valcárcel

ESTA mañana recibimos a tío Segundo. Lo esperamos cuatro horas, en medio de la gente que entraba y salía por montones, sentados en uno de los banquitos del aeropuerto. La gente nos miraba y decía cosas y yo pensaba cómo sería eso de montarse en un aeroplano y dejar detrás el barrio, los compañeros de escuela, mamá lamentándose de los malos tiempos y de los cafetines que no dejan dormir a nadie. Y después vivir hablando otras palabras, lejos del río donde uno se baña todas las tardes. Eso lo estaba pensando esta mañana, muerto de sueño porque nos habíamos levantado a las cinco. Llegaron unos aviones y tío Segundo no se veía por ningún sitio. Mamá decía que no había cambiado nada, que seguía siendo el mismo Segundo de siempre, llegando tarde a los sitios, a los trabajos, enredado a lo mejor con la policía. Que a lo mejor había formado un lío allá en el Norte y lo habían arrestado, que no había pagado la tienda y estaba en corte. Eso lo decía mamá mirando a todos lados, preguntándole a la gente, maldiciendo cada vez que le pisaban las chancletas nuevas.

Yo no había conocido nunca a tío Segundo. Decían que era mi misma cara y que de tener yo bigote hubiéramos sido como mandados a hacer. Eso lo discutían los grandes el domingo por la tarde cuando tía Altagracia venía de San Juan con su cartera llena de olores y bombones y nos hacía pedirle la bendición y después hablaba con mamá lo estirado que yo estaba y lo flaco y que si yo iba a la doctrina y si estudiaba, después de lo cual casi peleaban porque tía Altagracia decía que yo era Segundo puro y pinto. A mamá no le gustaba primero, pero después decía que sí,

GRANDMA'S WAKE

Emilio Díaz Valcárcel

WE welcomed Uncle Segundo this morning. We sat waiting on one of the benches at the airport for four hours while mobs of people came and went. The people were looking at us and saying things and I was thinking how it would be to ride in an airplane and leave behind the *barrio,* my friends in school, mamá moaning about the bad times and the cafés that don't let anybody sleep. And then to live talking other words, far from the river where we bathe every afternoon. That's what I was thinking about this morning, dead tired because we'd gotten up at five. A few planes arrived but Uncle Segundo wasn't to be seen anywhere. Mamá was saying that he hadn't changed a bit, that he was the same old Segundo, arriving late at places, and probably mixed up with the police. That he'd probably got in some kind of a jam up there in the North and they'd arrested him, that he hadn't paid the store and was in court. That's what mamá was saying, looking all around her, asking people, cursing everytime they stepped on her new slippers.

I'd never met Uncle Segundo. They said that he had my face and that if I had a moustache we'd be like made to order. That's what the big people argued about on Sunday afternoon when Aunt Altagracia came from San Juan with her bag full of smells and sweets, and told us to ask her for a blessing and then talked with mamá about how drawn and skinny I was, and whether I attended Sunday school and whether I studied, after which they would almost come to blows because Aunt Altagracia would say that I was Segundo through and through. Mamá didn't like it at

que efectivamente yo era el otro Segundo en carne y hueso, sólo que sin bigote. Pero una cosa, saltaba mi tía, que no saliera yo a él en lo del carácter endemoniado, que una vez le había rajado la espalda al que le gritó gacho y había capado al perro que le desgarró el pantalón de visitar a sus mujeres. Y mamá decía que sí, que yo no sería como su hermano en lo del genio volado y que más bien yo parecía una mosquita muerta por lo flaco y escondido que andaba siempre. Y después mamá me mandaba a buscar un vellón de cigarrillos o a ordeñar la cabra para que no oyera cuando empezaba a hablar de papá, de las noches en que no dormía esperándolo mientras él jugaba dominó en lo de Eufrasio, y mi tía se ponía colorada y decía que bien merecido se lo tenía y que bastante se lo advirtieron y le dijeron no seas loca ese hombre no sale de las cantinas no seas loca mira a ver lo que haces.

Eso era todos los domingos, el único día que tía Altagracia venía de San Juan y se metía a este barrio que ella dice que odia porque la gente es impropia. Pero hoy es martes y ella vino a ver a abuela y a esperar a su hermano, porque a él le escribieron que abuela estaba en las últimas y él dijo está bien si es así voy pero para irme rápido. Y le estuvimos esperando cuatro horas sentados en el banquito del aeropuerto muertos de sueño entre la gente que nos miraba y hablaba cosas.

Ni mamá ni tía Altagracia reconocieron al hombre que se acercó vestido de blanco y muy planchado y gordo, que les echó el brazo y casi las exprime a las dos al mismo tiempo. A mí me jaló las patillas y se me quedó mirando un rato, después me cargó y me dijo que yo era un macho hecho y derecho y que si tenía novia. Mamá dijo que yo les había salido un poco enfermo y que por lo que yo había demostrado a estas alturas sería andando el tiempo más bien una mosquita muerta, como quien dice, que otra cosa. Tía Altagracia dijo que se fijaran bien, que se fijaran, que de tener yo bigote sería el doble en miniatura de mi tío.

En el camino tío Segundo habló de sus negocios en el Norte. Mi madre y mi tía estuvieron de acuerdo en ir alguna vez por allá, que aquí el sol pone viejo a uno, que el trabajo el calor las pocas oportunidades de mejorar la vida . . . Así llegamos a casa sin yo darme cuenta. Me despertó tío Segundo jalándome por

first, but later she would say yes, that I was really another Segundo in the flesh, except without a moustache. But one thing, my aunt would snap, let's hope he doesn't have his fiendish nature, for one time someone called him "one ear" and he slashed the man's back and he also castrated the dog that ripped up the pants he wore for calling on his women. And mamá would say no, I wouldn't have her brother's high-flown disposition, 'cause I was more like a sick little mouse if you were to judge by the way I sneaked around. Then mamá would send me for a nickel's worth of cigarettes or to milk the goat, so that I wouldn't hear when she began to talk of papá, and of the nights she couldn't sleep waiting for him while he played dominoes in Eufrasio's, and my aunt would turn all red and say she had it coming to her and that they'd warned her plenty and told her don't be crazy that man's a barfly don't be crazy watch what you're doing.

That was every Sunday, the only day that Aunt Altagracia could come from San Juan and visit this *barrio,* which she says she hates because the people don't have manners. But today is Tuesday and she came to see grandma and to wait for her brother, because they wrote him that grandma was on her last legs and he said all right if that's the way it is I'm coming but I've got to leave right away. And we were waiting four hours at the airport, dead tired, while all the people looked at us and said things.

Neither mamá nor Aunt Altagracia recognized the man who came up dressed in white, looking plenty smooth and fat. He threw himself into their arms and nearly squeezed them both dry at the same time. As for me, he gave a tug at my sideburns and then stared at me awhile, then he picked me up and told me I was a real he-man and asked if I had a girlfriend. Mamá said that I'd been born a bit sickly and that from what I'd shown so far I'd turn out to be a sick little mouse. Aunt Altagracia said that they should take a good look, a real good look, for if I had a moustache I'd be the double in miniature of my uncle.

During the trip Uncle Segundo talked about his business in the North. My mother and my aunt both agreed that someday they would go up there, because here the sun makes one age ahead of time, and the work, the heat, the few opportunities to improve one's life. . . . We reached home without my being

una oreja y preguntándome si veía a Dios y diciéndome espabílate que de los amotetados no se ha escrito nada.

Tío Segundo encontró a abuela un poco jincha pero no tan mal coma le habían dicho. Le puso la mano en el pecho y le dijo que respirara, que avanzara y respirara, y no faltó nada para virar la cama y tirar a abuela al piso. Le dio una palmadita en la cara y después alegó que la vieja estaba bien y que él había venido desde tan lejos y que había dejado su negocio solo y que era la única, oíganlo bien, la única oportunidad ahora. Porque después de todo él vino a un entierro, y no a otra cosa. Mi madre y mi tía abrieron la boca a gritar y dijeron que era verdad que él no había cambiado nada. Pero mi tío decía que la vieja estaba bien, que la miraran, y que qué diría la gente si él no podía volver del Norte la próxima vez para el entierro. Y lo dijo bien claro: tenía que suceder en los tres días que él iba a pasar en el barrio o si no tendrían que devolverle el dinero gastado en el pasaje. Mi mamá y mi tía tenían las manos en la cabeza gritando bárbaro tú no eres más que un bárbaro hereje. Tío Segundo tenía el cuello hinchado, se puso a hablar cosas que yo no entendía y le cogió las medidas a abuela. La midió con las cuartas de arriba abajo y a lo ancho. Abuela sonreía y se veía que quería hablarle. Tío hizo una mueca y se fue donde Santo el carpintero y le encargó una caja de la mejor madera que tuviera, que su familia no era barata. Hablaron un rato del precio y después tío se fue donde sus cuatro mujeres del barrio, le dio seis reales a cada una y cargó con ellas para casa. Prendieron unas velas y metieron a abuela en la caja donde quedaba como bailando, de flaca que estaba. Mi tío protestó y dijo que aquella caja era muy ancha, que Santo la había hecho así para cobrarle más caro y que él no daría más de tres cincuenta. Abuela seguía riéndose allí, dentro de la caja, y movía los labios como queriendo decir algo. Las mujeres de tío no habían comenzado a llorar cuando dos de sus perros empezaron a pelear debajo de la caja. Tío Segundo estaba furioso y les dio patadas hasta que chorreaban, y se fueron con el rabo entre las patas, chillando. Tío movió entonces una mano hacia arriba y hacia abajo y las mujeres empezaron a llorar y dar gritos. Tío las pellizcaba para que hicieran más ruido. Mamá estaba tirada en el piso del cuarto, aullando como los mismo perros; tía Altagracia la abanicaba y le echaba alcoholado. Papá estaba allí, acostado a su lado, diciendo que esas cosas pasan y

aware of it. Uncle Segundo woke me up tugging hard at my ear and asking if I could see God and saying straighten up 'cause nobody pays attention to people who hang their heads.

Uncle Segundo found grandma a bit pale, but not as bad as they'd told him. He put his hand on her chest and told her to breathe, to come on and breathe, and he nearly turned the bed over and threw grandma on the floor. He patted her on the face and then claimed she was all right, and that he'd come from so far away and that he'd left his business all alone and this was the only—listen, you—the *only* chance right now. Because after all he'd come to a funeral, and nothing else. My mother and my aunt opened their mouths to yell and they said it was true, he hadn't changed a bit. But my uncle said the old woman was fine, look at her, and what would people say if he couldn't come back from the North for the funeral next time? And he said it plenty clear: it had to happen in the three days he was going to spend in the *barrio* and if not they'd have to give him back the money he'd spent on the trip. My mamá and my aunt had their hands to their heads yelling barbarian, you're nothing but a heretic barbarian. Uncle Segundo's neck swelled up, he started saying things I didn't understand and he took grandma's measurements. He measured her with his hands from head to foot and side to side. Grandma was smiling and it looked like she wanted to talk to him. Uncle made a face and went looking for Santo, the carpenter, and told him to make a coffin of the best wood there was, that his family wasn't cheap. They spoke about the price for a while and then uncle left to see the four women he's got in the *barrio*. He gave each one six bits and brought them over to our house. They lit a few candles and put grandma in the coffin where she could've danced, she was so skinny. My uncle complained and said the coffin was too wide, that Santo had made it like that just to charge more, and that he wouldn't pay a cent over three fifty. Grandma kept on laughing there, inside the coffin, and moved her lips like she wanted to say something. Uncle's women hadn't begun to cry when two of their dogs started to fight beneath the coffin. Uncle Segundo was furious and he kicked them until they peed and came out from under and left, their tails between their legs, yelping. Then uncle moved his hand up and down and the women began to cry and shout. Uncle pinched them so they'd make more noise. Mamá was stretched out on the floor, howling just like the dogs; Aunt Altagracia was

que la verdad era que la culpa la tenían ellas, que de no haberle dicho nada al cuñado nada hubiera sucedido.

Con los gritos, la gente fue arrimándose al velorio. A papá no le gustó que fuera Eufrasio porque se pasaba cobrándole con la vista. Llegaron Serafín y Evaristo, los guares, y tiraron un vellón a cara o cruz a ver quién comenzaba a dirigir el rosario. Lllegó Chalí con sus ocho hijos y se puso a espulgarlos en el piso murmurando sus oraciones. Las hermanas Cané entraron por la cocina mirando la alacena y abanicándose con un periódico y diciéndose cosas en los oídos. Los perros peleaban en el patio. Cañón se acercó a mamá y le dijo que la felicitaba que esas cosas, pues, tienen que pasar y que Diostodopoderoso se las arreglaría para buscarle un rinconcito en su trono a la pobre vieja. Tía Altagracia decía que en San Juan el velorio hubiera sido más propio y no en este maldito barrio que por desgracia tiene que visitar. Tío Segundo le decía a abuela que cerrara la maldita boca, que no se riera, que aquello no era ningún chiste sino un velorio donde ella, aunque no lo pareciera, era lo más importante.

Mamá se levantó y sacó a abuela de la caja. Cargaba con ella para el cuarto cuando mi tío, borracho y hablando cosas malas, agarró a abuela por la cabeza y empezó a jalarla hacia la caja. Mamá la jalaba por los tobillos y entonces entraron los perros y se pusieron a ladrar. Tío Segundo les tiró una patada. Los perros se fueron pero mi tío se fue de lado y cayó al suelo con mamá y abuela. Papá se ñangotó y le dijo a mamá que parecía mentira, que a su hermano hay que complacerlo después de tantos años afuera. Pero mamá no cejaba y entonces tío empezó a patalear y tía Altagracia dijo lo ven, no ha cambiado nada este muchacho.

Pero siempre mi tío se salió con la suya. Cañón estaba tirado en una esquina llorando. Las hermanas Cané se acercaron a mi abuela y dijeron qué bonita se ve la vieja todavía sonriendo como en vida, que bonita eh.

Yo me sentía como encogido. Mi tío era un hombre alto y

fanning her and sprinkling her with *alcoholado*. Papá was there, lying down at her side, saying that these things do happen and that it was all their fault, cause if they hadn't said anything to his brother-in-law nothing would have happened.

All that yelling began to draw people to the wake. Papá wasn't too happy about Eufrasio coming because he was always trying to collect debts with those hard looks of his. The twins, Serafín and Evaristo, arrived, and they tossed a coin heads or tails to see who would lead the rosary. Chalí came up with his eight children and sat them down on the floor and searched them for bugs while he mumbled his prayers. The Cané sisters came in through the kitchen looking at the cupboard, fanning themselves with a newspaper and saying things in each other's ear. The dogs were fighting outside. Cañón came up to mamá and said he congratulated her, 'cause these things, well, they have to happen and that God Almighty would fix things up so as to find a little corner on his throne for the poor old woman. Aunt Altagracia was saying that the wake would have been more proper in San Juan and not in this damned *barrio,* which she unfortunately had to visit. Uncle Segundo was telling grandma to shut her damned mouth, not to laugh, for this was no joke but a wake where she, though it mightn't seem so, was the most important thing.

Mamá got up and took grandma out of the coffin. She was carrying her towards the room when uncle, drunk and saying bad words, grabbed grandma by the head and began to pull her back towards the coffin. Mamá kept pulling her by the ankles and then the dogs came in and started to bark. Uncle Segundo threw them a kick. The dogs left, but my uncle went sideways and fell on the floor with mamá and grandma. Papá squatted down next to mamá and told her that this was incredible, that they should please their brother after all the years he'd been away. But mamá didn't give in and then uncle began to stamp his feet and Aunt Altagracia said, see, this boy hasn't changed a bit.

But my uncle still got things his way. Cañón was stretched out in a corner crying. The Cané sisters came up to my grandma and said how pretty the old woman looks, still smiling as in life, how pretty, eh?

I felt sort of shrunk. My uncle was a big strong man. I, mamá

fuerte y yo, lo dijo mamá, según ando ahora, no seré más que una mosquita muerta para toda la vida. Yo quisiera ser fuerte, como mi tío, y pegarle al que se metiera en el medio. Me sentía chiquito cuando mi tío me miraba y se ponía a decir que yo no me le parecía aunque tuviera bigote, que ya le habían engañado tantas veces y qué era eso. Y terminó diciéndome que yo había salido a mi padre escupío y que no se podría esperar gran cosa de me amontonamiento.

Cañón se puso a hablar con Rosita Cané y al rato se metieron en la cocina como quien no quiere la cosa. La otra Cané se abanicaba con el periódico y miraba envidiosa a la cocina y también miraba a Eufrasio de quien se dice que compró a los padres de Melina con una nevera. Melina se había ido a parir a otro sitio y desde entonces Eufrasio no hace sino beber y pelear con los clientes. Pero ahora Eufrasio estaba calmadito y miraba también a la Cané y le hacía señas. Se le acercó con una botella y le ofreció un trago y ella dijo qué horror cómo se atreve pero después se escondió detrás de la cortina y si Eufrasio no le quita la botella no hubiera dejado una gota.

El velorio estaba prendido y los guares seguían guiando el rosario, mirando el cuarto donde tía Altagracia estaba acostada.

Yo estaba casi dormido cuando me despertó la paliza que tío Segundo le dio a Cañón. Mi tío salió gritando que qué desorden era ése que se largaran si no quería coger cada uno su parte. Rosita Cané estaba llorando. Mi tío cogió la maleta y dijo que al fin de cuentas estaba satisfecho porque había venido al velorio de su madre y que ya no tenía que hacer por todo aquello. Salió diciendo que no le importaba haber gastado en pasaje ni en la caja ni en las lloronas, que miraran a ver si en todo el barrio había un hijo tan sacrificado. Ahí está la caja, dijo, para el que le toque el turno. Y salió casi corriendo.

Cuando me acerqué a la caja y miré a abuela, ya no estaba riendo. Pero noté un brillito que le salía de los ojos y mojaba sus labios apretados.

herself said it, will turn out to be just a sick little mouse, the way I'm going. I would like to be strong, like my uncle, and fight anyone who gets in my way. I felt tiny whenever my uncle looked at me and said that I wouldn't look like him even with a moustache, that they'd fooled him so many times, and what was this? He would end up telling me that I'd become the spitting image of my father, and that one couldn't expect much from someone with my looks.

Cañón began to talk with Rosita Cané and after a while they went into the kitchen, acting as if they weren't up to something. The other Cané was fanning herself with a paper and looking enviously towards the kitchen and also looking at Eufrasio who, they say, bought off Melina's parents with a refrigerator. Melina had left to give birth someplace else and since then Eufrasio just drinks and fights with the customers. But now Eufrasio was nice and calm and he was looking at the Cané girl and talking sign-language. He came up with a bottle and offered her a drink and she said heavens how dare you, but then she hid behind the curtain and if Eufrasio hadn't taken the bottle away she wouldn't have left a drop.

The wake was now going full-steam ahead and the twins kept leading the rosary, looking towards the room where Aunt Altagracia was lying down.

I was nearly asleep when the beating Uncle Segundo gave Cañón shook me up. My uncle was shouting and demanding to know what kind of things were going on and that they should all leave if each and every one of them didn't want to get their share. Rosita Cané was crying. My uncle grabbed his suitcase and said that all in all he was satisfied because he'd come to his mother's wake and that now he didn't have to go through it again. He went out saying that he didn't mind paying for the fare, or the box, or the mourners, and that in the whole *barrio* they wouldn't find such a sacrificing son. There's the coffin, he said, for whoever's turn it is. And he left, almost running.

When I went up to the coffin and looked at grandma she wasn't laughing anymore. But I noticed a tiny bit of brightness flowing from her eyes and wetting her tightly closed lips.

—tr. Kal Wagenheim

BRIEF BIBLIOGRAPHY

For those interested in further readings of Puerto Rican short stories, this bibliography lists some of the major sources in Spanish and English.

SPANISH

Cuentos puertorriqueños de hoy. Selections, prologue, and notes by René Marqués. Club del Libro de Puerto Rico, San Juan, 1959. 281 pages. Seventeen stories by eight authors.

El cuento. Ed. Concha Meléndez. Antología de Autores Puertorriqueños, III, Estado Libre Asociado de Puerto Rico, San Juan, 1957. Thirteen stories by six authors.

Antología de cuentos puertorriqueños. Ed. Paul J. Cooke, Monticello College, Godfrey, Illinois, 1956. Includes nine stories by six authors.

Revista Asomante, San Juan, Puerto Rico. The third issue of this magazine in 1956 includes eight stories by eight authors. Throughout its twenty-five years, *Asomante* has published many other Puerto Rican stories.

Revista del Instituto de Cultura Puertorriqueña. This quarterly magazine of the Institute of Puerto Rican Culture has published numerous stories.

El cuento en la literatura puertorriqueña por Lillian Quiles de la Luz. Editorial Universidad de Puerto Rico, 1968.

8 Cuentos Puertorriqueños. Libros del Pueblo Núm. 7. Instituto de Cultura Puertorriqueña, San Juan de Puerto Rico, 1968. Eight stories by eight authors.

ENGLISH

San Juan Review. A monthly magazine, published from February 1964 through November 1966, and available in many United States college libraries; published many Puerto Rican stories, including ten of the twelve stories published in this volume.

Caribbean Review. A quarterly which commenced publication in Hato Rey, Puerto Rico, in 1969, also published some stories.

From the Green Antilles. Ed. Barbara Howes, Macmillan, 368 pages, 1966. A large collection of Caribbean writing, including four stories from Puerto Rico.

REFERENCE BOOKS

Diccionaria de Literatura Puertorriqueña. Josefina Rivera de Alvarez. Ediciones de la Torre, 1955. Instituto de Cultura Puertorriqueña.

El cuento en la edad de Asomante: 1945–55. Concha Meléndez. In *Asomante* Núm. 1, 1955, San Juan.

Historia de la literatura puertorriqueña. Francisco Manrique Cabrera. Las Américas Publishing Co., New York, 1956

Figuración de Puerto Rico y ostros estudios. Concha Meléndez. Instituto de Cultura Puertorriqueña, San Juan, 1958.